I looked at the photo of the stone house for several minutes, sipping coffee, wondering what life in that little twelve-by-sixteen shack must have been like fifty years before, when a trip into town was an hour in a jolting Model A Ford, itself twenty or more years old by that time. Maybe Martin Holman had wondered the same thing and that was what had prompted him to take the photo in the first place.

"And whose windmill is this?" I said aloud to the quiet kitchen. That was another question for Johnny Boyd. Maybe he knew just where it was...and maybe he knew just why Sheriff Holman had wanted a photo of it.

I would have liked to talk to the rancher right then, but my heavy eyelids told me that it made sense to wait. The windmill wasn't going anywhere, and neither was Johnny Boyd. Come morning, he'd have half an army swarming around his ranch.

STEVEN F. HAVILL

OUT OF SEASON

WORLDWIDE.

TORONTO • NEW YORK • LONDON
AMSTERDAM • PARIS • SYDNEY • HAMBURG
STOCKHOLM • ATHENS • TOKYO • MILAN
MADRID • WARSAW • BUDAPEST • AUCKLAND

To Jerrold Flores,
who understands how important the
Don Juan de Oñate really is.

For Kathleen

OUT OF SEASON

A Worldwide Mystery/April 2001

First published by St. Martin's Press, Incorporated.

ISBN 0-373-26382-1

Printed in U.S.A.

Acknowledgments

For some of the technical information used in this novel, the author would like to extend special thanks to Virgil Hall and John Burns.

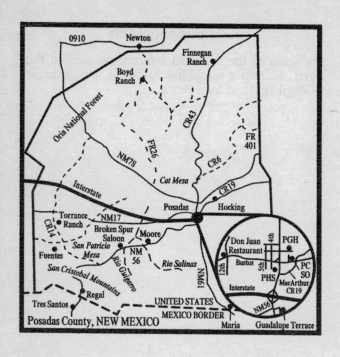

Posadas County, NEW MEXICO

ONE

My POLISHED-MAHOGANY desktop was almost the way I'd left it earlier that Friday afternoon—unmarred except for the computer terminal and its ancillary junk: the old leather-edged desk blotter, one black felt-tip pen, and an empty wooden in-and-out letter tray.

In an effort to call my attention to them, a sheaf of papers had been dropped into the middle of all that organization. I wasn't in the mood for paperwork, but as I sagged back into the comforting curves of my swivel chair, I recognized Sheriff Martin Holman's precise penmanship on a Post-it note spotted to the front of the first sheet.

I dug my glasses out of my pocket, slipped them on and saw that the papers were a Posadas County Sheriff's Department job application.

"I think you should talk with her," the sheriff's note said.

"Talk with whom?" I muttered aloud and scanned the first page of the application. "Well, for heaven's sake."

I leaned back in my leather chair and started reading at the top. So engrossed was I that the telephone buzzed half a dozen times before my hand drifted over to pick it up.

"Gastner," I said, still reading.

"Sir, this is Linda Real calling."

I let the application fall in my lap. "An unexpected surprise, too," I said. "How are you doing?"

"Fine. Sir, Sheriff Holman said you might be in the office this afternoon, and he said he'd pass my application along to you."

"I am, and he did," I said, and leaned forward, spreading the application out on the blotter. I rested on my elbows, frowning. "In fact, I was just going through it when you called." As I said that, I turned the page to read the section that included medical history and the attached physician's report. "I didn't know that you were back in town."

She chuckled. "I think my mother got tired of me hanging around," she said. "Anyway, I got kinda burned out in the big city. It's not very user-friendly."

"I can imagine."

"Do you think I could come in and talk with you? I know it's a Friday afternoon and all, but..."

"I think that would be a good idea, Linda," I said. I didn't bother to add that Fridays didn't hold much attraction for me one way or another. The clean desk was not the result of an end-of-the-week wrap-up with an exciting weekend vacation looming. All that tidy organization was just a momentary lapse, a giving-in to a brief episode of spring cleaning. In a week's time, I wouldn't be able to see the wooden surface. "Where are you now?"

"I'm at Estelle's."

"Ah," I said, sensing a conspiracy. Estelle Reyes-Guzman, the department's chief of detectives, had another week or so before she and her physician husband, Francis, left Posadas for the wilds of Rochester, Minnesota. "Have her bring you over, if you're both free." I glanced at the wall clock. "Better yet, let's meet for dinner." Only a limited number of opportunities remained for Estelle to feast on New Mexican green chili before she had to face raw fish, or sauerkraut, or whatever else the Minnesotans called food.

There was a pause. "Did you have a chance to read Dr. Guzman's report?"

"No. I see it, though. By the time we meet, I'll have the whole thing memorized." I kept my tone light.

"I'd really like to have the opportunity to respond to some of the things he said in that," Linda Real said.

I leaned back and stared at the ceiling. "Well, then, how about it? Dinner?" Somehow, talking between mouthfuls of food seemed more gentle than me sitting on one side of a big old desk with her on the other side, hands folded in her lap, looking wee and small.

"Yes, sir."

"Then I'll meet you at the Don Juan at about six. If Estelle can come, that's fine. Francis too, if he can make it. We'll see what we can do."

She thanked me and hung up, and I slipped the phone back in its cradle. Breaking bad news to a stranger was far easier than letting down someone whose life I had once held in my hands. I leafed through the application to the blue medical attachment, a requirement if positive answer was given for line 17: *Do you possess any physical limitation(s) that might compromise your performance in the position for which you are applying?*

Dr. Francis Guzman, the official on-call physician for our department, had been his usual plainspoken self, but I could imagine him trying to word the statement so that it told the unvarnished truth and at the same time, created a minimum amount of friction with his detective wife.

On Feb. 21, 1996, Ms. Real suffered extensive gunshot trauma to the head and neck, resulting in complete and permanent blindness in her left eye, and complete and permanent deafness in her left ear. Following a complicated and difficult convalescence, she continues to receive physical therapy for limited muscular movement and strength in the left shoulder.

In addition, a lengthy series of orthodontic reconstructive procedures are required to correct injuries to both upper and lower left dentition.

Although Ms. Real's recovery has been in many ways remarkable, it should be noted that her physical capacity, including strength, dexterity, endurance, and sensory perception, is well below standard for employment in a law-enforcement capacity.

Since the Posadas County Sheriff's Department routinely expects dispatch personnel to perform a wide range of duties, including some corrections and booking procedures, Ms. Real's physical limitations should be carefully reviewed prior to employment.

I tossed the application on the desk and sighed. I liked
Linda Real. When she had been on the staff of the *Posadas
Register,* she'd been eager, more accurate than most reporters
I had known, and a bright, smiling face during her daily
rounds.

Two years before, as the county neared budget time, she'd
embarked on a series of articles about the funding of various
agencies, including ours.

What should have been a simple evening ride-along with
an officer had turned into a nightmare. Linda caught a faceful
of double-ought buckshot, and the deputy with whom she was
riding was killed.

I knew that all the common sense in the world was telling
me that the Posadas County Sheriff's Department shouldn't
hire Linda Real. Sheriff Holman either hadn't been able to
make up his mind or just couldn't say no. Perhaps he thought
I would let Linda down more gently than he would—but there
was small chance of that.

I frowned and stood up. I was more than a little irritated
with Estelle Reyes-Guzman, too. She should have been able
to talk Linda down some other road. In fact, what had
prompted the young woman to even consider working for us
in the first place would no doubt have made a fascinating
psychological study. Estelle should have known better than to
encourage Linda, and Sheriff Holman should have just looked
them both in the eye and said "No." Now the mess was in
my lap.

Gayle Sedillos, our senior dispatcher, appeared in my office
doorway. On more than one occasion during the past few
days, I'd noticed the current issue of *Bride's* magazine on the
radio console. I didn't pester Gayle about it—and so far, I
didn't have a clue as to what appropriate wedding gift I was
going to find. Short-timer or not, Estelle would have to help,
that was all there was to it.

"Sir," Gayle said, "we just had a telephone call about an
aircraft in possible trouble. Tom Pasquale is on that side of
the county, and I asked him to head out that way for a look."

"By 'in trouble,' what did the caller mean?"

Gayle shook her head. "It was Mrs. Finnegan who called."

"Oh. That explains that." Charlotte Finnegan spent most of her waking hours "seeing things" and traveling to places that didn't exist. I didn't know if she suffered from Alzheimer's or was simply tuned in to an alternative universe. Whatever the case, her husband Richard was a man of infinite patience. They lived on a small ranchette just inside the Posadas County line on County Road 43, a desolate stretch of overgrazed country where Charlotte Finnegan could certainly do no harm.

"You might call Jim Bergin and ask him if there's been any traffic in or out of the airport in the last few minutes. Or if he's talked to any transient aircraft on the radio."

She nodded and started to turn away, then stopped. "The sheriff was going to leave a job application on your desk," she said. "Linda Real's."

"I saw it." I could see that she wanted to say something else, but I frowned one of my scowls and she changed her mind. Taking the electric razor out of the top drawer of my desk, I went to the rest room and chopped off the late-afternoon stubble and double-checked to make sure that I hadn't left a trail of lunch down the front of my shirt.

The lighting in the Don Juan de Oñate restaurant wasn't the best, but I wanted to look sharp if I had to do battle with a couple of women.

TWO

THE BATTERED, sagging booth seats in the Don Juan de Oñate restaurant had recently been replaced with genuine molded-plastic benches that were about as comfortable as sitting on ice. The goddam things were bright yellow. All Fernando Aragon needed now was a kiddy playland outside to complete the transformation.

I forgave Fernando all that because the food was unchanged. His wife Rosie and daughter-in-law Arleen still cooked the same amazing nuclear concoctions on which my system had depended for the past quarter century.

I slid across cold plastic and rested my right arm on the windowsill, tapping a nervous rhythm on the freshly painted white trim while I looked outside. There wasn't much to see other than asphalt and dust. The wind was gusting from the southwest, fitful and without a trace of humidity.

Bustos Avenue was already grimy and littered with tumbleweeds and ragweed tops, Posadas at its dismal, dry, early spring worst. In another few weeks, we'd be pounded by a storm that would dump a couple of inches of rain in an hour and the desert would sprout a new harvest of things with thorns, spikes, and pollen.

Within a minute, the waitress appeared and slid a cup of coffee across until it rested at my left elbow. She placed a basket of chips and a bowl of salsa in front of me and smiled. She was a lot prettier to look at than the dusty street and empty parking lot.

"Did you want to wait for the others, or order now, sir?"

"The coffee's fine, JanaLynn," I said. "Are you ready for the big wedding?" Sheriff Holman referred to the pending knot-tying as "the department event." He was probably right. Sergeant Robert Torrez, a thirty-six-year-old bachelor and fifteen-year veteran of the Posadas County Sheriff's Department, had finally proposed to Gayle Sedillos, our chief dispatcher. Gayle was twenty-eight and had been with us since she turned eighteen.

JanaLynn was one of Torrez's multitude of cousins, and I wouldn't have been a bit surprised if she were somehow related to Gayle as well.

"If it was up to Bobby," JanaLynn said, "they'd just elope."

"His mother would kill him," I chuckled.

"So would I," JanaLynn said and turned to go, adding, "I'll be back in a bit with a refill."

Three chips were all I had time for. Estelle Reyes-Guzman's van pulled into the parking lot, and I watched as she and Linda Real got out. I don't know what I had expected, but Linda's quick step matched Estelle's as they crossed the macadam. They impressed me as two women with a purpose, and I took a deep breath.

Before the incident, Linda Real had been a vivacious, raven-haired dynamo. She worked long, odd hours and, like the rest of us, was none too careful about what or when she ate. As a result, her face had few sharp angles and she chose loose-fitting clothes to suit her pudgy frame.

From a distance, it looked like she hadn't changed. She was wearing one of those slouch hats that would have been at home in the 1930s, pulled low and rakish. The wind tugged and fluttered the brim, and she clamped her right hand on the top of her head.

Then the corner of the building blocked them from view, but when they opened the outer door, the change in air pressure made the inner door thud loudly against its stops. I pushed the basket of chips a little farther away and wiped my mouth with my napkin. Linda's application rested in a manila folder on the bench beside me.

The two women appeared around the gold-embroidered velvet partition that divided the two rear dining areas. Estelle, her long black hair tied back in a ponytail, wore jeans, a University of New Mexico sweatshirt, and a light blue jacket...and she looked about eighteen rather than the thirty-one-year-old mother of two that she was.

I pushed myself along the yellow bench, but Estelle held out a hand. "Don't get up, sir" she said and slid all the way in on the other side.

I continued to my feet anyway. "I've got to collect a hug from this gal," I said. Linda Real grinned, a little lopsided perhaps, but game enough. Her perfume was strong and outdoorsy, and her hug lasted well beyond a perfunctory social courtesy.

"Have a seat," I said. "It's really good to see you." I watched as she slid into the booth beside Estelle. She didn't take off her hat. "JanaLynn's around here someplace," I added and sat down.

Indeed she was, and after she'd come and gone, I leaned forward and folded my hands in front of me. "So," I said to Linda, "what do you think about this one heading off to the wilds of Minnesota?"

She grinned at Estelle. "Exciting. What a change."

"Yeah," I said, and then to Estelle, I added, "Your mom's still doing all right?"

"She's fine, sir. She told me today that she's actually looking forward to the move."

"Remarkable woman," I said, still wondering how a tiny, elderly woman who, until a few months before, had lived alone in an equally tiny adobe house in rural Mexico, could find the strength to contemplate such a monumental change in life style.

"Tell me how you've been," I said to Linda.

This was no time for pretending, and I gazed at her steadily, taking in the details of her battered face. Linda remained silent, enduring my scrutiny. Both Estelle and I had been with her the day she'd been released from the hospital. After that, she'd gone home to Las Cruces to recuperate. Time had slipped by, and I hadn't seen her since then. Every now and then, I would receive a note from her and the tone was always upbeat. In the meantime, I'd had a surgical bout of my own and she'd sent me one of those funny, insulting cards that had made me laugh until I hurt.

She was a brave kid. Surgeons had managed to save the orb of her left eye, but the pupil was fixed and the iris dull. A dent the size of a quarter disfigured the outer corner of the orbit, with a heavy scar extending up into her eyebrow. The passage of time and some skilled makeup had blended most of the scarring on the side of her face and around her ear with her natural skin tone.

She didn't offer to say how she'd been, but I could guess

it hadn't been fun. "The application says that you're still facing more surgery."

Linda nodded. "Dental work," she said. She cocked her head slightly and her fingers traced a line down one side of her jaw. "They had to wire all this together. Apparently there were three or four pellets in a cluster, and they did a real tap dance. They busted off three lowers and two uppers. One of them went across and busted a tooth on the other side."

I grimaced. "When's the next round of surgery scheduled?"

"I've got two new permanent crowns waiting for me," Linda said. "There're a couple of procedures yet to go that involve building something that looks like the Brooklyn Bridge, but I think it's all on an outpatient basis." She didn't move her jaws much when she talked, but her diction was clear and precise.

"Those are what Dr. Guzman refers to as 'lengthy orthodontic procedures'?"

"Lengthy is in the eye of the beholder," Linda said easily.

"I think that what's at issue is the job description," Estelle said, cutting right to the chase. JanaLynn arrived with our food, and we waited while she placed the steaming, fragrant *burrito grandes* in front of Linda and me, and a taco salad for Estelle.

Linda Real hadn't lost her appetite, and even though she was forced to process the food entirely on the right side of her mouth, she attacked the meal with gusto.

"Job description?" I asked.

Estelle frowned as she worked loose a corner of the flower-petal taco shell. "If a dispatcher does nothing but dispatch, I don't think that a physical handicap matters."

"Depending on the handicap, of course," I said. "But let's look at the facts. Our department is a small one. Hell, not small. Miniscule. With twelve full-time employees to cover seven days a week, twenty-four hours a day, everyone has to be a jack-of-all-trades."

Linda started to say something, but Estelle leaned back and

put her fork down. "And you'll remember, sir, that's one of the things we talked about that needs to change."

"Sure enough," I said. I knew exactly what she was driving at, and in a normal world with normal budgets and legislators who had their heads screwed on straight, there would have been no argument.

"Especially where the dispatcher is concerned," Estelle pointed out.

I poked at my burrito and rearranged an ocean of sour cream. "If you were working dispatch, what'd be your job?" I asked Linda.

"Radio. Telephone. Fax. Computer. Some filing. Talking with walk-ins." She leaned forward eagerly, fork poised. "And I'd really like to continue working with photography. I think I can make a contribution there."

I nodded. "I have no doubt of that. And in a perfect world, those things you mentioned would be the bulk of what a dispatcher's job would be limited to. But this world is far from perfect. Sometimes the person working dispatch needs to tend to someone in the lockup. That's what Francis was talking about when he mentioned duties beyond the radio. And there are times when the officer working dispatch needs to assist in booking procedures, too."

"But always with another officer in that case, sir," Estelle observed. "And if the dispatcher needs to go into the lockup, it's just to check quickly on the general situation, not to enter the cells."

"I couldn't agree more," I said. "That's the way it should be. There should be nothing that takes the dispatch officer away from the communications console. I know that. And when it happens, we're setting ourselves up for disaster." I took a sip of coffee. "I'm sure you both remember Sonny Trujillo. The kid who choked to death in one of our cells? Gayle Sedillos was all alone when that happened. Granted, she probably shouldn't have been. But we were busy with another case, and we were shorthanded."

Estelle nodded and turned to Linda. "We get caught sometimes, Linda. We put ourselves in a position where we *hope* that the dispatch officer can get to the radio or telephone immediately. It doesn't always happen. It *hasn't* always happened."

Both women looked over at me and I shrugged. "Linda, you're an intelligent, gifted young woman. I have some idea about what you're going through. But you know, for the life of me, I don't understand what attracts you to the dispatch job. It's deadly dull ninety-nine point nine nine nine percent of the time. The starting salary we pay is less than welfare. On top of that, any new dispatcher will have to work graveyard…" I let it trail off and raised an eyebrow at her expectantly.

"I don't think I could explain why I want to do it," Linda said softly. "It's just something I'm comfortable with in my mind."

"Comfortable with…"

She nodded. "I've watched Gayle Sedillos work, and she seems so confident and professional. Part of a team."

I looked down at my diminishing burrito. "Let me ask you something straight-out." I put down my fork and pushed the plate away. "Does your wanting to work for us have something to do with the incident two years ago? With the shooting?"

"What do you mean?"

"Well, I think that if I'd been through what you have—and what you're still going through because of it—I'd sure as hell distance myself from anything to do with police work."

Linda bit her lip. "What happened to me could have happened anywhere, anytime. I could have walked into a convenience store at the wrong time. Or stopped my car at just the wrong intersection at just the wrong time. Or a thousand other scenarios."

"So you're not trying to put something right? Not trying to get back on the horse that bucked you off?"

"No, sir."

"There's a certain personality profile we look for, Linda. You mentioned Gayle Sedillos. She's about as good as they come. Levelheaded, commonsensical, quick-thinking, a good communicator.''

"I think I'm all of those things, sir."

"I won't argue that." I took a long breath. "And as you suggest, you've got some camera skills that we're going to need when Estelle leaves us. Let me ask you something else. In the event that the Posadas County Sheriff's Department were to hire you—"

JanaLynn appeared around the partition, pointed at me and then mimicked holding a telephone to her ear. "Hold that thought," I said. "Excuse me for a minute."

From the booth where we were sitting, I would have guessed that the restaurant was empty. As I walked around the first partition, I was startled to see a fair sea of heads as dinner-hour patrons picked up. JanaLynn reached under the counter by the cash register for the telephone and handed it to me.

"Gastner."

"Sir," Gayle Sedillos said, "Officer Pasquale reported that with binoculars he can see something that looks like it might be wreckage, and he's on his way to the site."

"How far off road?"

"He thinks at least three miles, sir. Over north of the Salinas Arroyo fork. He said he'd try to find a route to get him close enough to confirm before dark."

I glanced at my watch. "Any fire?"

"He says not, sir."

"Well, he doesn't have much time. Did you call Jim Bergin at the airport?"

"Yes, sir. Bergin said there was only one aircraft currently aloft in the area, and he's trying to contact it now."

"You mean a local flight?" I glanced out past the front doors as the wind scudded up the street.

"Yes, sir. Apparently Philip Camp departed Posadas at sixteen-ten for just a short ride. He hasn't returned."

"Phil Camp? That's Marty Holman's brother-in-law."

"Yes, sir. Jim Bergin said that Sheriff Holman went with Camp."

THREE

LINDA REAL wasn't finished with her meal, but she'd have to get used to interruptions. I wasn't sure why I invited her along, other than that it was as good a time as any to see what her instincts were.

She and I headed for the airport, and as we drove up Bustos Avenue toward County Road 43, I could tell by the way she sat, stiff-spined and leaning forward slightly, that she was eager to be doing something other than sitting and waiting for damaged cells to mend.

"Three-ten, PCS."

I nodded toward the mike. "Take it," I said.

Linda pulled it out of the bracket and promptly dropped it with a loud whack against the radio console. "Sorry," she said. "PCS, this is three-ten."

If Gayle Sedillos was surprised to hear something other than my gruff, monosyllabic radio response, she didn't let it show in her voice.

"Three-ten, be advised that three-oh-three will be on foot with vehicle disabled. He has a handheld, but it doesn't have the range to reach the repeater."

Linda glanced over at me. "Just acknowledge," I said.

She pressed the mike key and said, "Ten-four, PCS."

By the time we reached the airport, Jim Bergin had the main hangar open and had pulled his new Cessna 210 onto the apron. The fitful gusts rocked the wings and I grimaced as I parked behind the terminal. It was going to be a rocky ride, even with burrito padding.

"Jim doesn't have a police radio in the aircraft," I told Linda, "and the handhelds are useless at any distance and with all the engine noise. We'll be talking on the aircraft channel, on Unicom, back to the radio here at the airport. I want you on this end, and then you can patch back to Gayle by phone. All right?''

"Yes, sir," Linda said.

"Just transfer the messages word for word. Don't get creative.''

"Yes, sir.''

Bergin trotted over toward the car, glancing at his watch as he did so. Short, wiry, and intense, Bergin had eked out a living at the Posadas airport for twenty years. If the place had had to depend on transient av-gas customers for its economic survival, it would have been dead long before. And if Bergin's survival depended on prompt reimbursement by the county for flights like this one, he'd starve while he waited for the government check.

"I'm kinda worried, Bill," Bergin said as we shook hands. "They took off about two hours ago, just to do a little local sight-seeing. No radio response. You say one of the deputies has wreckage spotted?''

"He thinks he does, Jim. We don't know for sure." I shrugged. "It could be anything. Holman and his brother-in-law might have decided to skip over to Cruces or something like that.''

He shook his head. "I checked to make sure. They didn't do that." He looked up at the sky. Thin mares' tails stretched out from the southwest, their tips shredded by winds aloft. A gust ripped across the apron, pinging sand against the side of the Cessna. "This ain't going to be fun," he said.

"Let's get with it," I said, and added, "You know Linda Real. She's going to sit the radio down here, if that's all right with you.''

"Sure." He waved a hand toward the mobile home that served as the terminal. "It's open.''

When Bergin had predicted that the flight wouldn't be a pleasure ride, I'd chalked that up to his cautious nature. As far as I was concerned, the less time I spent in an airplane, the better, regardless of the weather.

The 210 kicked into life with a hearty rumble, and between

its vibration and the constant buffeting of the wind against its flanks, the aircraft felt like a living thing.

We taxied out and I looked down and watched sand and desert litter stream past the tires. The gusts were quartering across the tarmac, and Bergin kept full aileron correction cranked in to discourage the windward wing from lifting.

At the end of the taxi way, he let the Cessna weathervane, and we parked with its nose into the wind while he completed his checklist. When he was satisfied, he plucked the mike off the console.

"Posadas Unicom, this is Cessna four-niner Bravo November Mike departing the active straight-out to the east."

Linda's reply was immediate. "Ten-four, November Mike."

Jim looked over at me. "Ten-four?" he shouted with a grin. "That's one we don't hear much." He let the Cessna idle forward onto the runway, and with the yoke full over to the left to keep the wing down into the wind, he advanced the throttle. The turbocharged engine bellowed and we accelerated hard.

The little terminal building was about one third of the way down the seven-thousand-foot runway, and we were airborne long before that. The first updraft slammed the aircraft, and Bergin kept the climb angle moderate, building speed. I looked down just in time to see the landing gear on my side flop backward and disappear, and for a moment, my heart stopped.

"Where's the site?" Bergin shouted.

"You know where the Salinas Arroyo forks? Just south of Finnegan's place?"

Bergin nodded and banked to the north. I would have liked to have had a big, padded grab bar across my lap, like on one of those carnival rides. I sucked in my gut and yanked the shoulder harness tighter, then clamped my right hand on the dashboard.

As we cleared the mesa rim, an updraft kicked the Cessna so hard that we gained a thousand feet. Beyond the mesa, the wind was quartering from the northeast, and we flew crabbed sideways, the piñon and juniper scrub flowing by under my window.

What had turned into a major undertaking for Deputy Pasquale was a matter of minutes for us. The land sloped away from Cat Mesa, leveling out onto the flat, bleak prairie that stretched to the north, broken here and there by sharp out-croppings and vertical lava plugs.

Once clear of mesa influence, Bergin kept a thousand feet of air between us and the scrub below. The occasional herds of cattle ignored us. I could see dust and manure mixed into brown billows, kicked up where the cattle congregated for the night. The earth was bare, ribboned with narrow cattle trails that radiated out from the water tanks and windmills that dotted the landscape.

Off to the west, a clutter of buildings marked the southern corner of Johnny and Edwin Boyd's place. The Boyds' Circle JEB Ranch was huge, extending up to the patch of federal lands that split the county line to the north. It was country where ranchers really liked their neighbors...at a distance.

After leaving the village of Posadas, County Road 43 snaked north this way and that, up and around the east end of Cat Mesa. Crossing the ranch land north of the mesa, the road avoided the trap of Salinas Arroyo, just to the west.

Without the wind, the visibility would have been unlimited and someone with sharp eyes could have seen the evening sun wink off Tom Pasquale's patrol unit the moment the mesa was cleared. But we were flying through tan soup. The elegant, sophisticated Cessna felt like a 1953 Chevy pickup being flogged up a boulder-strewn wash.

"Lots of fun, eh?" Bergin shouted. He wasn't grinning at my discomfort. "There's a supply of bags in the pocket behind your seat, if you need 'em."

"That's not going to be a problem," I shouted back as another air pocket shook my teeth and wrenched my spine. "I'm going to need a chiropractor when we're done. I don't understand why they went flying in this kind of weather, anyway."

"Hell of a good question." He turned to scan a small hummock of oak trees that rocked by under the left wing.

The narrow strip of pavement that the county claimed as Highway 43 drifted to the northeast as the Salinas Arroyo picked up several tributaries. Bergin rested one hand on the dash and pointed straight ahead. "That's the fork," he shouted.

The Salinas widened and then, for no apparent reason, divided, with one tine swerving almost due west and the other running due north. Left in the middle was rumpled, inhospitable country with no easy access except for a handful of rough, two-track ranch roads. The main road to the Boyd ranch, County 9010, wandered west from its intersection with the pavement of County Road 43, crossing the Salinas and several other arroyos.

There were no bridges—arroyos formed and filled on their own vague schedules. When one got in the way, the two-track just plunged down one side and up the other, maybe with a little touch-up from a bulldozer if the arroyo was deep enough. As they crossed, ranchers got used to glancing upstream to make sure that a wall of water wasn't shooting down on them after a vagrant cloud had dropped its load.

Tom Pasquale had driven almost three miles west on County 9010, paralleling the smooth-sloping back of Cat Mesa. Then he had turned off the road, heading northwest across open prairie in what must have been a jouncing, kidney-bruiser of a ride.

After less than a half mile, another arroyo had blocked his path and he had tried to find his way across at what looked like a benign spot. His Bronco sat axle-deep in the sand, a target for the next rainstorm.

We flashed overhead, and Bergin initiated a sweeping turn to the east. I keyed the handheld and kept it against my lips when I spoke.

"Three-oh-three, three-ten."

By holding the speaker against my left ear, I could hear Pasquale's response clearly. "I'm about a mile and a half due

west of where the unit's parked," he said. "Right off your
right wing the way you're turning now."

Bergin continued the turn and then pulled back the throttle
and lowered a notch of flaps. It was like slowing an old pickup
from third gear to second...not much improvement, but some.

Even if I had known exactly where Pasquale was, I doubt
that I could have seen him. But Bergin did, and he dipped the
wings sharply. "He's right by that fence line." He pointed,
and I would have been more comfortable if he'd kept his
hands on the yoke. I didn't care where Pasquale was—he
wasn't the target of the search.

The radio crackled. "I think the site is about a mile or two
to the northwest," Pasquale shouted. "I'm going to make my
way over there. Let me know after you take a look."

Bergin peeled out of his tight turn and the engine sighed a
few RPMs slower. He extended the flaps another few degrees.
"Don't want to go too slow," he yelled at me.

I couldn't have agreed more. "Or too low," I said.

We flew west, methodically bucking the wind, until we'd
passed the main residence of the Boyd ranch. It was set into
the southeast-facing slope of a hill, with a fair-sized collection
of outbuildings dotted around it.

"You'd think maybe the Boyds would have seen or heard
something if a plane went down this close to their place."
Bergin shrugged and reached over to twist the throttle a quarter turn. "'Course, in this country, you just never know."

He banked the plane nice and easy and we started back
east, flying a mile north and parallel to our first pass. Back
and forth, east and west, we tracked, moving a mile farther
north each time, Bergin skillfully playing the wind.

On the fifth pass, when the Boyd ranch was hidden behind
the long swell of a cattle-trail-scarred hill, Bergin suddenly
stood the Cessna up on one wing, pushing in the throttle as
he did so.

I had a view of ground out the left window and solid sky
to the right. I braced myself and an inadvertent "Whoa!"
escaped. Bergin ignored me and continued his tight spiral,

throttle to the firewall and eyes glued out the side window. Finally he leveled off.

"Something down there, all right. Pretty good scatter." He pulled the throttle back and we sank into the wind. Five hundred feet above the prairie, he added throttle, picked up some speed and turned steeply again, reversing course. "Right over the nose," he shouted. "I'm going to make a pass with it on your side."

The Cessna slowed and Bergin tracked a straight line, letting the aircraft gradually sink. What from on high had looked like flat prairie now took on form and threat. Ahead of us, a swell of rock and scrub rose up, and if Bergin knew what he was doing, we'd skim over the trees with about a hundred feet to spare. I concentrated on watching the ground.

The northeast side of the rise was littered with junk in a long scatter, as if a giant had dumped a load of metal trash that winked in the late-afternoon sunlight. As we passed overhead, I saw several pieces tumbling in the wind, to be grabbed eventually by stunted junipers or black sage.

"That's it!" Bergin shouted and then added, "That looks like the aft fuselage and part of the empennage." He pushed in the throttle and we headed east, giving ourselves room for another turn.

This time even I could see one large piece on the side of the slope, resting amid a welter of torn metal. It was white with a blue stripe running under what was left of the registration markings.

"One more," Bergin said and turned to cross the site from north to south. "Let me see if I can make out the markings." From a hundred feet away, it wasn't difficult, even passing by at ninety miles an hour or more. "I can see the GVM," Bergin shouted, and leveled out. "And that's a Bonanza. Philip Camp was registered out of Calgary, Canada. A lot of times they don't use numbers up there. Just letters. If my memory's right, his registration was George Victor Michael Alpha."

I slumped back against the seat. "Make another pass, just

to be sure," I said, making a circular path with my index finger.

He did, and this time I saw the scarring of the earth and, many yards from the initial impact, a blocky, solid piece of wreckage that could have been an engine. West of the tail section, there was a dense collection of junk that was probably whatever was left of the main cabin.

I keyed the radio. "Tom, do you see where we've been circling?"

"Affirmative. You're about a mile or so northwest of me."

"Closer to two or three," I replied. "The wreckage is strewn across the northeast side of the rise. If you get here before dark, I don't think you can miss it. We'll orbit overhead until you've got things secured."

"Ten-four," Pasquale said. Bergin poured the coals to the Cessna and we spiraled upward, keeping the wreckage in the center of my field of view, off to the right.

I pulled the plane's mike off the dash. "Posadas Unicom, four-niner Baker November Mike. Linda, pick it up."

"Posadas, go ahead."

"Linda, give Gayle a call and have her contact the FAA in Albuquerque and advise them that we have an aircraft confirmed down. Make sure Estelle is at the office. She needs to put together a team to reach the site. The easiest way will be from the Boyd ranch and then on some of the cattle trails into the northeast. If she can come up with a helicopter from the state police, that's even better."

"Ten-four, sir."

"We intend to orbit the area until Officer Pasquale arrives and secures the site. Then we'll be returning."

"Ten-four, sir. Are there any other contacts I need to make?"

"Negative. We won't have any casualty confirmation until Pasquale reaches the scene. But tell Estelle that we don't see any sign of life down there. She'll know what to do."

"Ten-four, sir."

I hung the mike up and sighed.

"Hell of a thing," Bergin said. We hit a nasty stretch of

choppy air and we remained silent until it settled down. "Sun sets, it might calm down some. Another thirty minutes or so." He looked over at me. "I guess there isn't much doubt about whose plane that is."

"No," I replied, and that's all I could think of to say.

FOUR

THE SUN SET behind the San Cristobál mountains, the wind died, and the Cessna settled down to its job of boring a smooth hole through the air. The sky mixed with the western horizon to a dark, rich purple. The terrain lost its definition, with the hilltops blending into the sky. I sat glumly and watched the transformation.

Jim Bergin had clicked on the autopilot and dialed in a sweeping, four-mile-diameter turn. A thousand feet above the brush, we droned our patient circles as Tom Pasquale did all the hard work. I couldn't imagine stumbling across that arroyo-crossed, cholla cactus-studded landscape. One of the few consolations was that it was too early in the season for rattlesnakes.

At ten minutes after eight, the deputy reached the crash site. If I squinted hard enough, I could imagine that I saw the occasional flicker of his flashlight. A year before, Pasquale wouldn't have remembered something so simple as a flashlight as he eagerly charged into action.

I keyed the mike of the handheld. "What have you got, Tom?"

A burst of static followed, and then a hard-breathing Pasquale said, "Registration is George Victor Michael, and I think it's Alpha. Last letter, Alpha. It's pretty badly torn."

"Occupants?"

A pause followed, then, "I'm looking."

"Try more to the northwest, as the hill rises. Over near a rock outcropping." I closed my eyes and tried to visualize the terrain details, now replaced with the uniform charcoal wash of late evening.

"Ten-four."

We completed another orbit before he came back on the air. His voice was strained. "Three-ten, I've found what looks like part of the cabin structure. I think it's a section of the right side. One occupant is still belted into his seat." The radio fell silent for a moment. "Apparently the left front seat was torn from the structure at some point. I don't see it or any other occupants, if there were any. There's…there's a good-sized chunk of wing over to the left. Maybe over that way."

"Can you identify the victim strapped to the seat?" Pasquale had no way of knowing to whom the aircraft belonged, or who had been a passenger in it. I suppose I was putting off the inevitable as long as I could.

We waited through another pause, this time longer, before Tom Pasquale said, "That's negative, sir." His voice was close to cracking. "There's not enough here."

I felt a pang of sympathy for the kid. The prairie was a lonely enough place at night under the best of circumstances.

I muttered a curse, and when Bergin leaned over to hear me, I just shook my head. "More waiting," I shouted.

"I wish there was someplace I could touch down, but I'd sure hate to try it. There's that cow path over by the windmill to the west, but it's rougher'n I'd care to try, especially at night."

"No, that's not necessary," I said.

"I guess he needs to stay there, don't he?" Bergin asked. "'Til somebody can get out here?"

I nodded. "Let's go back." I keyed the handheld one more time. "Tom, we're returning to Posadas. There'll either be a chopper out here or a vehicle coming in from the Boyd ranch just as soon as we can manage it. Are you going to be all right until then?"

"Ten-four."

STEVEN F. HAVILL   29

I probably didn't need to say it, but I didn't want any screwups. "Don't leave the site, and don't touch anything," I said. "Just wait for us. And if someone from one of the ranches shows up, don't let them touch anything either."

"Ten-four."

The lights of Posadas winked into sight less than five minutes later as we cleared the mesa top. Bergin flew a conservative pattern, circling until he lined up on an eastbound final approach. I could see the lights of the terminal building, and as our tires squawked against the tarmac and we shot past the first intersection, I saw a fair collection of vehicles, including at least two from our department.

Bergin turned off the runway and gunned the engine, heading us back up the taxiway.

"I'll be around all evening," he said. "Just let me know what you folks need."

"I appreciate it," I replied. "I don't know if they've been able to round up a chopper or not." As we taxied across the broad apron, the door of the mobile home that Posadas Municipal Airport grandly called a terminal opened and Sergeant Eddie Mitchell walked quickly across to intercept us. He stopped and waited while Bergin spun the plane around against a blast of prop wash and then shut it down in front of the hangar doors.

I didn't realize how stiff I was until I nearly fell on my face getting out. Mitchell waited by the wingtip.

"Sir, Estelle's inside with Janice Holman and her sister-in-law, Vivian Camp."

I kept my voice down. "Who called them? I didn't authorize anyone to do that yet."

"They got worried that their husbands were overdue," Mitchell said. "They called and talked with Linda Real. She didn't tell them anything, but Janice Holman asked to speak with Jim Bergin. Linda told her that he was flying a charter and she didn't know when he'd be back. So the two women came on down." He gestured off toward the parking lot. "They saw your vehicle."

"What a goddam mess," I muttered, and walked to the terminal.

Janice Holman was standing with Estelle in the small pilots' lounge, looking at a wall map of New Mexico. Linda was behind the desk, radio and telephone at her elbow. The door to the rest room was closed, and I assumed that Vivian Camp was in there.

The sheriff's wife turned as I entered, and when she saw my face, she wilted, putting out a hand against the wall for support.

"Bill…" she started to say. Estelle put an arm around her shoulders.

"It doesn't look good, Jan," I said, and took her left hand. "What about the chopper?" I asked Estelle. "Any word?"

"We expect a departure from Las Cruces within the hour. Apparently there was some problem finding a flight crew."

I nodded and took a deep breath, still holding Janice Holman's hand. "One of the deputies is at the site now," I said. The door of the rest room opened and a dark-haired, chubby woman appeared, her face puffy, her eyes hollow and dark-rimmed. Vivian was younger than her sister, less angular, dressed in an expensive gray pantsuit.

"Was there any…any sign…" Janice Holman tried to say, and I brought up my other hand to hold hers in both of mine. Tom Pasquale had seen the remains of one body. If he hadn't been able to identify the man for whom he'd worked for three years, then the crash impact had been devastating.

"We're going to get out there just as soon as we can, Jan."

"But did he see anything? Anything at all?"

"It's going to be hard," I said. "That's rough country, and in the dark…" I shook my head. It wasn't the answer Janice Holman wanted to hear.

"Maybe it wasn't their plane," the sister said. She had slumped in one of the overstuffed chairs beneath the wall chart.

The sheriff's wife gripped my hands harder. "Is that a possibility, Bill?"

I looked at her for a minute and she could read the answer

in my eyes before I said, "Jim Bergin recognized the registration of the aircraft, Jan."

"But there wasn't a fire?"

"It didn't appear so," I said.

"Then there's always hope," Janice Holman said. She drew herself up, dropped my hands and covered her eyes with both hands.

"Why don't you sit down?" I asked gently, and Estelle ushered her to one of the other chairs.

Then Estelle stepped back and indicated the map on the wall. "Bob's on the way up with the other Bronco. He knows the country and said he thinks he can get within a few hundred yards of the crash site by driving all the way in to the Boyds' ranch, then cutting the fence here"—she tapped the map—"and following one of the cattle trails past the windmill, back east to the site." She looked at me. "He was going to stop at the ranch headquarters and pick up Johnny, if he's home. That way, the two of them can find the fastest route in."

"Did you get ahold of the Boyds on the phone?"

"Gayle said she'd keep trying. No one's been answering."

Looking outside, I saw Jim Bergin crossing the tarmac under the harsh light of the sodium vapors. He glanced skyward just as I heard the heavy drone of an airplane.

The radio came alive with the rapid, clipped lingo peculiar to pilots. I'd lived for forty years depending on radio communication and they still left me behind half the time.

"Bonanza niner-seven Gulf Alpha entering downwind zero-niner, Posadas."

Janice Holman and her sister reacted as if someone had slid a cattle prod under their seats. I guessed that they'd heard three magic words—Bonanza, Gulf, and Alpha. The plane was the right type, and the two letters began and ended with Philip Camp's registration.

"Oh, God," Vivian Camp said. She was on her feet and headed for the door, colliding with Jim Bergin as he entered. She lost her balance and he caught her, and for a moment, they did an awkward dance in the doorway.

"That's the UPS plane," Bergin said quietly, still holding Mrs. Camp's arm. "It comes in everyday at about this time."

As if to punctuate his remark, the voice over the radio barked something else about final for zero-niner, and we could see the bright landing lights coming in from the west. Vivian Camp wasn't willing to accept Jim Bergin's word. She stood in the doorway, clinging to the doorjamb and to Jim's arm until the Bonanza idled across the tarmac and slowed to a halt. The brown UPS van pulled up beside the plane even as the prop windmilled, and then stopped.

Vivian Camp turned away from the door, and the sobs came in great, gulping waves. She and her sister sat together, and Estelle knelt in front of them, covering their clasped hands with both of hers.

"Posadas Unicom, Bonanza niner-seven Gulf Alpha departing twenty-seven, straight out to the west." Bergin leaned across Linda Real and tapped the mike bar.

"No reported traffic, Ricky."

The radio barked two notes of squelch as the pilot keyed his own mike, and then we could hear the powerful surge of the Bonanza as it started its takeoff run.

"JetRanger Triple Eight November Mike inbound from the south. We've got the traffic in sight," another voice said, and Bergin looked across at me.

"There's your chopper," he said.

I breathed a sigh of relief, and as Estelle started to rise, I waved a hand. "Eddie and I will hook a ride out," I said. "You'll stay here?"

Estelle nodded. Janice Holman raised an agonized face and tried to say something, swallowed, and tried again.

"We should go along," she said.

"No, ma'am, you shouldn't. What would be helpful is to let Detective Reyes-Guzman take you back to the Public Safety Building. That's our communication center, and anything incoming will go through there." I tried to smile. "You'll be more comfortable."

That was a lie, of course. Neither Janice Holman nor Vivian Camp were going to be comfortable for a very long time.

FIVE

THE DOWNWASH FROM the rotors of the JetRanger tore up half an acre of New Mexico prairie as we settled to earth. A hundred yards ahead of us, caught in the harsh underbelly spotlights, stood Deputy Thomas Pasquale. Around him was the litter of what had once been Phil Camp's airplane.

A flash of light caught my eye, a set of headlights from a knoll a quarter mile to the west. If it was Bob Torrez, he'd damn near driven faster than the Bell JetRanger flew.

Eddie Mitchell hit the ground like a marine, followed by Donnie Smith, one of the state patrolmen assigned to the Posadas area. But I took my time, gingerly groping for solid footing before I released my grip on the thin door frame of the helicopter. Dr. Francis Guzman waited patiently behind me. Even as we stepped away from the chopper, the state police pilot was spooling the thing down into silence.

Pasquale walked toward us, head down against the wind and the treacherous footing. Mitchell joined him as he approached. "No survivors," the young deputy said when we were within earshot. "The pilot's over there, just a few yards from where the engine block ended up." Pasquale held up a wallet. "If this is his, then he's Philip Camp, out of Calgary, Alberta, Canada. I don't know who the passenger is. I didn't want to touch anything there."

"Philip Camp is Martin Holman's brother-in-law, Thomas," I said. "As far as we know, he and the sheriff were the only two on board."

Pasquale ducked his head. "The sheriff? You mean Martin Holman?"

I nodded and took Pasquale by the arm. "Let's go see."

Even as we walked the short distance toward the main

chunk of fuselage, I could hear vehicles in the distance. Four
sets of headlights appeared around the bottom of the mesa to
the west.

"Make sure they park behind the helicopter," I said to
Mitchell, and then Dr. Guzman, Pasquale, and I continued
toward the wreckage.

In the thirty years that I'd worked for the Posadas County
Sheriff's Department, I'd visited the scene of three air crashes.
That certainly didn't make me an expert. Within the next
twenty-four hours, investigators from the Federal Aviation
Administration and the National Transportation Safety Board
would arrive and begin their methodical sifting of the scene.
Maybe they'd have some answers for us.

I stood on a jumble of rocks, taking care to avoid the cactus. Within the range of my flashlight beam, the pieces of the
Beechcraft Bonanza spread out like confetti, making a cres-
cent-shaped scar at least a hundred yards long, maybe more.

Ahead of us, the chunk of the central fuselage was a tangle
of metal and tubing roughly the size of a small, imported
sedan that had been torn in half lengthwise. Neither wing was
attached, nor the tail aft of the rear cabin window. It would
take someone far more expert than I was to make sense of
the mess that remained. The windshield and its entire framework, including all of the cabin roof, were missing, as was
everything from the firewall forward.

"Christ," I muttered, and stepped closer so I could sweep
the flashlight beam over the wreckage. What was left of Martin Holman was belted to the right front seat, and the seat was
twisted and bent backward, mangled with the rest of the
cabin's right-side framework.

I felt a hand on my sleeve. "Let me do this, Bill," Francis
Guzman said. I nodded and held the light for him, then turned
my head so I didn't have to watch.

"Thomas," I said, "did you walk over to the east to find
the first point of impact?"

"No, sir," Pasquale said. His voice was shaking. "You
told me to stay right here, and that's what I did."

"Good man." I stood quietly and gazed off to the east. If

Philip Camp had been trying to land, the Bonanza would have been traveling in the neighborhood of eighty to a hundred miles an hour when it struck the rugged prairie. If it had hit flat, it would have been badly torn up. But it still would have been recognizable as an airplane.

If the plane had plowed straight in, or at a steep angle, the wreckage would have pulverized itself in a "smoking hole," as military pilots were wont to say.

As I stood in the dark and listened to Dr. Guzman's ragged breath behind me, I could imagine only one scenario that would have resulted in this kind of crash scatter: the Bonanza had struck the earth at a glancing angle, perhaps one wing down, at full speed—perhaps upward of two hundred miles an hour, maybe more. If that was the case, there could be a whole handful of explanations that were obvious, even to me. And an experienced pilot could provide far more, I was sure.

I had never met Philip Camp, and certainly had no idea of what kind of pilot he was—careful, careless, a hotdogger, a man who flew by the numbers, or a man who didn't pay much attention to detail. Martin Holman had mentioned in the previous week that his wife's sister and brother-in-law were planning a visit, but that had been the extent of our conversation. I didn't even remember the context of the discussion that had prompted the sheriff to mention the upcoming occasion.

"Let's look at the other one," Dr. Guzman said, and he waited for me while I made my way down off the rock pile.

One hundred and four paces later, we reached the remains of the pilot's seat. The frame was broken and the entire seat splayed out flat on the ground like a book facedown, its back broken. Thirty steps away lay most of Philip Camp's remains.

Headlights swept the area, and the cavalcade from the west pulled up in a vast cloud of dust. I could see Bob Torrez's county vehicle, along with one of the Posadas Emergency Rescue squad's four-wheel-drive Suburbans. Bringing up the rear was a pickup truck with a rack of lights across the roof, a spotlight on the driver's door pillar, and a large feed bin in the back. A dog perched on top of the feed bin, barking and dashing from one side to another.

The mutt was either well trained or tied, because when the truck jarred to a stop, it didn't leap off.

Doors slammed, but Sergeant Robert Torrez was the only person who left the group of vehicles and approached.

"Over here, Robert," I called and waved the flashlight. Torrez angled toward me, sweeping his own light from side to side as he approached.

"It is the sheriff," I said when he reached me. "Apparently just the two of them. Holman and his brother-in-law. Both dead."

"Well, my God," Torrez muttered and waved a hand back toward the vehicles. "The Boyds have a generator in the back of the truck if we need more light. Edwin said we're welcome to it."

"Light isn't what we need right now, Robert," I said. "We can take the bodies back, what's left of them, but beyond that, we're going to be waiting on the feds. Did Estelle say anything to you over the radio on your way out?"

"No, but I can't imagine that they'll be able to get investigators here much before mid-morning."

"Then all we can do is to secure the scene until they arrive," I said. "The first thing we need to do is to walk the crash track and locate the body parts."

Torrez made a little sigh, tucked his light under his arm and thrust both hands in his pockets. "That ain't going to be pretty," he muttered.

"Nope," I said. "But we don't want the coyotes, or the Boyds' dog, for that matter, making off with parts of the sheriff, either."

Torrez let out something that might have been a chuckle. I added, "And everything else stays untouched until the feds get here. Don't move a thing."

"Let's get to it," Torrez said.

"I want to use the radio in your truck first," I said. "Estelle needs to be tracking down what information she can from her end. The feds are going to want some answers when they get here…like what Philip Camp and Martin Holman were doing flying at this time of day, in weather like this."

"I didn't think the sheriff even liked to fly," Torrez said.

"He didn't. And his brother-in-law should have known better." I took a deep breath and turned back toward the wreckage. It was going to be a long night.

SIX

THE SUN CRACKED OVER the prairie to the east of us, cutting hard shadows across the scrub, arroyos, and rocks.

To the south, a herd of cattle had gathered, thinking in their own dull way that all the vehicular traffic during the night had been for their benefit, bringing in feed.

The livestock belonged to Johnny Boyd, and it was one more complication Boyd didn't need just then. Like everyone else, he was gaunt-faced and tired. He'd done more than his share during the night, moving with the rest of us as, like dark ghosts, we searched through the crash site, lights flicking this way and that.

Even his wife had returned half a dozen times with coffee, food, flashlight batteries. She had stayed near the truck each time, not wanting to venture out into the darkness. She knew what we were doing, and the last thing she wanted was to catch a glimpse of the contents of one of the black-plastic bags from the medical examiner's office.

I saw the cattle before Boyd did. He, Bob Torrez, and Donnie Smith were working carefully near the first point of impact a hundred yards to the east, getting ready to sweep their way along the strike path again now that the sun was far enough over the horizon to provide some definition for objects on the ground.

Watching my step on the rough terrain, I approached Boyd. A cigarette dangled from his mouth and he occasionally coughed short, choppy little spasms. He looked up and saw me.

"Those yours?" I asked and gestured toward the cattle.

"Sure enough," Boyd said and sighed. "This part of the prairie normally belongs to them." He grinned wryly and removed the cigarette.

"Are they going to move in closer? I'd hate to have them in here."

He coughed again. "Nah. I'll keep an eye on 'em. As soon as my brother and his boy get back, I'll have 'em drive 'em over beyond the windmill. There's a section fence there. We'll put 'em behind that." He stretched and put both hands on the small of his back.

"What happens now, you reckon?" he asked.

The smoke from his cigarette wafted past my nose. It smelled good. I hesitated, and even considered bumming one.

"The remains will go to the medical examiner," I said. "We'll get a preliminary report back in just a few hours. The details will take several days. Maybe a week. Maybe longer." I looked at Boyd. "Bob Torrez tells me you never heard the plane."

Boyd shrugged helplessly. "Never heard a damn thing."

I turned my back to the sun and looked across the swath cut by the wreckage. In each spot where a fragment of human being had been recovered, a small orange flag had been stabbed into the ground. Somewhere there was an expert who could tell me exactly what had happened—someone who could look at the trashed aluminum, steel, and plastic and tell me why the Bonanza had exploded itself and two occupants into fragments.

"The feds will be out later today. They'll pick through this bit by bit. It'll take time to reconstruct what happened, that's for sure."

"I didn't mean that," Johnny Boyd said. "I meant what happens with your department. Something like this throws a wrench in it, don't it?"

"I hadn't even thought about that," I said. "But I guess it will."

"Old Holman's been sheriff for quite sometime now, hasn't he?"

"Going on his ninth year," I said. "And I don't know what we're going to do. I suppose the county legislators will appoint someone until they get around to holding a special election."

"Hell of a note."

"Yes, it is."

"He leave much of a family behind?"

"Wife and two daughters. Both of the kids are in college."

"Hell of a note. Makes a man wonder sometimes. Here you are, goin' along just fine, thinkin' the sun's going to come up tomorrow like as it always has." He lit another cigarette from the butt of the first, then fragmented the butt between his thumb and index finger. "And then it don't."

I grunted something that Johnny Boyd could construe as agreement and let it go at that. Behind us, the sun was a full ball above the horizon, too bright to look at. And Martin Holman was pieces, flung through the rocks and cactus. For no constructive reason, the image of the Post-it note on Linda Real's application came to mind.

When Martin Holman had written that note, he'd been forty-three years old, happily married, well-thought-of in the community, and facing what he most loathed—making decisions that might create hard feelings within his department or within the community—or worse yet, create headlines in the *Posadas Register*. Sheriff Holman's decisions had involved personnel—some major realignments before summer's end.

Estelle Reyes-Guzman had announced several months earlier that she and her husband were moving to Minnesota—to a wonderful opportunity for Dr. Guzman and a major loss for us. Estelle carried the title "Chief of Detectives," but that was laughable. She was the *only* detective, the only person working in plainclothes except for the sheriff and myself.

Sergeant Robert Torrez was marrying our head dispatcher, Gayle Sedillos, and who knew what their future plans were. We all had expected them to live in Posadas until they were old and gray—but that was wishful thinking, and we knew it.

On top of that, September first was approaching—the date I'd set as my official retirement. I'd been undersheriff for the better part of twenty years, but my leaving was the least of Martin Holman's problems. The department had three sergeants—Eddie Mitchell, Howard Bishop, and Robert Torrez. Anyone of them could fill the position in a heartbeat, and any of the three could accomplish more in their sleep than I did in a day's work.

I was sure that Linda Real didn't consider herself a problem, but her application was in my folder, awaiting action. And Martin Holman's Post-it note was still lying on my desk blotter back at the office—perhaps the last thing he ever wrote before deciding to take an air tour of Posadas.

"Hell of a mess," I said, and patted Johnny Boyd on the shoulder. I walked back toward one of the department vehicles, deep in thought. If Martin Holman had wanted an air tour of his county, he could have asked Jim Bergin any day. He could have picked a nice, cool morning, when the air was silk.

I reached the Bronco and saw Tom Pasquale sitting on the back, the tailgate down and the spare tire swung wide, out of the way. His shoulders slumped, and he started to get up when he saw me. I waved a hand and shook my head. "Relax, son. There's coffee over in Boyd's truck, if you want it."

"No, sir," he said quickly. "Coffee and I don't agree." He wiped his mouth and looked off into the distance.

"Are you all right?"

"Yes, sir." The light wasn't really good yet and I couldn't see the expression in his eyes. But I knew that if Tom Pasquale had been "all right," he'd have been in motion, his natural state of affairs. "I guess I need to hook a ride back to the office before too long and do something about my unit, sir."

"Your unit?"

"The other Bronco. It's still out in the arroyo."

I chuckled and leaned against the vehicle. "That's the least of our problems, that's for sure. Forget it. I'll have one of the county wreckers go out and haul its sorry carcass out of the sand. Don't worry about it.''

Tom Pasquale nodded, relieved that he didn't have to move just then. Another pair of vehicles had arrived, sending up dust plumes from the new road that had been cut across the Boyd property. Most of our department was accounted for. Estelle was back at the office, and if someone robbed a bank, she and Gayle Sedillos would have to handle it, with Linda Real lending some unofficial help.

''Do you know what he was doing out here?'' Pasquale asked. He pushed himself to his feet. He was a head taller than I am, forty years younger, and he outweighted me by forty pounds. As bad as he felt just then, I could see he was hungry for answers, and that was a good sign.

''No idea, Thomas.''

''I don't understand why he and his brother-in-law would be flying over this place, anyway. There's nothing here.''

''Just sightseeing, maybe.''

Pasquale shook his head in disbelief. ''What's there to see? The sheriff hated to fly almost as much as you do.''

I looked at him sharply. ''How do you know that?''

He ducked his head. ''Well, that's what everybody always says. If he wanted to tour, I can't imagine him choosing to do it in the weather we had yesterday.''

''So what else comes to mind, son?''

''His brother-in-law just got done flying all the way down here from Canada. And Sergeant Mitchell said that Camp had been flying planes for twenty-five years. I can't imagine he'd be so eager to jump in a plane and tour Posadas County just before dinner. He'd be tired. The weather was bad.'' He shook his head doggedly. ''It just doesn't make sense, is all.''

''So Camp was a veteran pilot?''

''Sergeant Mitchell said the two wives were talking about that. That's why they couldn't believe that anything bad could have happened.''

''Well,'' I said, ''something did happen. It's that simple.''

Pasquale nodded and looked off toward the horizon. He

took a deep breath and hitched up his Sam Brown belt. "Sir, when the feds get here, may I ask to be assigned to them?"

"I'll mention it to Sergeant Torrez, Tom."

He turned and looked at me. "I screwed up a lot over the years, and it was Sheriff Holman who finally gave me a chance and hired me on. I'd like to be a part of finding out what happened out here."

"I'll talk with Torrez," I repeated, and didn't bother mentioning that the single biggest roadblock to Pasquale's hiring had been myself. When the kid finally had proved to us that he had a head on his shoulders, I'd approved his application.

Sheriff Martin Holman had been willing to give Tom Pasquale a chance; he'd sounded willing to do the same for Linda Real. He'd had good reasons for both, I was sure, since no man that I knew hated the thought of making an incorrect decision more than Marty Holman.

There were dozens of reasons that should have kept Martin Holman from sliding into that Bonanza on that choppy, blustery afternoon at Posadas Municipal Airport. Tom Pasquale was right. We needed to know the one compelling reason that had pushed Martin Holman and his brother-in-law into the air.

SEVEN

JANICE HOLMAN hugged me, wordlessly, for a long time. I looked over her shoulder at her two daughters, Ellie and Tracie. They were trying their hardest to be brave and thoughtful and considerate for the sake of the two dozen or so people who cluttered the Holman living room just then. Except for the long faces and tears, it could have been a gathering for a political brunch.

Despite Sheriff Holman's continual fight with them over

nickels and dimes during the rest of the year, two of the county legislators—Tobe Ulibarri and Sammy Carter—stood now by the sofa, each uncomfortable and stiff, each balancing a coffee cup for want of anything better to do.

Janice shifted position with a loud sigh and half turned so that she could put an arm around Estelle Reyes-Guzman. The three of us remained motionless for another thirty seconds or so, and everyone else in the large living room left us alone.

"Janice," I said finally, "we need to talk with you and Vivian, if you can manage a few minutes." Estelle turned to intercept one of the Holmans' neighbors who couldn't help but press in at the wrong moment. The detective engaged the woman in quiet conversation while we pulled away.

Martin Holman's wife nodded and leaned close. "Let's try the back porch," she said. She almost managed a smile. "I think Vi is out in the kitchen."

The mid-morning sun hadn't touched the redwood arbor over the back porch, but the air was warm and soft. In a moment, Estelle and the two women stepped out. Janice Holman immediately walked over and took my hand in hers, as if afraid I might stray away more than a step or two.

Her eyes, red-rimmed and puffy, nevertheless bored directly into mine. "We won't know what caused this for some time, will we?"

"No," I said. "We're expecting investigators from the National Transportation Safety Board this morning. If there are answers, they'll find them."

She nodded slowly, reaching out as she did so to take Vivian Camp's hand as well.

"We need to know if there was any particular reason why Martin and Philip went up yesterday afternoon," I said. "It would help if you can remember anything they talked about, anything at all. Was it just impulse or what?"

Janice Holman closed her eyes, whether against the pain or just to help herself think—or both—I couldn't tell.

"The only thing I can remember," she said, "is that Martin had been telling Phil that there was only one little corner of the county he'd never seen from the air." She shrugged helplessly. "Phil and Vi were planning to leave tomorrow for home, so maybe it was just one of those spur-of-the-moment things."

"You don't remember anything specific, then?"

She shook her head.

"Do you remember when he said that? About there being a part of the county he wanted to see from the air?" It seemed to me that the comment in itself was unusual. I'd known Marty Holman for a decade, and flying was far from being a passion with him—or even a passing interest. On the rare occasions when I'd requisitioned Jim Bergin's charter services for the department, Holman had always blanched at the cost.

She shook her head again, but Vivian Camp said, "We were out to dinner Tuesday night, and Philip and I had been talking about all the trips we'd taken around the country. Martin said that he didn't care anything at all about flying, but that he'd managed to tour most of the county." She blinked. "He said it for a joke. We'd traveled the whole country, and he'd managed to cross the county."

Estelle Reyes-Guzman had settled on the corner of a large planter, her hands clasped in her lap, shoulders hunched forward as if she were chilled. "Janice, yesterday afternoon, before the two men went down to the airport, did they mention to you, or to either of you, why they were going flying at that moment? Or where they were going?"

"Phil was saying that as the sun went down, the air would get smoother," Vivian said. "That's all I can remember him saying." She wiped at her left eye. "I wasn't paying any attention."

Janice squeezed my hand. "Could they have talked to Jim?"

"Jim Bergin said he was caught up doing something when they came in and that he exchanged only a word or two with them over the radio as they taxied out. Apparently Phil said something about being back within the hour."

Estelle shook her head, gazing off into the distance. "How long had you folks owned that airplane?"

Vivian flinched, and I saw the muscles working in her jaws.

"We bought it new in nineteen eighty-four. Phil was proud of the fact that in fifteen years, he was the only pilot who had ever flown it."

"It was like new, then."

"'Pampered' would be a good word," Janice said, and I was surprised at the lightness that she could force into her voice. Vivian didn't disagree with the assessment.

"And you've been down here before on different occasions?" Estelle asked. "Visiting family?"

"At least once a year," Vivian said.

"So there was no particular reason why Phil would want to show Martin anything about the plane. No new paint job, no new special avionics, nothing like that?"

She shook her head, and Estelle added, "The sheriff had been up in that airplane on other occasions?"

"Yes. Several times. Last year we flew to Phoenix for a weekend."

"I remember that," I said.

"Did you have any trouble of any kind with the aircraft on the flight down from Canada?" Estelle asked.

"None," Vivian Camp said quickly. "Not for an instant."

I looked down at the porch floor and frowned.

"Tell me what you're thinking, Bill," Janice said.

"I don't know what to think," I replied and took a deep breath. "Janice, the NTSB people will want to talk to you both, too. I'll make sure they call first. But it'll be helpful if each of you can think back to the conversations you had in the past day or two. Anything at all that can give us a clue."

"God," Janice Holman said heavily. "What I'd give to be able to tell you something."

"I know," I said, and squeezed her hand. "It's going to be rough. But we'll do all we can. I'll be by off and on, but you call me at anytime if there's anything I can do."

Estelle and I drove away a few minutes later, leaving Janice Holman and Vivian Camp to cope with their houseful. Thinning the numbers by two was probably the most helpful thing we could have done for them.

Estelle's dark face was set in a frown, her black eyebrows furrowed, as we drove out of the neighborhood.

"I think we need to find out why they went sightseeing late in the afternoon of a rough day when they had no need to do so, when there wasn't the attraction of a new plane, or of a first-time ride or anything like that. When Martin didn't even particularly like to fly," I said.

"And the feds will be looking into Phil Camp's record, too," Estelle said quietly.

"Sure. I'm no crash investigator, but it's obvious to me that the plane hit the ground at a shallow angle, traveling at high speed. Maybe the sort of thing that would result from buzzing the ground. Hotdogging." I glanced over at Estelle. She was still frowning.

"Do you have time now to run by and talk with Jim Bergin?" she asked.

"That's where I was headed next," I said. I glanced at my watch.

But the airport manager had no magic answers for us. Although he hadn't talked to either man before the Bonanza departed on its last flight, he had watched from the far end of the big hangar while Phil Camp did his preflight inspection.

"I've met Phil Camp a number of times," Bergin said, leaning back in his swivel chair, his left hand resting on top of the radio console. "He's always impressed me as a careful, considerate pilot. I watched 'em when they took off, because it was so bouncy. Camp didn't do anything fancy. No steep climbs, no turns out of the pattern halfway down the runway, none of that shit that we see all the time."

"Could the crash have been caused by engine failure, do you think?" I asked.

Bergin grunted. "That was a good, strong airplane. But things break. The crash could have been caused by one of ten thousand things. But if the engine had quit out there over the prairie, someone as experienced as Camp would have had ten dozen places to pick for a landing spot. And even if he miscalculated his approach and dumped it into a bar ditch or something, that airplane still would have been traveling at only eighty or ninety knots when it touched down. On top of that"—he waved a hand as he groped a cigarette out of his pocket with the other—"the wind was kickin' and he'd have been headed into that. So subtract twenty knots, and his actual touchdown speed would have been fifty, sixty knots." He took a deep drag and exhaled. "And that Bonanza was flat humpin' when it hit the ground. It wasn't mushing in for a landing. No siree."

"I can't see Phil Camp or Martin Holman wanting to chase coyotes," Estelle said.

Jim Bergin shot her a quick glance. "That's the usual way pilots get in trouble," he said. "Too low and too slow. He wasn't slow. How old a man was he?"

"Camp? I think fifty-two or three, maybe. He was older than Holman by a bit."

"Heart attack, maybe," Bergin said. "Who the hell knows? That plane had one of those swing-over control yokes. If Camp had died suddenly, he could have fallen forward on the yoke, maybe. Holman would have had hell trying to get him off and swinging the yoke over so he could use it—assuming that he knew how." Bergin shook his head and gazed out the tinted window at the asphalt. "The feds will find some answers for you. It's probably something so simple we'll be surprised we didn't see it." He grinned. "They'll take their own sweet time, of course."

His telephone rang and he twisted to pick up the receiver. I was about to say something to Estelle when Bergin said into the phone, "Yes, he's here. You want to talk to him?" He grunted something else and then handed me the phone. "Sam Carter," he said.

I took the receiver. Carter had seen me at Holman's only moments before and could have talked to me then.

"Gastner," I said.

"Bill, Sam Carter. Listen, can we get together sometime today for a few minutes?"

"Well," I started to say, but Carter interrupted me.

"It's really important. I know you're busy, but if you can spare just a handful of minutes, I'd appreciate it."

"I guess," I said without much enthusiasm. "Estelle and I are about wrapped up here."

He said something I didn't catch, then added, "I mean, can I meet with just you? I need to talk to you personal-like."

"I'll be at the sheriff's office in a few minutes. You want to stop by?"

"How about my office in an hour?" he said quickly, and I didn't see the point of arguing.

"See you then," I said and handed Bergin the phone. "Jim, thanks. I'm sure this place is going to be the center of the storm for a few days."

"I'll be here. You need anything, you just holler."

As we got back into the car, I said, "I wonder what Sam Carter wants."

Estelle shrugged and left it at that. I added, "That's going to be an interesting conversation." One corner of her mouth twitched just a bit, and the crow's-foot by the corner of her left eye deepened for an instant.

"I can tell you right now what he's going to say," she said.

"I'd rather wait and let it be a surprise," I told her. "We'll compare notes later. Keep the heat on the medical examiner's office for some preliminary results. And then you and I have to find a quiet corner and do some serious talking ourselves."

She nodded, and we drove the rest of the way back to the Public Safety Building in silence.

EIGHT

THE ELECTRONIC EYE saw me and snapped open the big glass doors of the Trust Super Market. The place was quiet and smelled of bleach and floor wax, and then, as I took a few steps in, the other odors—most of them from a display of baked goods off to my left—wafted over to greet me.

The first in a line of four checkout registers was to my right, and Taffy Hines was working there, bent over a large bound volume of computer printouts splayed over the conveyor.

"Is Sam around?" I asked, and Taffy looked up quickly. She was fortyish, a bleached blonde, and had the sort of facial wrinkles that hinted at too many cigarette breaks.

"He's out back," she said and gestured down an aisle.

I walked between chips, soft drinks, and bottled water for several yards, heading toward the dairy case and the white, windowless door beside it.

Before I reached it, Sam Carter rounded the corner, his lean face set in grim lines.

"Glad you could come by," he said, shaking my hand. His grip was dry and limp. "Let's find us a quiet corner."

He led me through the door by the dairy case and then up a short flight of stairs. His office was cramped, with only enough room for a single large folding table, two chairs, and the junk that made his business go. He pushed a pile of papers out of my way so I had a place to prop an elbow.

He stopped fussing finally and settled into his old-fashioned swivel chair. What would appear to customers to be the polished mirror over the meat-display case was actually his office window. He had a good view of the place, and I could look out and see, fifty yards away, Taffy Hines still mulling over the computer readout.

"So," I said.

Carter leaned forward with both forearms on his knees. He cocked his head at me, one eyebrow up. "Did you ever imagine something as terrible as this?" he asked.

I shook my head.

"God," he said, and leaned back in the chair, gazing out the window at his customerless store.

He turned his head and regarded me. The index finger of his left hand strayed to his mouth and he bit the nail. "I talked to Tobe this morning," he said, "and to Hewitt earlier."

Hewitt Stewart was a third county commissioner.

"We're calling a special meeting for Monday afternoon at one. We'd sure like for you to be there."

I nodded slowly. "I can do that, I guess. It's going to be an awkward time, Sam."

"Federal boys be in town sometime today?"

"Yes."

"And no telling how long they'll be involved, is there?"

"No."

He nodded quickly. "That's really no concern of mine, or anyone else's outside of your bailiwick. And that's not why I asked you to drop by. Let me get right to the point."

He leaned forward again, brow furrowed. "This goes no farther than this room," he said. I raised an eyebrow and didn't reply.

"The county commission wants to appoint you in Sheriff Holman's place until elections."

I looked at Carter quizzically and then asked, "Why would they want to do that?"

Surprise flickered across his face, and the fingernail went back between his teeth. "It's the only thing that makes sense to us just now," he said.

"I'm retiring in September," I pointed out. "And the department has three good sergeants. You could appoint anyone of them and you wouldn't lose a minute's sleep over your choice. Bob Torrez is senior, and he's smart, steady, and a good leader. Howard Bishop is no ball of fire, but he's honest and thorough. Eddie Mitchell's got his rough edges, but he'd do the job." I shrugged. "The last thing the county needs is a sixty-eight-year-old warhorse with enough health problems to keep the county hospital solvent."

"I can't imagine Bob Torrez would take it any too kindly if we passed him by for one of the others," Carter muttered.

"He'd get over it. And if he's got any political ambitions, he keeps 'em to himself. But he's your natural choice."

"What about Estelle Reyes-Guzman? You don't think she'd jump at the chance? Hell, she didn't lose that last election by too much. If you didn't want the job, wouldn't she be next in line? And the way you two work together, you'd probably recommend her.''

The tone of his voice told me what his real worry was, and I took a deep breath.

"If she were staying in Posadas, sure. And a better sheriff you couldn't have. But her husband has taken a job in Minnesota. It's a hell of an opportunity for them. I don't think she's about to stay behind just so she can be appointed to fill in until the election. I think one stab at politics was enough for her, anyway.''

Estelle had run against Martin Holman in a surprisingly genteel and civil race, and the loss she'd taken at the polls had told both of us that Posadas County wasn't ready for a female Mexican sheriff.

Carter leaned back again, relaxing. He held up both hands. "Let me tell you what the others have in mind. And I agree with 'em. This all hit us pretty fast, you understand. But it's a concern. The commission wants you to fill in until November. That gives everyone who wants a shot at the office time to run through the primaries this June, and to go about it without rushing into something they might regret.''

"And gives you folks time to find a candidate you like,'' I said with a smile. I wondered who he and his political cronies had in mind, but I didn't care enough to ask. Martin Holman had certainly been a good, straight-arrow Republican, a member of all the right service clubs. On top of that, he'd turned out to be a quick study. I knew I was going to miss him, and I knew I didn't have the energy left to train a replacement.

Carter shrugged. "Politics is politics, Bill. The county sheriff's position is one of the most important ones there is. With all the civil litigation and so forth, we've got to have someone in there who knows the ropes.''

"If you want my advice, Torrez is your first choice. Then Bishop. Then Mitchell.''

"If one of them wants to run for the office, then that's fine,'' Carter said. "But until that time, the county commission wants to appoint you. You know Martin Holman's policies better than anyone else. You know what he was trying to accomplish. Nothing else makes sense.''

"I'm no administrator, Sam. I'm a cop. I don't even do the civil legwork for the department. Holman always did that, along with Sergeant Bishop and Deputy Mears.''

Carter leaned forward, reached out and touched my knee. "Then think of it this way if you want to get right down to cases. Who does more road patrol work, you or Bob Torrez?''

"He does, of course.''

"And who does more road work, you or Eddie Mitchell?''

"Mitchell, hands down.''

"You supervise them, don't you?''

"Sure.''

"Does it make sense, in a county as strapped as this one is for both personnel and funds, to take one of those two boys off the road and tie him behind a desk? To ask one of them to learn the ropes of a job he's never done before? Hell, you've filled in for Marty Holman before, when he went on vacations and such. And a decade or so ago, you filled in for Eduardo Salcido, when he had his heart attack.''

I frowned. "All right, so I'm the expendable one.''

"That's not what I said," Carter snapped, "but if that's what it takes to talk some sense into your head, think of it that way. The young kids belong out on the road. You've got twenty-five years' experience, and hell, you've been undersheriff for fifteen or twenty years. Do the county a favor and fill in for us. Just until after the November elections.''

I shrugged, seeing no reason to play coy. If Carter and the other commissioners had an ulterior motive in moving so quickly, before Martin Holman's shattered bones were even off the autopsy table, that was their affair.

"All right," I said.

Carter nodded vigorously. "Just for the sake of continuity, if nothing else. I'll sleep a lot better, that's for sure.'' He smiled and stood up. "I know you're busy. But come Monday, if you can breakaway for a few minutes, we'd appreciate it. If there's anything we need to do, you be sure to tell us at the meeting Monday.''

We shook hands and I left the Trust SuperMarket Grocery. Maybe Sammy Carter would sleep better. But after the previous twenty-four hours, I'd have cheerfully traded any possibility of early retirement for one decent night's sleep. Now I wasn't going to get either one.

NINE

A GUST OF WIND drove sand into our faces, and Vincent Buscema tucked his head and closed his eyes.

"Wonderful," he muttered. To his left, a piece of torn aluminum began a slow, easy roll toward the east. "Secure that, son," he said, and Tom Pasquale jumped like he'd been shot. Buscema looked at me out of squinting eyes. "This is going to be holy hell," he said. Wind tore at his jacket, snapping the nylon around his waist and flattening the large NTSB letters across his back...I could see the curve of his shoulder blades and spine through the fabric.

He turned and looked off to the southeast, where a small party of federal investigators and two Posadas County sheriff's deputies were working. "At least we know something," he said. "We've got the exact initial-impact spot, and the markings on the prop tell us that the engine was putting out power at the time of impact." He hitched up his collar. "If they can find the missing propeller blade tip, we'll know a little more."

"You'll tear down the engine?" I shouted over the wind.

Buscema nodded. "That's going to take some time." He thrust his hands in his pockets. "Compared to a jumbo jet or something like that, a Bonanza is a pretty simple airplane, Sheriff. It's usually not hard to pinpoint a problem if mechanical failure was to blame. What we're going to do"—he pivoted at the waist to look back into the wind and the sun—

"is make as thorough a survey of this site as we can before we move anything. Establish the angle of impact, probable direction of flight, all those simple things."

He grinned at the expression on my face. The jumble of junk in front of me didn't look "simple," even if the wind stopped shifting it around, but I was willing to take Buscema's word for it.

"And then we take a look for the obvious things." He held up an index finger. "Number-one cause of all crashes is pilot error, Sheriff. That's number one. It's a good bet that Philip...what was his name?"

"Camp. Philip Camp."

"It's a good bet that Mr. Camp made a mistake. That's what the statistics tell us. If the weather had been really bad, with low ceiling, crap like that, I'd be willing to bet next month's wages on pilot error. But this is a bit more complicated. It was clear and windy—not perfect flying weather, but still, not so bad. What we know for sure is one big, fat, humongous fact." He paused and I raised an eyebrow to prompt him.

"He was flying too goddam low. The airplane hit the ground at a shallow angle. Not enough to skip like a rock across water, but pretty shallow nevertheless." He shrugged and tucked a hand in his pocket. "If he'd been cruising along at ten thousand feet above the ground, this kind of violent scatter crash wouldn't have happened." He made a corkscrew motion with his other hand. "Let's say something really bizarre happened. Let's say he was trying to show his brother-in-law how he could do a barrel roll. He gets all crossed up, and the end result is that the plane sheds a wing. Or a serious chunk of empennage. What comes down is a ball of junk. Not smithereens like this."

Buscema turned his back to the wind and pulled his cap down tight on his head. "I'll be willing to bet that they were flying fast and low. You know why?"

"Because the sheriff wanted to look at something. That's the only reason I can think of that explains why they'd be over here. Philip Camp had no reason to be curious. The sheriff might have.''

"That's right. You know Martin Holman and his work better than anyone, Mr. Gastner. You told me that he didn't like to fly. He didn't like to spend county money. So he could have driven out here, couldn't he?''

I nodded. "He could have," I said, "but my guess is that time was a factor. He saw an opportunity and decided to con a free ride out of his brother-in-law. They could do in a few minutes what would take most of the day by ground vehicle.''

"And what the hell was there to see, anyway? Dust, open prairie, and an occasional herd of cattle. Hell of a thing to die for.'' Buscema paused. "And you said he had a camera with him?''

"Yes. It's been recovered. One of our deputies is processing the film.''

"Well,'' Buscema said in dismissal, "don't hold your breath.'' He wrenched the bill of his cap down again. "Now, a lot of people will fly low to get out of mountain chop. You get down a little closer to the ground, right over the tops of the trees, and there's better visual reference.'' He grinned. "It's more like riding in an old freight wagon on a bouncy road. But you've got stuff in your visual horizon and you're less apt to get airsick. Way up high, you get to feeling sort of detached when you're bouncing around. See what I mean? And it still doesn't tell us why they were over here, or what they were doing.''

He took a couple of steps to his left and knelt down to look at a tangle of instrumentation and engine controls. "What we need to do is stick with what we do know. The remains of the cockpit controls make a few things pretty clear.''

He pointed first at one twisted piece and then at another.

"There were no flaps dialed in. She was flying clean. Trim was where we'd expect it to be for level cruise flight. Cruise throttle setting, too. Not maximum, not pulled back for descent. Just cruise, running right at sixty-five percent or a little better. Nothing unusual about manifold pressure settings, at least judging by the position of the controls. Prop in cruise pitch. Gear up and locked. Plenty of fuel, and fuel selector in the expected place. In fact, why he didn't make a fireball after impact is only God's guess.''

"Everything normal," I said. "You don't think that maybe the plane could have shed the tip of the propeller while in flight?"

"No, I don't. I might be wrong, but the odds of that are a long shot. If that's what happened, he would have slammed in some engine-control changes to take care of the vibration. And let me tell you, that would be enough to shake the engine right off its mounts in nothing flat. So, if he had half a brain and that's what happened, we'd expect to see the throttle pulled out to stop, and if he had the time, maybe the prop pitch messed with one way or another. But that's not what we've got.''

He touched a toggle switch. "At least not at first glance. The autopilot was disengaged, so the pilot was doing the flying.'' He looked off to the east again. "Where does the woman live who first reported the problem?"

"Charlotte Finnegan." I pointed toward a rugged knoll a mile distant. "Her ranch is another four miles or so beyond that, right on the county road.''

"And she told you that she saw an aircraft in trouble?"

"That's what she told the dispatcher. And last month, she told the dispatcher that she'd heard two tractor-trailer trucks collide head-on just down the road from their ranch, too. What she really heard was a piece of tin blow off one of the shed roofs and hit the kitchen wall.''

"Ah…I see. One of that kind. But this time she didn't explain what 'trouble' meant concerning the airplane?"

"No."

"Have you talked with her since?"

"No. I haven't had a chance.''

"Then we'll want to do that. In fact, how about if we do that right now? Milliman will keep after this. I've got a hunch that the airplane isn't going to let us in on any secrets. Maybe the medical examiner will." He glanced at his watch. "Is your man pretty prompt?"

"My man?"

"The coroner. Is he going to make us wait, or is he on top of things.?"

Doctors Alan Perrone and Francis Guzman were handling the initial examination for us, and it was clear that Vincent Buscema didn't know either one of them.

"We'll know the results as soon as they're in," I said.

"Then let's go chat with this Finnegan lady." He gestured at the hill. "It's just a few minutes over there. This is a good time."

I grinned. "There're no 'few minutes' about anything around here, Vincent. And if we're going to talk with Charlotte Finnegan, I'd like to take my chief of detectives with me."

"Where's he at?"

"She. And she's at the medical center, where the autopsy's in progress. We can pick her up there and head on out. It means some backtracking, but if we want to talk with Mrs. Finnegan, we'll want Detective Reyes-Guzman along, believe me."

"What, she's a Mexican woman?"

"Mrs. Finnegan? No. She's just not the sort of person you'll want to deal with by yourself. You'll need the backup."

Buscema looked puzzled, but let it go at that.

TEN

IN THE PREVIOUS twelve hours, there had been enough vehicular traffic to wear a well-marked road across Johnny Boyd's property. I could follow the route in my sleep, and just then, that didn't sound like such a bad idea.

I drove south along the fence line to a gate in the barbed

wire that Boyd had cut for us and waited while the federal investigator struggled with the wire closure and then walked the gate to one side to let me drive through.

He grunted back into the Bronco and slammed the door. "Does this wind ever stop out here?"

"Sure," I said. "It'll get so still that the windmills won't turn for an hour at a time."

"That's something I'd like to see," he said and peered out the side window as we skirted the first series of stock tanks, the water brimming over the rims as the eight-foot Aermotor blades spun in a steady blur. The area around each tank was pockmarked by the hooves of the cattle into a thick, rich goo about the color of chocolate pudding.

"Gets hot out here in the summer, I bet," Buscema said.

"Beyond hot," I told him.

For another ten minutes, we thumped along an east-west fence, dodged to the south again to cross a rugged arroyo, and then followed the base of a small mesa until we reached an established dirt road that shot due north from the Boyds' home to another windmill.

By the time we had driven a quarter mile on their ranch road, the fine dust had sifted into the vehicle, pungent and cloying in the back of the throat.

The road led straight to the Boyds' ranch house, and we kept the speed down while driving through their yard. Just behind the barn, we thumped across a cattle guard and pulled up onto the graveled surface of County Road 9010. This was barely a track and a half wide, but in comparison to jouncing across the open mesa, it was a boulevard.

We drove due east and before long, reached the intersection with County Road 43, the paved arterial that would take us to Posadas.

I paused at the stop sign and pointed to the left, toward the north. "The Finnegans live up that way about a mile. Remember the last cattle guard?" Buscema nodded. "All the land on this side of that fence line belongs to Richard Finnegan. On the west side, it's Johnny and Edwin Boyd's."

"Big spreads," Buscema said.

"With not much on them," I replied and pulled the Bronco out onto the county road. Buscema hefted his briefcase onto his lap and snapped it open. For the next several minutes, he was engrossed in his paperwork.

We were still three miles north of Posadas, humming along on blessedly smooth pavement, when the mobile phone beside me chirped.

"Hi-tech stuff," Buscema said as he watched me fumble the thing to my ear. With my other hand, I turned on the radio. "Gastner."

"Sir, this is Linda."

For a moment, my mind went blank, but experience had taught me not to bother fighting it. "Linda who?" I asked.

"Linda Real, sir. Gayle has been trying to raise you on the radio and I've been working the phone."

"We've been out of range on both counts," I said. I didn't bother to add that the radio hadn't been turned on until that moment. "What's up?"

"Estelle said it's important that you swing by the hospital at your first opportunity, sir."

"She's got some news for us?"

"I don't know, sir. That's all she said. She did say that if we weren't able to reach you by"—she paused—"seventeen hundred hours, we should send a deputy up to the site for you."

I glanced at the clock on the dash. We'd saved a deputy a long, rough ride by six minutes. "We're just coming down the hill past the mine. ETA about six minutes."

"I'll inform her, sir."

"Thanks." I dropped the phone on the seat and glanced at Buscema. "Something from the hospital. I don't know what."

Less than a mile from town, another department vehicle passed us northbound. It was Sergeant Mitchell, flying low. As he passed us, the radio squelched twice, and even before I had time to wonder where he was bound, I saw his four-by-four slow abruptly, turn around and charge after us.

"Three-ten, three-oh-seven."

I picked up the mike. "Three-ten."

"Three-ten, did you copy the message from three-oh-six?"

"Ten-four. We're heading to the med center now."

Buscema glanced at his watch. "Are your boys usually this eager?" he asked.

"They better be," I said.

"Are most of the deputies locals? Homegrown?"

"Some are. Some not. Sergeant Mitchell, the hot-rod in our rearview mirror, spent about five years in Baltimore."

"Now that's a little cultural shock," Buscema said. "What keeps him here?"

"I don't know," I said. I grinned at him. "The peace and quiet, maybe." We entered the village and turned southwest on Pershing. I knew the hospital's layout intimately after hundreds of visits over the last decade since the facility's construction, and knew exactly how to save time and steps. I parked in an "Ambulance Only" slot near the emergency-room door. Mitchell pulled in beside me.

Estelle Reyes-Guzman was waiting for us. I introduced her to Buscema, and the federal agent's eyebrows shot up for just a second before he nodded brusquely and recovered his composure.

"Francis is waiting in X-ray," Estelle said, and we followed her down the polished, antiseptic hallway, made a shortcut through the kitchen and then took the back door to X-ray, avoiding the waiting room out front. I trailed Estelle and Buscema and noticed that the federal agent kept close watch on Estelle's every move.

Dr. Francis Guzman was on the telephone when we entered his domain, and he glanced over at the four of us, holding up an index finger while he finished his conversation. "Sure," he said and then hung up.

"This is Vincent Buscema from the National Transportation Safety Board," I said. They shook hands and then Francis looked across at me. He was handsome in a rugged, bearded sort of way, and his dark eyes shared the same deep inscrutability as his wife's.

"Dr. Perrone is still working, but I wanted you folks to see this prelim," he said and stepped over to a polished counter.

He picked up a small plastic bag and handed it to me. I took it and rearranged my bifocals so I could see the specimen, or at least pretend that I could. It appeared to be a chunk of brass, no more than an eighth of an inch on a side, roughly rhomboid-shaped.

"What is it?" Buscema asked.

"If I had to guess," Francis said, "I'd say that it was part of the jacket from a rifle bullet."

The silence that followed was so intense that I could count the gentle pulses of the air-conditioned breeze out of the ceiling vents.

"No shit," Buscema said finally.

"Look here," Francis said, and with one hand on my elbow, he pulled me toward the long clipboarded viewing wall. Several X rays were fastened in place—vague, shadowed portraits of mysterious inner-body parts.

"There's more," Francis said, and he touched the first X ray with the tip of his silver ballpoint pen. "As nearly as we can determine so far, the path of the bullet—or whatever it was—was at a steep angle upward. The piece you're holding"—he turned and nodded at the plastic envelope—"is one of two pieces that ended up right here. The other fragment is actually quite a bit smaller."

"And where's that?"

"The track looks like it came up and unzipped the descending aorta, right below the heart. There's a tear there that's nearly four centimeters long."

I frowned and leaned closer, trying to make sense of the shadows and highlights. "I don't understand," I said. "Who was shot?"

"Mr. Camp."

I looked at Francis in astonishment. "You're trying to tell me that Philip Camp was shot? He was shot in his own airplane?"

Francis nodded. "It appears that way, sir."

"By who?" Buscema asked, and immediately grimaced, realizing it was a stupid question. He waved his hand and then tapped the X ray. "You're saying that you found bullet fragments? Is there anyway you could be mistaken?'' He reached over and took the plastic bag from me, peering closely at the specimen. ''It sure as hell is.''

''And even if it's not from a bullet as such,'' Estelle said, ''it's a piece of a projectile that was traveling fast enough to penetrate a considerable distance as it was fragmenting.''

''Did you look at any of those pieces under a stereoscope?'' I asked, and when Estelle nodded, I added, ''And what did you find?''

''I'm sure the fragments are from a bullet. One of them has what look like rifling marks. Really pretty clear. Eddie agrees.'' I glanced at Mitchell, and he nodded soberly.

''Where are the rest?''

''Deputy Abeyta is with Dr. Perrone now, down in Autopsy. He and Eddie were cataloging each fragment as it was found. When I was sure of what we had, I sent Eddie up after you.''

I leaned against one of the polished stainless-steel tables. ''So you're saying that Philip Camp was shot,'' I said. If I said it enough times, maybe I'd believe it. ''What about Martin Holman?''

Francis shook his head. ''Nothing yet. Nothing has shown up in X ray. Nothing at all.''

''So,'' I said, ''from the ground?'' I stood up and advanced on the X ray once again. ''Nothing else makes sense.''

''It looks like one bullet. It struck Mr. Camp low in the back, just above the pelvis. My guess is that's where some of the shattering took place. At least two pieces continued on for some distance, stopping where you see them in the X ray.''

''And if the aorta was opened up, death would have been instantaneous,'' Buscema said flatly.

''Just about. Seconds at most.'' Francis held his thumb and index finger two inches apart. ''You've got a tear that long. He wouldn't have had time to do more than take a couple of breaths. That little piece of brass is like a fragment of a razor blade. Just unzips the artery.''

''He collapses forward, and down the plane goes,'' Buscema said. ''It fits. Before the passenger has time to realize what's happening or to lunge for the controls. *Bam!*''

"Jesus Christ," I muttered. "Eddie, I want you and Abeyta to put this thing together. Be goddam sure nothing gets misplaced. You get all the fragments and make a composite. I want to know what this goddam thing was. If it was a bullet, I want the caliber, manufacture, grain weight, everything. Rifling twist, everything."

"Yes, sir," Mitchell said, and Buscema handed him the plastic bag.

"It had to come from the ground," I said. "Do you see any other way?"

Buscema shook his head. "There's no other way that makes sense," he said. "We need to know where the plane was struck. If a high-velocity rifle bullet punched through the aluminum skin, it wouldn't be deformed or deflected much. But if it hit frame members, or cables, or the frame of the pilot's seat, it very easily could be."

"The entrance hole in the victim's back was extremely small," Francis said. "It wasn't the sort of wound I'd associate with being struck full-on by a high-velocity bullet."

"So it was a fragment to begin with," Buscema said, and Francis nodded.

"Then we've got three big jobs, Mr. Gastner," the federal agent said. "One, we need to put that airplane back together and find out just what the hell happened. Reconstruct where and how that bullet hit the airframe. It's a comparatively small plane, but that's still going to take time. Does the county have a vacant hangar we can use?"

"We'll find one."

"The second thing is to determine what kind of bullet it was. The Bureau has resources that you don't, so I wouldn't waste anytime before calling them in on this."

"I've already done that," Estelle Reyes-Guzman said.

"Good," Buscema nodded. "You got the bullet, and we find out where and how it hit the airplane. That leaves just the big one."

"Who fired it," I said.

"And why," Estelle added.

ELEVEN

SAYING WHAT we had to do was a hell of a lot easier than doing it. What Vincent Buscema wanted first was a telephone, and while he barked orders to whoever was on the other end, I sent Eddie Mitchell down to the airport to secure a hangar.

The vacant hangar was the easy part. The Posadas Municipal Airport had enjoyed a spurt of growth and activity back in the early 1970's, when Consolidated Mining still believed that ore-rich deposits were available under the rugged slopes of Cat Mesa. Those glory days lasted for about a decade.

Three hangars now stood empty, and Jim Bergin handed over the keys to what he called CMCO-2. The sixty-by-hundred-foot hangar had once housed Consolidated's Gulfstream Jet, a couple of executive cars, and the hulks of half a dozen odd pieces of mining equipment that hadn't made their way to the Consolidated boneyard up on the hill.

The machinery still remained, but there was plenty of floor space, blow-sand streaked, to lay out the torn pieces and chunks of Phil Camp's Bonanza.

As soon as Buscema was off the telephone, he beckoned Estelle and me and we followed him into one of the doctors' conference rooms. "First things first," he said and closed the door. "That crash site has to be secured for the night."

"We'll have deputies up there," I said, "and, I assume, some of your people as well. Everyone will stay on-site."

He nodded. "Weather looks all right, so that's a help. You got us a hangar?" I nodded. "Good. Now, here's the problem. We can't just pitch stuff into the back of pickup trucks and haul it down to the hangar like loads of trash."

"I can appreciate that," I said.

"I've got a detailed, low-level aerial photo being processed of the crash site," Buscema said. "It's actually a composite." He framed a long, rectangular space in the air with his hands. "Over the top of that, we lay a clear plastic grid. Each square on the plastic grid gives us a square meter. That way, we can mark where each piece is found on the crash site. Where it comes from."

"And then it's tagged, and then it's moved," I said.

Buscema nodded. "Exactly. It's a pisser of a process, but in a case like this, it's the only way we're going to make sense of what might have happened. Toss a homicide into an air-crash equation and all kinds of rules change."

He took a deep breath and stood for a moment with his hands on his hips, regarding the tile floor. "Fortunately," and he said finally, "this isn't three hundred tons of shattered Boeing 747 that we're handling. In comparison, it's a little pip-squeak of an airplane that won't take us long to move or to tag. And we're starting off with a known fact, which helps just a whole hell of a lot. We know, with as much certainty as we know anything in this crazy world, that a bullet from the ground—or maybe from some other, unseen aircraft— took out the pilot. And then the plane scattered over two hundred yards of prairie."

It was the first time I'd heard anyone mention the possibility of a second aircraft, and I looked at Buscema with surprise. "You really think there might be a second plane?" I asked.

"No, I don't. Not a remote chance in hell."

Estelle let out a long sigh. "It could be anything from a youngster firing a wild shot with a hunting rifle to..." She hesitated, searching for the extreme.

"Terrorists shoot down airplanes," Buscema said. "Or try to." He shrugged. "But not in the countryside outside of Posadas, New Mexico, I wouldn't think. Not unless your Philip Camp or Martin Holman were very interesting to someone as targets."

Holman would have been pleased, I thought, to have someone even briefly entertain the idea that he was something other than a former used-car salesman who had enjoyed a reasonably successful run as sheriff. International conspiracies had a nice ring of intrigue that would have puffed him up with pride.

I shook my head. "The odds of hitting a low-flying aircraft with an intentional rifle shot are pretty slim," I said. "I'm not saying it's impossible, but damn near. If someone wanted to kill either of the two men, there'd be easier ways to go about it. And who the hell would know where they were flying, in any case?"

Buscema nodded. "I agree. The books are full of all kinds of weird incidents that support this being an accident. Some hunter lets fly at a treed raccoon; the bullet misses the 'coon and connects with the Bonanza a thousand yards distant. Stranger things have happened."

"There aren't many raccoons up on that mesa," I said, and as I spoke, both department pagers chirped. Estelle glanced at the display.

"I'll get it," she said and stepped across to the corner table to use the telephone.

"But there's a witness to the plane in trouble, and we need to talk with her," I said as Estelle made her call.

"You think we can be out there before dark?" Buscema asked, and I nodded at Estelle.

"Just as soon as she gets off the line."

When Estelle hung up the telephone, she turned to me and said, "Bob Torrez said that they found one of the department cameras at the crash site. The sheriff had the camera with him."

I frowned. "What was the other camera they said they found, then? One was sent down earlier with Tom Mears."

"It belonged to the Camps. And there were no exposures on it."

"And this one? Any film used?"

"Bob said the counter is on seventeen. And unless someone didn't follow procedure, there's always a fresh roll of film in the camera, ready to go. That means they took sixteen shots before the crash."

"Lots of if's," I said, remembering Martin Holman's tendency to let procedure slide. "The camera and film are on their way down?"

Estelle nodded. "They should have it processed in an hour. Then we'll see."

I started toward the door. "While we're waiting, let's use the time to pay a call on Charlotte Finnegan," I said, beckoning Estelle.

Vincent Buscema jabbered on either the radio or the cellular phone most of the way north on County Road 43, organizing the logistics of the operation that would transfer the remains of the Bonanza to CMCO-2.

We supplied night quarters in the form of the departmental RV for the officers who would sit the wreckage overnight, one of the benefits from a drug bust the year before. The thirty-two foot motor home, ironically nicknamed "Holman's Hilton," would make for a far more comfortable second night for Tom Pasquale and the others who elected to remain at the site.

County Road 43 wound its way up past the village landfill, the remains of Consolidated Mining's boneyard and headquarters, and then through a long stretch of bleak ranch land before turning eastward to link up, well outside of Posadas County, with the state highway to Glenwood and Reserve.

By the time we passed the intersection with the ranch road that cut west toward the Boyds' place, the sun had set behind the bulk of Cat Mesa. I gestured off to the west. "All this land, up to the back side of Cat Mesa, belongs to Richard Finnegan. Either that or he leases it."

"Bleak," Buscema said. The road started its long curve to the east.

"The entrance to Finnegan's ranch is just ahead," I said. "There's a cattle guard on the left." Estelle slowed the car.

"What the hell is there for cattle to eat out here?" Buscema asked, and I laughed.

"Not much. I doubt they can support more than one steer on two hundred acres."

The patrol car thumped over the cattle guard and we saw

the small iron sign, pocked here and there with bullet dents, with the name "Finnegan" cut out with a torch.

"She says she saw the aircraft from somewhere around here?" Buscema twisted in the seat, looking south to the back side of Cat Mesa.

"Apparently. It wouldn't take long to cover that distance in a plane."

"A hundred eighty miles an hour gives you a mile every twenty seconds," Buscema mused, then added, "No telling."

The Finnegans' ranch house was a well-worn mobile home, its paint baked to faded dust by the unrelenting sun. The roof was dotted with discarded tires, black donuts that kept the flimsy metal from peeling off when the wind started to howl.

The location was picturesque in a way that Dante might have appreciated. The mobile home was butted up against a rock slide from the small mesa behind it. It looked like it might be rattlesnake heaven, a great place for kids to play.

A single elm, still alive because its roots were probably wrapped around the septic system, grew scraggly by the front door, its thin, lacy limbs just starting to show some buds.

Other than that, the nearest vegetation was creosote bush and a few token specimens of bunchgrass. The predominant crop was sand, and even that was too coarse to be of any commercial use.

Scattered here and there around the homestead were outbuildings of various sizes, shapes, and stages of repair. Three enormous rolls of black-plastic pipe rested against an old Dodge four-wheel-drive pickup. The truck didn't look as if it had moved in a decade, but the piping was new, no doubt part of the never-ending projects meant to move water across the bleak landscape to a spot where it might do some good.

One lean-to housed a late-model Ford Taurus. The slot next to it was empty. Estelle pulled the car to a stop behind the Taurus.

"This place in August must be something else," Buscema muttered.

"Delightful," I said. "It gets hot as a blast furnace, but at least"—I paused to turn to Buscema and grin—"it's a dry heat."

"That's nice to know," he said. We got out of the car, and only when the last of the three car doors had slammed did the blue heeler pup by the front stoop push itself to its feet and saunter out to greet us. As if to demonstrate that it really didn't care who we were or what we wanted, it walked right past us to the right front tire of the car.

While I knocked on the door, Vincent Buscema stood with his hands on his hips, surveying the horizon. He stretched out an arm and pointed to the southwest. "So it's about ten miles or so, as the crow flies, to the south rim of Cat Mesa."

"That's close," I said.

"Huh," Buscema said, and thrust his hands in his pockets.

I rapped on the door again, but heard no movements inside.

"This might be them," Estelle said. I looked past her and saw a pickup truck. The light was too poor to distinguish the make and model, but its ubiquitous shape was silhouetted against the dust cloud it left behind as it followed in our tracks from the highway.

The dog pried itself away from our car tires and greeted its family as they got out of the truck, its tail practically slapping the sides of its face. I recognized Richard and Charlotte Finnegan by shape, if nothing else. He was squat, broad, and flatfaced, his ruddy skin cooked to blotches and scabs in places where the sun could sneak a peek around the shade of his Resistol.

Charlotte reminded me of the long-suffering schoolmarms in those old black-and-white photos taken on schoolhouse steps around the turn of the century. She had probably been pretty as a girl, but time had flattened and angulated her.

Richard Finnegan let his hand drift along the top of the Ford pickup's front fender, as if he were fearful that he might stray too far from its company in the presence of strangers.

"Howdy," he said.

Charlotte Finnegan beamed a radiant smile that thirty years before would have been a stunner. "Well, hi now," she said and waved. She walked over to Estelle as if she were half an hour late for an appointment, extending both hands to the detective.

"I'm so sorry," she said, her voice dropping. "Just so sorry."

Estelle nodded and held both of Charlotte Finnegan's hands in hers. "We appreciated you calling us, Mrs. Finnegan," I said. "This is Vincent Buscema, from the National Transportation Safety Board. He'll be investigating the crash." Charlotte reached out one hand and took Buscema's, but she still held on to Estelle's left hand.

"So what the hell happened?" Richard Finnegan asked. He shook hands with me, and his grip was enough to make me flinch. His skin was hard and rough. He dug a cigarette out of his shirt pocket, and the mannerism was a perfect replica of Johnny Boyd's habit.

"That's what we're here to find out," Buscema said. He disengaged his hand from Charlotte's. She and Estelle stood side by side, hand in hand, like two old friends. "Ma'am, when did you first see the aircraft?"

"Let me show you," Charlotte said, and she started off around the end of the trailer, dropping Estelle's hand only when they reached the deep shadows near the hitch.

"You ain't going to be able to see anything from there, Charlotte," Richard said. But his wife ignored him. Standing at the end of the trailer, Charlotte indicated what was apparently a small flower bed, tucked between the aluminum of their home and the limestone of the rocks behind.

"It'll be cool enough here during the summer," she said with considerable delight. "I've never been able to have a nice garden, but I really think this will work. Don't you?"

I realized she was talking to me, and so I replied, "I'm sure it will. Is this where you were when you first saw the plane yesterday?"

"No," she said. "I was standing out by the car."

"Maybe you'd show us," Buscema said.

We walked back around to the front of the trailer, and Charlotte turned and started for the front door. "How about some

coffee?'' she asked, with the satisfaction of the habitual coffee
drinker who knows that the time is perfect.

''Sure,'' I said. Vincent Buscema stopped in his tracks and
looked back at me. He held up a hand as if to say, ''Well?''

''Charlotte,'' Richard Finnegan said gently, ''they want to
know about the plane yesterday.''

''Oh,'' Charlotte said. She reached out a hand to Estelle
again, and the detective wrapped an arm around the woman's
shoulders.

''Do you remember how high up it was when you first saw
it?'' Estelle asked quietly, and Charlotte frowned.

Estelle turned her around so that they were facing southwest. ''When you first saw it, was it up like so?'' Estelle lifted
her free hand and held it at a steep angle, pointing at an
imaginary aircraft well above the horizon, then dropped her
arm down so she was indicating a level just above the distant
trees on the back side of Cat Mesa. ''Or down low?''

''It came along from that way,'' Charlotte said, sweeping
her hand from the west. ''And right over there''—she pointed
to a spot in the sky as if we would be able to return to that
particular bit of air space at will—''it turned right up this way,
then went back to the west.'' She frowned and ducked her
head. ''And you know, it did that four or five times. Just great
big circles like that.''

''When you called the sheriff's office, Charlotte, you said
something about the plane having trouble. Do you remember
that?''

''Oh, yes,'' she said. ''Now Richard tells me that it was
the sheriff who was in that airplane.''

''That's right.''

''Well, that's horrible,'' she said, and I agreed.

''Could you tell that the plane was in trouble?'' Buscema
asked.

''It just reminded me of the county fair,'' Charlotte said
and nodded firmly, diving her hand down and then up sharply.

''That's what the airplane did?''

''That's what it did. Just like one of those rides at the fair.

Swoop. And almost over on its back. *Swoop.* And that's when I went in and called town.''

"The pilot was doing stunts, like?" I asked.

"And then he swooped right down behind that little mesa there." She pointed almost due west.

"She told me that it was backfirin' pretty bad," Richard Finnegan said. "You tell 'em about that, Char."

But Charlotte just seemed puzzled. She turned to look at Estelle, and the detective joggled her shoulders as if she were holding a sleepy child. "Did you hear something?" she asked the woman.

"Backfiring, as in engine troubles?" Buscema asked. "Or backfiring like maybe something else?"

"She ain't going to remember," Richard said. "Maybe it'll come to her. If it does, I'll holler to you."

"Richard," I said, "did you see anything? Did you ever see the plane?"

He took a deep, final drag of the cigarette, dropped it beside his boot and ground it into the sand. "Wish I had," he said. "I got home about six from Belen." He turned and gestured toward the rolls of black pipe. "Man could spend a fortune on that stuff. Went downtown earlier today and that's when I heard what happened. Quite an uproar. I was going to drive on over there today and see for myself, but then I got to seein' all the cars and such and figured it'd be better just to stay the hell out of the way."

Buscema drew a business card from his wallet and handed it to Richard Finnegan. "We appreciate your help, folks. If you think of anything else, give me a call, will you? You can reach me either through that number there or at the sheriff's office."

Charlotte Finnegan was reluctant to have us leave, and she'd forgotten about the offer of coffee. I felt a pang of sympathy for her as she flustered, but Estelle gave her another hug and promised to come visit again when she had time.

As we thumped across the cattle guard, Buscema said, "She's been around the block a few times, hasn't she?"

"Yep," I said. "They had two kids, a boy about sixteen

and a daughter who was twenty-one or so. They lost 'em both within two weeks of each other about five or six years ago.''

"Nineteen-ninety," Estelle prompted.

"Nine years ago, then," I said. "Time flies. The boy was working on a windmill and got hit by lightning. The daughter was working as a counselor at a church camp and drowned during an outing over at Elephant Butte Lake.''

"Christ," Buscema said. "No wonder she's come unglued." He rolled down the window. "She saw something, though. Maybe it'll come to her. But no matter. She's not what I'd call a credible witness.''

"And it won't be the first time gunshots have been confused with the backfiring of an engine," Estelle said.

TWELVE

VINCENT BUSCEMA caught a ride up to the crash site, and Estelle and I went to my office. With the flurry of activity nonstop since the crash, we hadn't had time to find a quiet corner to sit down and take stock.

As I walked past the front desk, Ernie Wheeler lifted a hand and then beckoned to me with a clipboard.

"Gayle Sedillos wanted your okay on this, sir," he said, "but I haven't been able to catch you since I came on shift. I've penciled Linda Real in to sit this shift with me." He extended the clipboard toward me.

"Fine," I said. "Where is she now?" It was six forty-five, and thirty-six hours or more without a catnap were beginning to take their toll. My temper was short and my belly was screaming for a long, quiet dinner at the Don Juan.

"Tom Mears needed a matron for a few minutes. Aggie Bishop wasn't home, so I asked Linda if she wanted to do it.''

"A matron for what?"

"Mears did a routine traffic check and it turns out the driver—Bea Kellogh, remember her?" I nodded. "She was about passed-out drunk. Apparently she had stopped just off MacArthur Street and was parked in an odd sort of angle, and Mears happened by. She had her thirteen-year-old daughter with her. Mears figured it'd just be easier to take them home, but you know how it is. Linda was handy, so it seemed okay."

I handed the clipboard back. "It's not okay on several counts, Ernie," I said, and he frowned. "First of all, Linda doesn't work for us."

"Oh. I thought she was hired on."

"No. We're talking about it." Before he had a chance to bring it up, I added, "She filled in on the airport radio earlier yesterday because it was just a relay job. Any civilian could have done it." I turned to walk back toward my office. "And second, we don't have time to run a taxi service for goddam drunks right now. If you're going to use her, use her here."

"I guess Mears just thought that he didn't want to spend time right now with a DWI bust. 'Specially since she'd parked it." He shrugged.

I waved a hand. "When Linda comes back in, tell her I want to talk with her. But give Estelle and me a few uninterrupted moments first."

Estelle had collapsed in one of the leather chairs in my office, hands folded over her stomach, head back and eyes closed.

I shut the door behind me. She opened her left eye and regarded me as I crossed to my desk and plopped down in the chair behind it.

"Of all the goddam things I could have predicted, this is about the last," I said and heaved a huge sigh. "It just goes to show that when you think you have everything all planned out, you'd better think again."

"What had you planned?" Her voice was quiet and distant.

I chuckled and leaned back so that I could lift a leg up and rest my boot on the edge of the desk. "You're leaving next week, I turned in my retirement effective September one, Robert's getting married, Linda's waiting in the wings. I figured payback time. I could just dump all that in young Martin's lap and let him figure out what the hell to do.''

Estelle put both hands over her face, her fingertips rubbing her eyes. After a few seconds, she moved her hands just enough so she could stare at the ceiling. "What will you do?" she asked.

"Sam Carter asked me to take the sheriff's job until the election next fall." If I thought that would surprise Estelle, I was mistaken. She didn't reply, but nodded, just a tiny inclination of the head, eyes still closed. I wanted an answer, so I asked, "Does that make sense to you?"

"It's the best idea Mr. Carter has had in years," she said.

"I want you to be undersheriff, Estelle."

This time, she opened her eyes. Her right eyebrow went up in that expression I'd come to know so well. She took a deep breath and pushed herself up in the chair. "Sir, we're leaving Posadas next week. We've already started packing. Mama has been practicing driving her wheelchair back and forth from her bedroom to the front door in anticipation." Her delightful smile lit up her face.

"I know you're going," I said. "I know that." I swung the other boot up and crossed my legs. "I was a little irritated today when Sam was in such an all-fired hurry to make sure I took the job. He didn't want you to have it, or any of the three sergeants. I don't know what his agenda is."

"I do," Estelle said, her grin even wider. "Sam Carter's brother-in-law is Sam Carter's agenda."

"Why don't I know who this brother-in-law is?"

"He lives in Deming, sir. He's retiring from the state police in July."

"I see. You think he's going to move here and run for sheriff?"

"Yes."

"And how do you know this tidbit?"

"Martin Holman told me a week or so ago. The man's

name is Ellison Franklin. At one time he was chairman of his county's Republican Club."

"That would have put him head-to-head with Martin in the primary," I said. "But that would have been three years from now. After this mess, the field is wide open."

"Right."

"So. None of that matters, since I'm not running in the election in November to fill the office and you'll be in Minnesota. I want you as undersheriff for the rest of the week. How's that for an offer?"

She chuckled, leaned forward, rested her elbows on her knees and ran both hands through her thick black hair. "Is this just to tweak Sam? Make him nervous? Are you sure his bigoted little heart can take it?"

"It's for selfish reasons, mainly," I said. "If you're undersheriff, I won't have to spend ten seconds training you. Any of the others will flounder some, and we don't have time for that. And think of it this way: do this for me and you can write 'undersheriff' on your resume when you go job-hunting up in Genesee County, Minnesota."

She smiled again and shook her head. "Maybe I can avoid job-hunting for a while," she said. "Remember, Erma's not going with us." Erma Sedillos, our senior dispatcher's younger sister, had been a full-time nanny for the Guzman clan for three years.

"But—" I began and stopped when my telephone buzzed. "Sure," I said, and hung up.

Bob Torrez was at my office door before I had a chance to explain what the call was. In his hand was a manila folder, and trailing behind him was Linda Real.

"Sir," Torrez said, "we've got the prints from the camera."

I beckoned them in. "And how's Mrs. Kellogh?" I asked by way of greeting Linda. She looked heavenward.

"Soused. We just dropped her and her daughter at their house. The car was off the right-of-way, so we just locked it and left it there. The daughter said it wouldn't be a problem to come and get it later."

"Wonderful."

"And then I came back and heard about the film. I helped Sergeant Torrez get the prints ready. Sir, the department needs a new print drier. The old one is shot."

"Uh-huh," I said and glanced at Estelle. "So, Robert, what have you got?"

He had already opened the folder on my desk, and he handed me an eight-by-ten print. Linda Real reached across and pointed. "The surface gloss is blotched here and there. That's the old drier," she said.

"Thank you." I leaned over so that I could focus the correct part of my bifocals on the print.

"That's the first one on the negative," Robert Torrez said. Estelle came around behind me so she could see the photos at the same time. "It looks like his brother-in-law posed by the airplane."

"That is Philip Camp, sure enough," I said. I reached out a hand for the next one. Instead, Torrez handed me a set of three.

The terrain in the photos was rugged, and in the first of the three, I could see the road cutting through the trees. "That's taken from just beyond the mine," Torrez said.

"And the others are from on top," Estelle added.

"An aerial tour," I muttered. "What the hell was he doing?" The next four photos were of prairie—open, rolling prairie. At least, that was my guess. "Are these out of focus, or is it me?"

"Some of them are really bad," Linda said.

"That," Torrez said, tapping one of the photos with his index finger, "is Boyd number-two. One of Johnny Boyd's windmills and stock tanks. I recognize the sharp turn of the two-track just to the south of it."

"I don't even see the windmill," I said. "Where is it?"

Torrez pulled a pen from his pocket and used it as a pointer. I grimaced and shook my head. "I'll take your word for it."

"And this looks like the country just to the north of where the plane eventually crashed," Torrez said. "This black line is one of the boundary fences. Or a section fence. Something like that. It's a fence, anyway. And those''—he leaned close and jabbed at the tiny figures with the tip of the pen—''are cattle.''

''Whoopee,'' I said. I straightened up, and my back popped with an audible crack. ''You need to tie these things down and go over them inch by inch with the stereo viewer. I can't see much detail, but maybe you'll turn up something. There's no reason for Martin Holman to be taking aerial photographs of creosote bushes and cattle on a gusty, bumpy after-noon...or at any time, for that matter. We need some hint of what he was about. That's half of it.''

Torrez glanced at me, questioning.

''The trouble here, folks,'' I said to the three of them, ''is that the odds of there being any connection—any at all—between what Martin Holman was trying to see yesterday af-ternoon and the bullet that killed his pilot are slim and none.'' I picked up one of the photos again and looked at it. ''Unless there's something here that we're not seeing.''

''Maybe we could blow up each negative, a little at a time. You've got a pretty good enlarger in the darkroom,'' Linda Real said.

''Why don't you do that,'' I said. ''That film is evidence, so make sure it stays in the department's possession at all times. It doesn't leave the building for any reason, and it doesn't leave your possession unless it's locked in the evi-dence locker.'' I reached out a hand and took Linda's in mine. It was tiny—and clammy with excitement. ''Which means that as of now, your soul is ours, my dear. Welcome aboard.''

''Thank you, sir.''

''You may regret it, but for now, you're welcome. And I want to be able to see every grass blade by midnight.''

''I can do that.''

''I know you can. And while you're waiting on the chem-icals, cruise through a catalog and find a new drier.''

She grinned, gathered up the prints and folder, and shot out the door.

''And now,'' I said, ''let's see if we can find out what Martin Holman was up to.''

THIRTEEN

NO ONE HAD BEEN in Martin Holman's office since he'd left it sometime after three o'clock the day before. I didn't know that for a fact, of course—it was just the immediate feeling I got when I opened the door and stepped inside.

I felt as if I were intruding. I stopped and took a deep breath, then felt Estelle's hand on my shoulder.

"It's always easier if it's a stranger, isn't it?" she said. She reached over and turned on the lights.

I grunted and shut the door. "I wish to hell I knew what to look for." I walked across to Holman's desk. He could have stacked a few more papers on it, but it would have been a trick.

"Maybe one thing we have going for us is the sheriff himself," Estelle said, and I glanced across the desk at her. She had walked around and was standing by the empty chair.

"Meaning what?"

"Well, as far as I know, Martin Holman didn't work on cases by himself. I don't recall him ever mentioning a case to me where he had initiated the file. He routinely turned things over to deputies when he got calls personally."

"True. Half the time he didn't know what to do, anyway." I waved a hand. "Yeah, I know, that's unkind. But it's true. It seems to me that a good place to start is to inventory every scrap of paper on this desk...his telephone logs, whatever is on that thing." I nodded at the computer. Toasters were floating across the screen, patiently waiting for their owner to return.

Estelle tapped a key, and the toasters disappeared, replaced by a page of finances. She leaned close and read for a few seconds. "This is that federal grant he was working on to hire two full-time civilian employees."

I scanned the desk. "An orderly avalanche," I mused. I settled on three initial piles. The first included routine county documents like budget transfers, time sheets, and purchase orders, along with the myriad catalogs that vendors liked to send to law-enforcement agencies. One was for photography equipment, and I tossed it to one side on the remote chance that I would remember to give it to Linda Real.

In a second pile, I put the small messages that Holman routinely scribbled to himself. He had been an avid fan of Post-it notes. The little yellow things were ubiquitous throughout the county building.

A third pile was reserved for documents and papers that weren't immediately obvious in nature—and there weren't many of those.

I sat down in Holman's chair and pulled myself close to the desk. Estelle still leaned over the computer, cruising down through the various file names. I picked up one of the pink "While You Were Out" slips.

"He had a call from Doug Posey at one-thirty." I peered at the slip. "Apparently Marty was still out to lunch. Gayle has checked here that Posey was returning a call." I put that slip down by my elbow. "Are you aware of any complaints we've had that might include the Department of Fish and Game?" Posey didn't spend much time in Posadas. The village—even the county—wasn't the center of a sportsman's paradise, and the state critter cops had more productive hunting grounds elsewhere.

"The last time I can recall was when Posey asked our department for backup when he was busting those Mexican big shots who were hunting turkey down by Regal Springs. That doesn't mean there hasn't been other activity."

I picked up another slip of paper, also with Gayle Sedillos' writing. "And a note to call Sam Carter," I said. "Politics, politics." I paused, resting my forearms on the desk. "You know what's wrong with all this, don't you?" I shuffled the remaining slips and laid them out on the desk like playing cards, and my eyebrows furrowed. I picked up a slip dated the previous day and read the message again.

I almost didn't hear Estelle say, in response to my question, "We're assuming there might be some connection between the incident that brought the plane down and the reason they were flying out there in the first place."

I laid the slip down on top of the others. "And what if there isn't? And the odds are all in that favor, by the way."

"I don't think there is any connection, sir." She straightened up and regarded the index on the computer screen. "But this is what bothers me. There are a limited number of people who live anywhere near that quadrant of the county. The shot must have been fired in fair proximity to the crash sight. As Francis said, Philip Camp couldn't have lived long with his heart pumping blood through a two-inch tear in his aorta. And there is no evidence that suggests that Sheriff Holman was able to grab the control yoke and do anything with it. He certainly didn't swing it over to his side."

"What a terrifying ride downhill that must have been," I muttered.

Estelle walked around the desk and approached the big map of Posadas County that was framed on the wall. She placed her hand over the area north of Cat Mesa. "Charlotte Finnegan said that the plane was flying a repeating pattern in this area." She traced with her index finger eastward along the back of the mesa to the blue line that indicated County Road 43, running north-south. "First this way, then circling north to within easy sight of the Finnegans' place, then back to the west again...toward the Boyds' place." She put her hands on her hips and turned to look at me.

"Those are the only two ranches in that immediate area, sir. There're federal lands scattered about, and some state sections. And then there's Newton, that little settlement just out of the county, about eight miles north of the Boyds'. Maybe four or five houses there, at the most." She turned and put one finger on the map over Finnegan's ranch and another finger over Boyds'.

"Those two places mark the north boundary, on the east

and west ends, of the pattern that Charlotte said the plane was flying.''

"And to the south is just the back side of the mesa,'' I said. "That's Forest Service land.''

"And so far, they haven't found any sign of campers up there, or kids from town, or anything else. There's a family right about here''—she tapped the map—"around by Parson's Bench, cutting on a commercial firewood plot. Last night I asked Dale Kenyon and his staff to cover that area in case someone might have seen the plane go down. Dale says the folks cutting wood were the only ones up there as far as he knows. They didn't remember seeing anything.''

"And if they were listening to a chain saw, they wouldn't have heard anything,'' I said.

Estelle frowned, regarding the wall map for a long minute. Her lower lip was pooched out in an expression that she must have learned from her two kids. "You know what bothers me?''

I grinned. "You'd be surprised if I said 'yes,' wouldn't you?''

She shot a quick glance at me, and the right eyebrow went up. "What?''

I shook my head. "I was just sitting here thinking that if Charlotte Finnegan actually did hear what she said she heard—and that might be open to question, too—then the gunshots had to come from somewhere west or southwest of where she was standing. If what she calls backfiring was actually gunshots, that is. The wind was kicking hard and the sound wouldn't carry against it much. I don't know the physics of it, but it seems to me that wind noise would cancel a lot. The gunshots, if that's what they were, couldn't have been too far away.''

"Exactly,'' Estelle said, and she turned back to the map. "If Charlotte heard them while she was standing here, then it makes sense that they came from somewhere over this way.'' She drew her hand westward, stopping with her palm over the Boyd ranch.

"I talked to Johnny Boyd,'' I said. "We spent most of the

night and day together. He said he didn't hear a thing." I reached out and picked up the telephone message that had stopped me in my tracks. I held it out to Estelle. "Take a look," I said, "and then let's talk about coincidences."

Estelle crossed quickly to the desk and took the slip.

"Maxine Boyd," she said.

"Logged in at ten forty-six yesterday," I said. I leaned back and clasped my hands behind my head. "Now we know what the odds are. The odds say that Martin Holman had a reason for what he was up to. It wasn't just a joyride."

"Well, sure he had a reason," Estelle said, puzzled.

"No, not 'sure,' sweetheart. Martin had more than a few faults, like most of us do. One of those faults was that he occasionally got the bee in his bonnet that he was a cop. I'm sure you'll remember that on more than one occasion, we all had cause to be nervous. The worst moments were when Martin took it upon himself to check out a patrol car and go public." I smiled without much humor.

"You think he was acting on impulse?"

I shrugged. "It's happened before. It's a very human frailty." I reached out and took the note from Estelle. "Let's see if Linda has found anything and then look into this." I opened the door and damn near collided with Ernie Wheeler.

"Sir," he said, "Mrs. Holman's on line two for you. She sounds pretty upset."

FOURTEEN

WHEN I PICKED UP the telephone, Janice Holman was in the middle of an argument with someone else, and she wasn't doing much of a job covering the receiver.

"I'll do what he says I should do, and that's it," she said, and the vehemence of it surprised me. "I just don't care. I really don't. And neither should you."

Uncomfortable with eavesdropping, I said, "Janice? This is Bill Gastner."

"Oh, God, I'm glad I was able to find you," Janice Holman said. "Hang on just a minute, can you? I need to find a private nook somewhere." Her tone held an even blending of desperation and the old Janice Holman sense of humor.

Estelle mouthed something and made camera motions with her hands. "I'll be in the darkroom with Linda," she said, and I waved at her.

"I'll be there directly," I said.

I heard more voices, a couple of them shriller than they probably needed to be, and then the thud of a door.

"You still there?" Janice asked.

"I'm still here. How are you holding up?"

"It's a nightmare, it really is," she said, then paused for a moment, and I didn't rush her. "I don't know how we're going to manage, Bill. I really don't."

"And I'm afraid I'm not going to make it any easier for you," I said.

"Oh, there's nothing you can do, Bill. There really isn't. Just be a friend, that's all."

"That I'll be, Janice. But there's some unsettling news."

The phone went silent, and then she said, "I don't see how I can be unsettled anymore than I already am." She came close to a chuckle.

"Janice, Philip Camp was hit by a bullet fired from the ground."

"He *what?*"

I took a deep breath and repeated myself. "It's beginning to look like a single bullet struck the underside of the airplane. A fragment struck Philip and he died almost instantly."

"My God..." Her voice trailed off.

"I haven't called you because I wanted to come over and tell you in person."

"I called you, didn't I?" Janice sighed. "But I guess both

Vivian and I needed to know. I appreciate knowing, Bill. I know it's hard for you, too."

"Most likely it was an accident of some kind. A careless shot by a hunter. There was nothing wrong with the aircraft, and no pilot error evident at this point. Nothing your brother-in-law did that caused the crash."

"My God," she said again. "Hit by a bullet..."

"He would have remained conscious for only a few seconds," I said, wishing I could say the same for Martin's final, desperate moments.

"Poor Martin," Janice murmured.

"When we know more, I'll be by. In the meantime, is there anything I can do to make it any easier?"

Her sigh was loud and heartfelt. "Do you know Leo Burkhalter?"

"Of course I know Leo," I said. "He's president of the New Mexico Sheriffs' Association this year."

"Well, he called not long ago. I think there's something about the English language he has difficulty with, Bill."

"How so?" Leo Burkhalter was sheriff of a county that actually included a couple of cities and a population that was both large and diverse enough to create some interesting crimes. He'd won his share of awards and had worked his way up through the ranks for twenty years before being elected sheriff.

There was another pause. "God, this is so hard to say," Janice Holman said, her voice small.

"Take your time, sweetheart."

"He called to tell me that he was taking care of all of the arrangements. For..."

She hesitated, and I said quietly, "For Martin's funeral, you mean?"

"Yes."

"Well, that should be a load off your mind."

"Bill," she said, and this time there was some steel in her tone. "I do not want some big, lavish, garish affair with a string of police cars ten blocks long and a bunch of young men all grim-faced with little black ribbons over their badges, and then someone, and it'll probably have to be you, handing me a folded flag.''

I murmured something noncommittal. Janice had pegged it just about right. I hadn't thought about the service yet; in fact, I might have been justly accused of avoiding the issue. A bunch of sleepless hours might have been an excuse, but the truth was that I didn't do funerals well, especially those where I might be required to say something intelligent and heartfelt.

"It's something of a fraternity," I said, feeling ridiculous saying it. I didn't have enough fingers and toes to count the times I'd grumbled about Martin Holman "playing cop," even though on an equal number of occasions, I'd been the first to admit that he'd had a hell of a steep learning curve. If I wanted to be fair to him, I could readily admit that he'd earned the awful tribute of a long line of patrol cars, all their lights winking as they idled to the cemetery.

"What would you like, Janice?" I asked. "There is starting to be some evidence that he died doing departmental work. We're beginning to see several reasons why he wanted to fly over that area.''

"I've gathered that already," she said with acid that surprised me. "And that was something I wanted to mention to you, too. In the press of things, I forgot to tell you that yesterday morning Maxine Boyd called here, trying to get ahold of Martin. He'd gone off somewhere with Philip, and when they returned for lunch, I forgot to tell him about it. About the call.''

"Do you know what she wanted? Did she say?"

"No, and it didn't sound particularly urgent, either, if you can judge by the sound of someone's voice over the telephone. I just told her I'd give Martin the message and that he'd call her. It doesn't take a rocket scientist to figure out that there may have been some reason for him to want to fly over the Boyds' ranch. Maybe she got ahold of him at the office.''

"That's apparently what happened. Estelle and I are going out to the Boyd ranch later tonight.''

"You be careful," she said.

"We always work best at night," I said lightly. "But listen. Do you want me to call Sheriff Burkhalter for you?"

"Will you?"

"Of course I will. What do you want me to tell him?"

"Well…"

"Janice, you can do whatever pleases you. Don't worry about what people think."

"Neither Martin nor I were particularly religious. I guess you know that."

"Yes."

"He did tell me once that if anything ever happened to him, he'd like his remains buried in the family plot with his mother and father."

"That's in Iowa, I believe," I said.

"Drew's Ferry, Iowa. I guess what I'd like is a quiet family memorial there. The girls said that would be fine with them."

"All right. Is there any kind of service you want here in Posadas? Martin lived here for a long time…since he was in high school, as I remember. Thirty years or more. In fact, he went to at least one grade here with my oldest daughter. I'm sure there are many folks who would like the opportunity to pay their respects."

"Something small and private," Janice Holman said. "Just friends from the community. Maybe at the First Baptist Church. I like Jeremy Hines, the pastor there. No one else. And nothing 'fraternal.'"

"If that's the way you want it, it's fine."

"I don't know why this is so important to me," she said.

"It doesn't matter why, Janice. It's your call. You don't have to explain yourself to anyone. Least of all, to me."

She paused again and then said in a rush, "No uniforms, please. Can you promise me that?"

"Yes."

"Will you say a few words?"

"Yes. Of course." I chuckled. "That might not be the wisest decision you've ever made."

She actually laughed, and the laugh ended in a short, gulping sob. "Bill, Bill, Bill," she moaned, and then she found her solid self-control again. "Martin would probably have been concerned that you'd offend one of the politicians."

"I'll try not to disappoint," I said.

"Tuesday at ten, then," she said. "That will be all right with all of you?"

"Of course," I said. "And I'll call Sheriff Burkhalter right now, before I forget, or before he makes plans that are difficult to change."

"Thank you, Bill. And please keep me posted."

"Count on it. What are your sister's plans, by the way? Has she decided on anything yet?"

"We've just now begun talking about it. She really doesn't know. She'll be flying back to Calgary, of course, and I suppose there will be some sort of service there. I just don't know yet. Neither one of us is very good at this."

"I don't think anyone is," I said, adding silently, "least of all myself."

"I'll tell her about the preliminary cause of the crash," Janice said. "But you'll remember us if you find out anything else?"

"Sooner rather than later," I promised.

FIFTEEN

LEO BURKHALTER was puzzled, but finally I could hear the shrug of surrender in his voice.

"Whatever Mrs. Holman wishes," he said. "You don't want me to call her?"

"If you want to make a brief call expressing condolences, that's fine. You might tell her that you talked to me and that whatever she decides is fine with you."

"Well, it isn't fine with me, but I suppose I can do that.

What I meant was, do you think I could talk her into something appropriate?''

I laughed. ''What's appropriate, Leo, is what Janice Holman wants. Not what you and I think she should want.''

''Did she say why she wouldn't go for any formal contingent of officers?''

''No. And I didn't ask. It's none of my business. Or of yours, either.''

''God, I'd forgotten how grouchy you can get, Bill. All right, that's the way we'll play it, then. By the way, is the commission going to appoint you as interim sheriff?''

''I guess. They say that's what they're going to do. I told the chairman that I'd fill the spot until November.''

''They didn't ask Detective Guzman?''

''Nope. They should have, though.''

''Damn right. No offense, but your county government's got the brains of pissants. And while I've got you on the line…you're listed as a supervisor on an application that we received not long ago, so I don't see the harm in asking. Tell me about an officer of yours. One of your sergeants. Edward Mitchell.''

''Well, son of a bitch. He applied with you?''

''Uh-huh. He lists June first as a date he's available.''

''He's one of our best, Leo. And right now, I can't spare him. Do me a favor and stall on that application for a while. Are you shorthanded?''

''Aren't we always? Anyway, he's my top choice. I got a bunch of applications, but they're all either misfits, rookies just out of the academy, or halt, lame, and blind. I could use somebody with Mitchell's experience and training.''

''So could I, Leo. At the rate things are going, we'll have two people working come fall—me and the dispatcher.''

''You'll survive. What the hell happens in Posadas, anyway?'' Burkhalter said.

''Well, for one thing, the coroner dug a chunk of high-velocity brass out of the gentleman who was flying Holman's plane. That's why they went down.''

''No shit?''

"No shit."

"What, did Holman shoot him? As I remember, you did something like that once, if I'm not mistaken."

"Nothing like that. The bullet came from the ground."

"Christ. Just a stray shot, eh?"

"Looks like it."

"What a goddam waste. Well, if there's anything I can do to help, you just holler."

"Stop pirating my best and brightest, for a start."

Burkhalter laughed. "He's the one that applied. I didn't recruit him. Do me a favor and cut him loose as soon as you can, all right?"

I promised all kinds of cooperation I didn't feel like delivering, and when I hung up, I damn near cracked the plastic of the phone. With a curse, I pushed myself out of the late sheriff's chair. "This is a really fine week," I muttered, and yanked open the office door.

The darkroom was down in the basement, a cool fortress full of dust-covered pipes and endless cartons of obsolete documents. Where plaster had fallen away, the walls showed the old, square-cut limestone that formed the foundations.

I rapped on the darkroom door with a knuckle and waited. After three minutes, I was ready to rap again when I heard the door bolt draw back. Estelle looked out around the black-rubber curtain that hung inside the door as extra protection against stray light.

"What did you find?" I asked.

"Linda still has a couple more to print, but let's take the ones we've got," she said.

"Do they show anything?"

"Well, that depends," Estelle said, and I followed her back upstairs.

She spread the collection of eight-by-tens on my desk. With two exceptions, they were sharp and clear. "The camera moved on these," Estelle said, handing me the first two. "From that distance, the focus would be set on infinity. Everything should be clear and sharp, but he couldn't hold the camera still against the jouncing of the plane. They're the first two on the roll, so he took them early in the flight and maybe didn't use a high enough shutter speed. All of the others are clear. Like maybe he made some adjustments when he realized how rough the ride was."

I picked up another photograph, a composition in muted shades of gray. "So what's this? It looks like prairie."

"It is," Estelle said. "If you look right there, just to the west of the two-track, you'll see a little area with what looks like livestock."

"Sure enough. Pictures of cows."

Estelle grinned and handed me another. "This is an enlargement of just that area, from the two-track west to the cows."

"I'm surprised at the quality," I said.

"A good camera and high enough shutter speed to compensate for most of the bouncing around," Estelle said.

"And those aren't cows, either."

"No, sir, they're not."

"They're antelope. See that one?" I pointed at one animal that had twisted its head around, probably at the sound of the airplane. "Nice set of horns, and its white butt stands out clear as can be. But so what? The range is full of them. Maybe Martin had decided to take up hunting and he was casing the place." I handed the photo back to Estelle. "What else is there?"

"Several shots of open prairie, with a fence running east-west. The fence is so clear you can almost see the barbs on the wire."

"And the range is full of fences, too." I turned the photo this way and that. "And that looks like sheep fencing. There's a grid pattern. Maybe it's just the light."

"And finally this photo, taken looking west. There's some glare from the side window."

"That's the Boyd place?"

"Yes, sir. I think so."

I sat down, still holding the last picture. I looked at Estelle. "Huh," I said. I wagged the photo at her. "This is what we've got. Maxine Boyd tried to reach Martin yesterday morning at home. He was out, and Janice offered to take a message. Mrs. Boyd apparently didn't think it was important enough, or she didn't want to tell a third party. She called Martin's office sometime later and did talk with the sheriff.''

Estelle nodded and slid the photos into a bundle. ''And the sheriff tried to contact Doug Posey, of Fish and Game. He wasn't successful, but Posey later returned the call.''

''And then Martin talked his brother-in-law into going for an airplane ride,'' I said. ''All of the other photos just show prairie? You got fences and antelope, probably cattle, too. No other features?''

Estelle separated one photo from the pack. ''This one has a windmill, fences, cattle, and trees.'' She handed it to me. The windmill's shadow was stark against the soft background.

''Did Linda do a blowup of this?''

''She's going to,'' Estelle said.

''The windmill's not in operation,'' I said and pointed. ''See how its rudder is turned over to the side? And it looks like the tank is dry.'' I squinted and tried to pick out detail. ''The cattle really stomp the ground to nothing around those water holes, don't they?'' I said. ''And what's this?'' I pointed at a dark outline, partially obscured by a rock outcropping north of the windmill.

''It looks like the remains of an old building,'' Estelle said. ''Linda was going to try for an enlargement of that and the windmill area.''

''And then these pointless pictures of prairie. Open land and fences. That's all that's here.'' I leaned back in the chair and stared at the ceiling. ''Martin, what the hell were you up to?''

SIXTEEN

ESTELLE REYES-GUZMAN tricked me into a few hours of fitful rest. As an enthusiastic insomniac, regular sleep had eluded me for years. Over time, I'd stopped fighting the fashion that said sixteen hours awake followed by eight hours unconscious was the norm. And I didn't do those nifty little "wolf naps" of fifteen to thirty minutes that some folks use to recharge their batteries. Instead, I tended to plod along, working as best I could until I fell flat on my face from complete exhaustion. It was a system that seemed to work for me.

Unfortunately for others around me, I often made the mistake of thinking they wanted to partake of the same schedule.

When I suggested again that we drive up and talk to Johnny and Maxine Boyd, Estelle looked at her watch, an uncharacteristic hesitation that prompted me to look at mine.

"We'd be up there at about nine-thirty," I said, and Estelle grimaced.

"I need to go home for a few minutes, sir. We were up all last night and I haven't seen *los niños* since yesterday. They're going to forget I'm their mother. And if she doesn't get some time off, Erma is apt to go insane."

She grinned. "And much as she adores them, I don't think Mama would last long with those two all by herself."

"Let me holler at Linda, too," I said. "She's got to be dead on her feet." I followed Estelle out of Martin Holman's office. Ernie Wheeler was still working dispatch, and he was leaning forward, his fingers poised over the mike's transmit bar.

"Posadas, three-oh-seven." Eddie Mitchell's voice was quiet and crisp.

Ernie tapped the bar. "Three-oh-seven, be advised that one-eight-niner Baker Mike Nora is registered to Patrick Salazar, Three-twenty East Bustos, Posadas. No wants or warrants."

"I knew that," Mitchell muttered, a rare departure for him from standard airwave protocol. "Three-oh-seven is ten-eight."

"He's tired, too," I said as Wheeler signed off with the repeated number gibberish that the FCC demanded.

Wheeler turned to regard Estelle and me. "Eddie's been up on the hill working around the lake and in that area, hoping maybe there was someone camping that we missed in an earlier sweep."

The lake was nothing but a deep, black-water-filled hole, the remains of an old quarry just up the hill beyond Consolidated Mining's operations. It was a popular party spot, despite the Forest Service fence and half a dozen signs warning of imminent danger to life and limb if anyone took a plunge into the cold water.

"Call him in and send him home," I said to Wheeler. "Tell him I said so."

I heard quiet footsteps behind me and turned to see Linda Real. She held another fistful of photos. She managed a game smile, but I could see she was among the walking dead herself.

"You might want to look at these," she said and handed the photos to me.

"I might. I might also want to get some sleep. You can do the same. The feds will be here in full force tomorrow, transferring the wreckage to the hangar. I need people bright and in gear come morning."

I tapped her on the shoulder with the photos. "That's a condition of employment, Linda. Your first sixteen-hour shift is over. We'll see you here at eight sharp."

She started to say something about the pictures, pointing toward one of them. I held them away from her.

"Linda..." and when I was sure she was hearing me, I added, "Go home. Now. Just forget explanations. Just turn around"—I took one shoulder and urged her in the proper direction—"and walk out the door. Get in your car, go home, and get some rest. It's that easy."

"Well said, sir," Estelle murmured, and I glanced sharply at her. She grinned at my mock reproof. "I'll see you here in the morning," she added. "We'll run up to the Boyds'."

And my advice to others turned out to work pretty well. I

took the pictures home, dropped them on the kitchen table and started the coffeemaker. While it popped and gurgled, I spread out the photos. With a powerful twinge of regret, I realized just how much I would have liked to ask Martin Holman what had attracted his attention to this scrubby section of prairie.

And I had to give him credit. Aerial photography was not easy without the proper equipment. It was hard to stick a camera against the Plexiglas of the aircraft's cabin and shoot past the reflection, the haze, the bouncing. Even without a magnifying glass, I could count the vanes on the windmill. The rudder was latched to the side, braking the mill and keeping it stationary. On the rudder, the name of the manufacturer was clearly legible.

The windmill's sucker rod drew water up and into a pipe that fed a circular stock tank. The tank looked to be about twelve feet in diameter and perhaps three or four feet deep. The shadow cast by the west wall of the tank cut a dark line across the other side. I squinted hard, couldn't make out the detail, and grunted to my feet. I rummaged in one of the kitchen utility drawers and found one of several magnifying glasses that I owned—all of which took turns being lost somewhere in the house.

With that, I could see that the tank was less than a quarter full. "Huh," I said. The area around the windmill was beaten flat by cattle hooves.

A second photograph showed what had been not much more than a dark shadow in the first print. Sure enough, off to the northwest of the windmill were the remains of an old stone building. The roof itself had caved in, exposing the top of the stone walls and the ends of several of the roof beams.

The county—in fact, most of the state—was dotted with similar structures, some built just after the First World War, some thrown together as late as the 1950s. In almost every case, the homesteaders had found that the vagaries of the New Mexico climate made their lives miserable. It would have been more pleasant living as a street person somewhere. And in almost every case, it was the lack of water that drove them away.

In good times, a twenty-foot-deep, hand-dug well in a lucky

spot might produce bountiful water for a little while. Then it
would take the expense of drilling fifty or sixty feet, and a
windmill to suck the water to the surface. And finally, if the
ranchers had the money and the patience, the major well-
drilling rigs would smoke down through hundreds of feet of
rock, sometimes finding usable water, sometimes not.

I looked at the photo of the stone house for several minutes,
sipping coffee, wondering what life in that little twelve-by-
sixteen shack must have been like fifty years before, when a
trip into town was an hour in a jolting Model A Ford, itself
twenty or more years old by that time. Maybe Martin Holman
had wondered the same thing and that was what had prompted
him to take the photo in the first place.

"And whose windmill is this?" I said aloud to the quiet
kitchen. I didn't recognize it, but that meant nothing. That
was another question for Johnny Boyd. Maybe he knew just
where it was...and maybe he knew just why Sheriff Holman
had wanted a photo of it.

I would have liked to talk to the rancher right then, but my
heavy eyelids told me that it made sense to wait. The windmill
wasn't going anywhere, and neither was Johnny Boyd. Come
morning, he'd have half an army swarming around his ranch.

SEVENTEEN

THE NEXT MORNING, Estelle surprised me by suggesting that
we drive to the Boyds' ranch by way of Newton, the tiny
hamlet in the neighboring county that was due north of the
Boyds. Straight lines were usually my habit in getting from
point to point, but if my chief of detectives wanted to approach the ranch from the back by circling in from the north,
that was fine with me.

The traffic up to the crash site would be heavy, both coming
and going. We'd eat a lot less dust by slipping in the back

door. We drove out of town on County 43, but before that route started its long climb up the mesa past Consolidated and the lake, we turned west on State 78, the main arterial that ran past the airport.

The state highway angled northwest, and in another twenty miles, we were out of Posadas County. In ten more miles, we passed the sign for the Petros Farmers' Market and then Estelle slowed for the right turn onto a narrow, paved lane that led along the base of a series of rolling, low hills to the tiny hamlet of Newton.

What Newton's claim to fame had once been, I didn't know. Maybe it grew out of feeble attempts at mining. There was certainly no timber close by. Perhaps it was one of the myriad little villages that had once been active trading centers scattered across the state, places for the various dryland farmers to bring their produce or livestock. There wasn't much left to trade anymore.

On the outskirts of Newton, perched on a mound of reddish dirt fill capped with asphalt, was the new post-office building, a little modular structure that would have looked right at home in Ohio. The Circle JEB ranch paid rent on P.O. Box 17.

Beside the post office—and separated from that federal property by a row of wrecked cars, a fair-sized collection of used irrigation pipe, and three or four tractors that would never again rumble to life—was a store labeled only as "Baca."

I knew Floyd Baca, and knew that he had taken over the family business from his father just after World War II. Floyd Baca had seen more than seventy New Mexico summers as the sun baked Newton silent each day. I didn't know what kept him there, and wouldn't have presumed to ask. Besides, I'd spent nearly thirty years in Posadas without much excuse. Few folks claimed that town as the center of the universe, either.

In addition to the post office and Baca's, downtown Newton included Our Lady of Sorrows Church, sitting back from the highway and almost touching the cinderblock corner of the Newton Community Center. Scattered around the nucleus were a dozen homes in various stages of disrepair, at least half of them empty. From the center of that village, we were just about eight miles north of the Boyd ranch.

We turned south on County 805, a road that was wide and level and paved as far as the village limits—about a hundred yards from the Baca store.

After two miles of smooth, well-crowned gravel, we reached a small sign announcing the northern boundary of Posadas County. The metal signpost had been nicked by the road grader sometime in the recent past, no doubt as it was turning around to return to Newton. The county sign hung askew, pointed down at the greasewood. Ten paces beyond, securely on Posadas County turf, was another sign, this one promising that "County Maintenance Ends."

Despite the warning, the road was in good condition, and in another mile we reached an intersection where two narrow lanes met the main road, one from the southeast and one from the northwest. In the center of the right-hand island of bunchgrass stood a small, neatly lettered sign that pointed south along the main route and read, "Boyd 2 Miles."

"You could get around this way from Posadas pretty fast if you had to," I said. We passed through a low basin where the greasewood and Klein's cholla along the road were as high as the car. Dust seeped inside and I could taste the fine, powdery grit.

"You're going to miss all this come next week," I said, and Estelle turned and smiled at me.

"Yes, I am," she said, and I didn't doubt for an instant that she was telling at least a partial truth. I thought she might elaborate, but in typical Estelle fashion, she let the three-word response do all the work.

"Leo Burkhalter tells me that Eddie Mitchell has applied to his department," I said.

"Yes," she said.

I looked at Estelle in surprise. "You knew already? When did you hear that he was going?"

"Well, it's a huge department, compared to ours. And apparently they have an opening where he'll be working Homicide. It's a lateral transfer for him. He'll go in there without losing his sergeant's status.''

"And when," I asked again, "did you hear all this?"

"He told me last week. But only that he had applied. I didn't think he'd heard yet one way or another."

"Huh," I said, feeling just a tad hurt. "There's nothing formal so far, I don't think."

Estelle read my mind and said, "He didn't want to tell you until he knew for sure he was going."

"Well, I suppose it makes sense. There'll be lots of opportunities for him in a larger department."

"And more regimented," Estelle said. "I'm not sure I could work for Mr. Marine."

"Burkhalter? He's all right."

Estelle grinned. "In a very, very strait laced sort of way. He's full of himself, as Mama would say."

"I was in the Marines, you know."

"Yes, sir. But when you retired from the military, you didn't take it home with you."

"I see," I said, not seeing at all. I reached out a hand to the dashboard as we thumped across a cattle guard and pulled under the arched, wrought-iron gate of the Boyds' Circle JEB Ranch.

"Plus, there's the university campus there," Estelle added. "Eddie wants to work on his degree in criminal justice, and that's pretty hard to do in Posadas."

"I didn't know he wanted to do that, either," I said. "But I don't know why it would surprise me."

The road curved around a wart in the prairie, an out thrusting of limestone that sported a thick blanket of small barrel cacti. Just over the rise, one of Boyd's windmills was clattering along at a great rate, and I could see the sunlight flashing silver off the gentle stream of water that trickled into the large stock tank.

Their house tucked under a grove of elms, about the only tree that seemed willing to put up with the scorching summers and dry winds of winter. If not appearing actually prosperous,

the place looked as if there was at least a little hope in its
owners' lives.

Avoiding the ubiquitous adobe tones, the Boyds had
painted the house a clean white with startling blue trim. The
red-metal pitched roof would simmer most of the time, but
the wind wouldn't rip it off and the sun wouldn't blister it to
bits. One vehicle, a white-and-blue pickup truck, was parked
in the yard.

"The welcoming committee," I said as the first wave of
dogs emerged from the various shadows around the house.
Two heelers led the pack, followed by a black-and-white, one-
eyed something and—looking incongruous out here in the
middle of the cacti and cattle—two German shepherds,
tongues lolling dangerously toward beckoning cactus thorns.

"You get out first," I said gallantly. One of the heelers
jumped up and put its grimy paws on the door. I could imagine its sharp claws tearing scratches across the expensive
county decal. With good sense, Estelle hesitated. All the tails
were wagging, so we were probably safe.

A lanky, stooped individual appeared on the front porch,
whistled sharply, and the dogs retreated without a backward
glance. He waved a beckoning hand at us in greeting.

We got out of the car, and the breeze was brisk and warm,
enough to suck the moisture right out of a dog's nose in the
brief seconds between tongue swipes.

"Good morning," the man said and stepped off the porch.
One of the heelers advanced a pace or two behind him, and
the man turned and muttered something. The dog retreated
back into the shade. One of the shepherds emerged to circle
around us, nose down and ears akimbo.

"Don't worry about him none," the man said. "He's too
gaddam dumb to figure out what to do." He extended a hand
to me. "Name's Edwin Boyd. You're Undersheriff Gastner,
if I remember right."

"Good to see you," I said. I couldn't remember ever actually meeting Edwin Boyd before, beyond a quick glimpse
in a grocery-store parking lot at one time or another. He was
taller than his brother, just as lanky, clean-shaven, and leath-

ery-skinned. He wore a cap that had collected enough diesel fuel and grease and dust to disguise the logo above the bill. "This is Detective Estelle Reyes-Guzman."

Edwin Boyd's eyes twinkled as he extended a hand to Estelle. "Certainly a pleasure to meet you," he said and touched the bill of his cap with his free hand. "We got us plenty of activity today, haven't we?" He spoke with great care, as if feeling the need to be mindful of what he said.

"Yes, sir," I said. "We wanted to breakaway for a bit and talk to you folks, if we can. Away from the hustle and bustle." I smiled ruefully. "Away from all the feds."

"You got that right," Edwin said. "I took a drive this morning out to just west of where they're parked. Haven't seen so many black jackets in some time." He gestured toward the house. "Come on in, then. You figure they got everything they need to do the job?"

"I expect so," I said. "If not, you can bet they'll sure as hell ask in a hurry."

"'Spect so," he nodded, and closed the door. The house was quiet and dark. "How about some coffee?"

"That'd be nice," I said.

"Let me put some on. It won't take but a minute."

I looked up at the heavy beams that supported the painted ceiling boards. The logs were glossy with varnish but looked old and worn smooth. "The pitched room was added later, I bet," I said to Estelle. "I wonder when this place was built."

"The fireplace was put in during the fall of nineteen fifty-two," she said, pointing at the scratched date just below the mantelpiece. "So before that."

She moved over and looked through the glass doors of an elaborate gun cabinet. I joined her. The muzzles of more than a dozen rifles and shotguns gleamed from inside.

"That's interesting," she said, her gaze intent on the first three guns in the row. I recognized the M-1 Garand that stood in the number-one slot, its bayonet lug looking clumsy and angular in comparison with the slender barrels of the various sporting arms.

"I used to shoulder one of those," I said. "Worth some money now."

"And thirty-ought-six is a good, all-around caliber for ranch work," Estelle added. "And a modern version," she added, indicating the third gun in line. "Recognize it?"

The rifle was black, with lots of sharp corners and doo dads, including a long, heavy clip that hung down just in front of the trigger guard. "Maybe a Heckler and Koch. I don't know. I haven't kept up with that stuff."

"It looks to be the same size bore as the ought-six," Estelle said. "If it's foreign, it might be the NATO round. Three-oh-eight."

"You interested in hardware?" Edwin Boyd asked. I half turned, startled. I hadn't heard him return from the kitchen.

"It's all kind of neat," I said and pointed at the assault rifle. "What's that thing?"

Edwin peered through the glass as if he were looking at the collection for the first time. He reached out and turned the small key that was in the lock, then opened the door.

"Oh, that's the boy's. Some damn thing." He hefted the rifle out of the case. "Some foreign thing. But I tell you what, it's hell on wheels. Accurate as I've ever seen and spits 'em out just like that." He handed me the rifle. I was surprised at its weight.

"Quite a piece," I said and popped the clip. The brass of the loaded rounds gleamed in sharp contrast to the black metal of the weapon. "Whoops," I said.

"Oh, I doubt that there's one in the chamber," Edwin said, unperturbed. I pulled back the bolt, stiff against the recoil spring. He was right.

"He's at school in Cruces," Edwin volunteered. "I don't guess he has much need of that on campus, even though I hear things get wild there once in a while."

"What is this, a twenty-round clip?" I said, turning the clip this way and that.

"Don't know," Edwin said. "I never checked. 'Course, I don't have much use for something like that."

I handed the rifle to Estelle and held the clip so that what window light there was played on the cartridges. I could see the pointed noses of only three rounds, and I thumbed them out into my left hand. Sure enough, three was the magic number. "Really slick," I said and pushed the ammo back into the clip. "But you know, I was in the Marines, and that old M-1 is more my style." I handed the clip to Estelle. "You mind?"

"Have at it," Edwin said. He reached across and hefted the Garand by the barrel, handing it to me.

"Replacing these with the M-16 was a mistake," I said, running a hand up the long wooden stock.

"Wouldn't know," Edwin chuckled. "I did me some time in the Navy and spent most of it up close and personal with a paring knife. Still can't look a potato in the eye." He chuckled again.

I pulled back the bolt of the Garand, and sure enough, its magazine was full. I pressed the top cartridge down and eased the bolt forward so that the round wasn't stripped off the clip and into the chamber. "Nice piece," I said and returned it to the rack.

"Let me check that coffee. You take anything in it?"

"Nope," I said. "And the detective doesn't drink the stuff, so it's just you and me."

"Some lemonade, maybe?" Edwin said to Estelle, but she shook her head politely.

"I'm fine," she said. When Edwin left the room, she held the assault rifle out toward me. "How hard is it to hit something like a low-flying plane with something like this?" she asked quietly.

"For me, impossible except by dumb luck. For a marksman who's in practice, just difficult. But if the shooter's seriously trying to hit the plane, you do what antiaircraft gunners do. You don't aim at the plane. You just put a curtain of fire *in front* of the plane and let him fly into it."

"Where do you suppose the other seventeen rounds are?" she mused, and then sniffed the barrel. "Not used recently, anyway. Unless it's been cleaned thoroughly, and it doesn't smell like that, either." She leaned the gun back in the cabinet just as Edwin appeared with two mugs.

"Johnny or Maxine around this morning?" I asked as a mug was handed to me.

Edwin Boyd took a tentative sip of the coffee. "Johnny's over at the crash site, or at least that's where he said he was going. Maxine went into Posadas. You probably passed her on the highway. You came by way of Newton?"

"Sure enough."

"What kind of vehicle is she driving?" Estelle asked.

"She's got the Jeep today. That blue Wagoneer. I think it's an eighty-two. You know, one of them tanks. She was probably at the post office or some such or you'd have seen her. Me, I'm nursing a bum knee for a day or two. Sprained the hell out of it yesterday."

I looked around to sit down and settled into an old leather-padded straight chair by the fireplace. "What did you hear on the afternoon of the crash?" I asked.

Edwin looked apologetic. "Wish I'd been here. I was over to Drury, getting the hitch on the truck fixed. By the time I done this and that, and ate dinner, I didn't even get back here until close to ten o'clock."

"Maxine told you what happened?" Estelle asked.

"Yeah, that's who I heard about it from. I drove over close enough to see the lights and the helicopter and all. I figured I'd be in the way. Then later, Johnny came and we both run the cattle out of that section." He grimaced. "That's when I wrenched my knee. Can't work in the dark so good."

"Earlier in the day," I said, "did you see any aircraft in the area?" Edwin shook his head. "Nothing anytime at all?"

"No. But then I don't pay much attention to that sort of thing. What was the sheriff lookin' for, anyway? Did you ever find out?"

"No idea," I said.

"And no word yet about what actually caused the crash in the first place," Edwin said.

It wasn't a question, so I didn't offer any information. I placed my coffee mug on the end table and pushed myself to my feet. "Apparently Maxine called the sheriff's office some-time yesterday. She even tried to reach Sheriff Holman at home."

Edwin Boyd frowned. "Huh," he said, and looked down at the wooden floor.

I could see he wasn't planning on being a fountain of un-solicited information and it would be easier just to talk to Maxine Boyd about her telephone calls.

"Thanks for the coffee," I said. "I'm sure you'll be seeing us around more than you'd like in the next few days."

Edwin waved a hand. "Now don't worry about that. You folks got a job to do, same as anyone else." He walked behind Estelle and me as we left the house. His truck, the one we had seen when we arrived, was a late-model GMC three-quarter ton, parked in the shade of one of the elms.

The rear-window gun rack carried a single Winchester le-ver-action rifle, probably a .30-30. I didn't mention the gun, but I saw Estelle's gaze take it in.

When we were back in the patrol car, I said, "He appar-ently doesn't favor the modern stuff," referring to the rifle. "But he can probably shoot a coyote in the eye at a hundred yards."

"I really want to talk to Maxine," Estelle said. "There's every possibility that she didn't drive into town just to go shopping for groceries."

EIGHTEEN

I LICKED DUST off my lips and regarded Estelle Reyes-Guzman as she drove back toward Newton.

"What are you thinking?" I asked.

We thumped from gravel to pavement at the same time we caught a first glimpse of the "Baca" sign as we came around

a row of abandoned, flat-roofed buildings that marked the last
vestiges of Newton's suburbs.

"You've always told me that it's the little things that finally
come together to finish a puzzle, sir," she said. "Something
was important enough to Maxine that she tried to contact
Sheriff Holman twice yesterday, once at home and once at
the office. To me, that's important."

"And there are a hundred explanations, too," I said. "Anything from door-to-door bible salesmen to a family spat that
turned ugly."

"But she didn't say anything last night at the crash site."
She glanced over at me and then turned the car into the small
parking lot in front of Baca's. As she pushed the gear lever
into park, she said, "She and her husband were there most of
the night. You said so yourself. She could have talked to you,
or to one of the deputies, anytime she pleased. She could have
called me at the office in Posadas. She didn't do any of those
things."

"Maybe the problem resolved itself, whatever it was."

"Maybe. This is the other thing that bothers me. A shot
was fired from the ground. If the shot was intentional, it might
have been one of a hail of bullets. Maybe only one struck the
plane. Maybe it was a single, well-placed shot."

"A single, extraordinarily lucky shot," I said. "Or it might
have been an accident."

"It might have been. But so far, no one has turned up
anyone who was in that area at the time. It seems big, maybe,
but the general area where Philip Camp's plane was circling
was really pretty small. It's logical that the shot was fired by
someone who slipped out of the area without being seen, or
it was fired by someone in the area who just isn't talking."

"I can understand that whoever it was, he might be reluctant to jump forward and volunteer that information," I said.
"If there was a passel of kids from the various ranches, then
that's a possibility. But the population of that area includes
the Boyds...that's Johnny, Maxine, and Edwin. Their only
son is in Las Cruces, at school."

Estelle opened her door, but made no move to get out of

the vehicle. "And the Finnegans have no children," she said. "Geographically, the only other family who lives within any reasonable distance is the Kealeys. The road into their ranch is on down east of here. Their place is just outside the Posadas County line. In order for any of them to be in the vicinity of the crash site, they'd either have to cross the Finnegans' or the Boyds' place."

"Unlikely," I said.

Estelle swung her door wider and turned sideways, as if to slide out. She stopped, one hand on the door and one on the steering wheel. "There's something there, sir. I know there is."

"Meaning what? That Martin Holman was overflying the area because of something that was concerning Maxine Boyd? Something that she wanted to talk to him in particular about?"

"Yes."

"And the next connection to consider is whether the person who fired the shot knew who his target was."

Estelle slid out of the car. "That's going to be the tough part," she said. "I'm going to find some iced tea. Do you want anything?"

I shook my head. No sooner had Estelle gotten out of the car and closed the door than the radio squawked, and she halted in her tracks.

"Three-ten, Posadas. Ten-twenty."

I picked up the mike. "Isn't that Linda?" I asked, and Estelle nodded. "And why does she want to know where we are? Gayle should have said something. She knows better than to ask that over the air." I frowned and pushed the button. "Posadas, this is three-ten."

"Three-ten, can you ten-nineteen?"

"Can I?" I mumbled without keying the mike. "Ten-four, Posadas. ETA about twenty-five minutes."

"There's a woman here who said she needs to talk to you, sir." I looked heavenward, wishing that Gayle Sedillos was standing more firmly at Linda Real's elbow. "A Mrs. Boyd."

I swore and rapped the mike against the dashboard sharply. "Ten-four," I said, trying to keep my voice even.

Estelle was in the car and pulling it into reverse before I'd slammed the mike back in the bracket. "She's trying, sir," she said.

"Goddam broadcast our business all over the county," I said and shook my head. "She should have used the phone, anyway."

The car hit the pavement with a chirp of tires. "And it might be nice," I added, "if we didn't poke along, now that the entire world knows what we're doing."

From Newton to the Posadas County Public Safety Building was 34.7 miles. We had covered two thirds of that distance when the radio barked again.

"Three-ten, Posadas."

"Now what?" I muttered and fumbled the mike off the bracket. It was Gayle Sedillos on the air, sounding crisp and formal.

"Three-ten, cancel ten-nineteen. Subjects have left the office."

"Ten-four," I said, puzzled. Estelle slowed the car a bit and I looked at her. "She apparently didn't want to talk to us very badly."

As we passed the Posadas Municipal Airport on the outskirts of town, I saw activity near the hangar, but my attention was drawn away as a blue-over-white Jeep Wagoneer drove past us headed west.

"That's Maxine Boyd," Estelle said and slowed to pull onto the shoulder so she could do a U-turn. We had to wait for an oncoming pickup truck to pass before we could swing around. Johnny Boyd was at the wheel of the truck. As he drove by, he smiled and lifted a forefinger in greeting.

With a protest from the tires, Estelle turned around and accelerated, pulling in close behind Boyd's truck. I could see a handful of oncoming traffic in the distance, and for almost a mile, Boyd drove as if he were unaware of our presence.

Finally, at a turnout for one of the State Highway Department's stockpiles of crushed stone the brake lights on Boyd's truck flashed and he pulled over. I expected Estelle to do the same, but instead, she accelerated past, and in another half mile, we were on Maxine Boyd's back bumper. There we stayed for several minutes.

"She knows you're here," I said as the woman showed no inclination to stop.

Estelle nodded and looked in the rearview mirror. "And so does her husband." Sure enough, Johnny Boyd's truck trailed us by a dozen car lengths.

"If she doesn't stop, we'll just follow her back to the ranch," Estelle said.

"Stop her right here, if you want to," I said.

Estelle shook her head. "I don't want to use the lights, sir. I want to keep this as friendly as possible."

"The Boyds are friendly," I said. "As long as it's coincidence that they're both downtown at the same time."

"That's what I was thinking," Estelle said. "Let's just be patient and see what happens."

What happened was that Maxine Boyd ignored us until we reached Newton. Then she pulled into the parking lot in front of Baca's. Estelle parked on the far side of the Wagoneer, and Johnny Boyd swerved in so that he was angled toward the Wagoneer, fender to fender.

Mrs. Boyd didn't get out of the Jeep, but her window was rolled down. Johnny Boyd eased himself out of the pickup and sauntered around the front end, then leaned an elbow on the hood of the Wagoneer. The body language wasn't lost on me. If we wanted to talk to his wife, he'd have to move.

"How you doing?" I said. Without it being offered, I walked over and took up position with my elbow on the Jeep's hood, too. Estelle was messing with paperwork in the patrol car and hadn't gotten out.

"I hope you folks got more rest than we have," I said and pushed my Stetson back on my head. "We needed to see if anything's jogged your memory"—I turned and nodded at Maxine Boyd as well—"if you folks heard anything the afternoon of the crash. If you heard anything unusual. Even earlier in the day."

"Unusual? Like how?" Johnny Boyd asked. He fished a cigarette out of his pocket and lit it.

"Well, we've had at least one report saying the engine on that plane was backfiring pretty badly. That gives us a little something to go on. It looks like they might have been having trouble of some kind."

"If they did, I never heard it," Boyd said. "You know, I never saw that plane go down. I was up here in Newton just about that time. Right inside the store here. I didn't know what all the ruckus was until the traffic started to show up and cut tracks through my pasture."

"Was your wife home?" I asked. Estelle had gotten out of the car and had her clipboard in hand. The expression on her face was thoughtful as she walked around the back of the Wagoneer.

"Well, yes, she was home," Boyd said and turned. By that time, Estelle was at the driver's-side window of the Wagoneer. She unclipped a photograph from the board and handed it to Boyd, resting the clipboard on the windowsill as she waited for him to look at the photo.

"What's this?" he asked and turned the photo against the glare from the sun.

"We were wondering if you could tell us where that windmill is," Estelle said. "And, ma'am, if you were home, we need to know if you saw or heard anything unusual."

Maxine Boyd shook her head. "I had that darn old television on," she said. "And now I sure wish I hadn't. But I did, you know."

"So you didn't hear the aircraft at all?" Estelle asked. Maxine glanced at the clipboard and shook her head.

"Well," Johnny Boyd said, "this here is the windmill out by what we call the block house. It isn't in this picture, but just off to the north"——he held the photo toward me and indicated with a stubby index finger—"there's the remains of an old stone building. Damn thing was built to last forever, thick as those walls are."

"From your place, where would that be?" I asked.

"East and a bit north. It's over on the back side of Dick Finnegan's place." He shrugged and handed the photo back to Estelle. "There're old windmills all over. Most of 'em have had the guts pulled off the tower. This one here, though, it still pumps from time to time.'' He grinned ruefully. ''There ain't just a whole lot of water 'round about.'' He glanced at his wife. ''So what's the significance of that? You want pictures of old windmills, I can show you a couple dozen.''

''We don't know yet,'' Estelle said. She hesitated as if weighing just how much she should say. ''This photo was taken by Sheriff Holman during that flight Friday afternoon.''

Boyd grunted. ''Maybe he was a collector of windmill pictures.''

''I don't think so,'' I said.

Estelle had handed the photo to Maxine Boyd, and the woman frowned as she studied it. ''This is where Dick was trying to dig that pond isn't it?'' she asked her husband.

''No, not there. He was thinkin' of putting one in over at William's Tank. But he gave up,'' Johnny said shortly.

''Gave up?'' I said.

Boyd shrugged and took the photo from his wife. He glanced at it briefly again and handed it to Estelle. ''Dick wastes his time in all kinds of strange ways,'' he said. ''There wouldn't have been any water to put in the tank even if he finished digging for it. I guess after a few hours on the dozer, he reached that same conclusion. The way this soil is, it would never have held water anyway. He'd have to line the tank somehow. Bentonite, or plastic, or something. Not worth the trouble for what little water that mill puts out.''

''Wasn't he going to—'' Maxine started to say, but Johnny Boyd cut her off.

''I understand that they're going to put that plane back together,'' he said. ''Down in one of those hangars at the airport.''

''That's right,'' I said. ''They're transporting the wreckage this morning.'' I grinned. ''The detective and I thought it might be a good idea to stay out of their way.''

''What do they expect to find?''

''That's just it,'' I said. ''None of us know what we're looking for. We'd kind of like to have some woodcutter come out of the trees and say, 'Hey, I saw the whole thing.' But I don't think that's going to happen."

Boyd snorted in derision and stamped out his cigarette. "If you found somebody who'd tell you that, nine times out of ten they'd get it all screwed up, anyways."

"You're right, but it's more like ninety-nine out of a hundred," I said.

"Who told you about the backfiring thing?" Boyd asked. "Or is that privileged information?" He smiled thinly and rummaged in his shirt pocket for another cigarette.

"Mrs. Finnegan," I said, and Johnny Boyd's reaction was immediate.

He looked heavenward, then at his wife and grinned. "Christ almighty," he said and shook his head, chuckling. "She might have told you that the airplane was being chased by a squadron of UFOs, too. Her elevator don't go all the way to the top floor, that's for damn sure." He pointed the cigarette at Estelle's clipboard.

"That the only picture the sheriff managed to take?" he asked.

"No," Estelle replied. "There are others, but they don't show much of interest." She paused and then said, "Fence lines, that sort of thing."

"Huh," Boyd said. He slapped a hand on the fender of his wife's Wagoneer. "Well, if you need anything, you folks just holler. There's almost always someone to home. I guess maybe you talked to Edwin already."

"Yep," I said and glanced at Estelle. "He was in Drury at the time of the crash, so that's not going to help much. And who knows," I said, pushing myself away from my leaning spot on the Jeep's fender, "we may never know just what happened, or why."

Boyd chuckled. "I'll tell you one thing that's for damn sure true. If you keep those feds around here long enough, they'll make up a story that fits, whether it's anywhere close to what actually happened or not. You know how that goes."

"They've got a job to do, like everyone else," I said.

"Yeah, well," Johnny said, then shook his head with disgust and dropped the subject. Estelle had turned and apparently said something to Maxine, because the woman nodded briefly before Estelle walked back to the patrol car.

"You just keep 'em away from me," Johnny said, and I regarded him with interest.

"They'll talk to you if they think it's necessary, Johnny. That's just the way things go," I said.

The last thing I wanted was to enter into an argument with Johnny Boyd about federal agencies. When it came right down to it, what he thought one way or another didn't matter much. So I settled for, "Thanks, folks," and a tip of my hat. As I settled into the car, Estelle was rummaging around in the back seat. Both Boyds had pulled out and left Baca's parking lot by the time she slid back into the front seat.

She held the clipboard out to me. On it, in inch-high letters, she'd printed neatly: *Do you need to talk to me privately?*

"She nodded that she did, twice," Estelle said. "So she knows something that either she doesn't want her husband to hear or that he already knows and doesn't want to tell us."

"Maybe so," I said.

"And one other thing," Estelle said as she tucked the clipboard back under the stack of paperwork that filled the center section of the front seat. "No one told him that we'd been talking to his brother."

"Lucky guess," I said. "I wouldn't be surprised if he's got a scanner in that rig of his. Half of the ranchers do, along with CBs, cell phones, and God knows what else. If he heard my estimate of how long it was going to take us to get back to the office and then saw us coming in on the state road, he could have put two and two together."

"I wish *we* could," Estelle said and slapped the steering wheel in frustration.

"So how are you going to arrange to meet with Maxine Boyd?"

"First I'll try the obvious thing. I'll give her a phone call."

"That's not too private."

"It'll work. The phone's in the kitchen. I'll call right at dinnertime." She lowered her voice an octave. "Hubby at table, eating steak." She turned to me and grinned. "He won't get up to answer the phone. She will."

I grimaced. "You read too much psychological stuff."

"It works, though. Watch."

NINETEEN

NEIL COSTACE was leaning against the counter in the dispatch room, idly reading the daily call log, when Estelle and I entered the Public Safety Building. He turned and saw us, and his lips came close to a smile. But the rest of his face was sober, even grim.

As I approached, the FBI agent straightened up and extended his hand. His grip was firm. "Bill," he said, and nodded at Estelle. "Walter Hocker, one of our special agents who works out of Oklahoma City, is up here with me."

I looked around. "Fine. Where is he?"

"He's using the telephone in the sheriff's office."

I nodded and said to Gayle Sedillos, "When he's finished, tell him to join us." I indicated the door to my own office, and as Estelle and Costace filed past me, I turned back to Gayle. "And I need to see Linda Real, Eddie Mitchell, and Doug Posey." I smiled at her. "In any order."

"Linda's working downstairs, sir," Gayle said, and made hand motions to indicate a camera.

"As soon as she can break free," I said, and walked into my office and closed the door. I'd worked with Neil Costace several times before on cases that interested the Federal Bureau of Investigation. He had a law degree, but never let it get in the way.

"Bring me up to speed on this fine Sunday morning," he said, and sat down on one of the straight chairs. "I understand from Buscema that the pilot of the aircraft was killed by ground fire.'' He made it sound like an incident in a war zone.

"That's correct. It appears that one bullet struck him low in the back, traveled upward and unzipped his aorta. It also appears that the bullet was fragmenting when it struck him, so it's going to be interesting to see just where it struck the airframe of the Bonanza. That should tell us something.''

"No ground witnesses?''

"Maybe one,'' I said. "We have a woman...come here and let me show you.'' I stepped to the wall map of Posadas County. "She and her husband live right here. The Finnegans. She's the woman who made the initial call reporting an aircraft in trouble. She told us that she saw it flying in big circles in this area here, and then she claims that she heard sounds that were like an engine backfiring.''

"Backfiring?''

"Right. And that's what the sounds, if she heard them at all, might have been. So far, there's no obvious evidence of mechanical failure in the aircraft's engine, but we won't know definitely for some time.''

"Yeah, yeah,'' Costace said with impatience. "They'll have to tear it down. Weeks and weeks. But you're saying the sounds that the witness said were of backfiring could have been the gunshots responsible.''

"Yes.''

"Weather?''

"Windy, gusting out of the west-southwest at twenty knots or more.''

"So regardless of the source of the 'backfires,''' Costace said, "that noise had to have been fairly close to the witness in order for her to hear it, even downwind.''

"I would guess so.''

"And no one else was seen on the ground?''

"No. We've had people scouring the mesa, the forest roads, everywhere. But remember that we didn't locate the crash until nearly dark, and we didn't arrive at the scene until well after dark.'' I stopped and took a breath. "And we didn't know about the bullet fragment until yesterday around mid-morning. So the odds of the shooter still being in the area are slim to none.''

Costace crossed his arms over his chest. ''And the wounds that killed the pilot were such that you don't think he could have flown for any great distance after being struck?''

I shook my head. ''If what Mrs. Finnegan tells us is correct, the plane was flying normally, then she heard the noises, followed immediately by erratic flight patterns. Then it disappeared from view behind a mesa, so she didn't actually see the crash.''

''How reliable is she, do you think? You just sounded like her version of events might not be the most accurate.''

''If she's not actually mentally ill, Charlotte Finnegan is a hairsbreadth from it. I'm not sure how much of what she actually sees is real or what she imagines.''

''Husband? Other members of the family?''

''Only her husband, and he wasn't home at the time.''

''Huh.'' Costace rubbed a hand through his close-cropped hair. ''And Buscema says that...'' He let his voice trail off as the door opened. A short, stumpy man in jeans, knit golf shirt, and a light blue jacket stepped into the room. He didn't bother to knock, and he pushed the door shut behind him. He carried a slender black-leather folder.

''Bill, this is Special Agent Walter Hocker. Walt, Undersheriff Bill Gastner. And this is Detective Estelle Reyes-Guzman.'' Hands were pumped, and Hocker regarded Estelle with interest.

''Isn't your husband one of the docs over at the hospital?'' His voice was quiet and husky, right on the edge of being hard to hear.

''My husband is a physician, yes,'' Estelle said.

''He's doing the autopsies?''

''Yes. He's working the autopsies with Dr. Alan Perrone, one of the assistant state medical examiners.''

''Ah,'' Hocker said. He stood with his hands on his hips, feet planted. He transferred his attention to the top of my desk, but it was clear that he was preoccupied with his own thoughts rather than actually interested in my housekeeping.

While he gathered his thoughts, I walked around behind the desk and sat down. "So," I said, and folded my hands on the blotter. Hocker jerked out of his trance, squared his shoulders, and sat down on the edge of the desk, dropping his leather folder beside him.

"Buckmaster…no, what's his name?"

"Vincent Buscema," Costace prompted.

"Buscema." Hocker looked up at the ceiling and closed his eyes for a couple of seconds, as if he were playing private memory tricks. "Buscema. Right." He nodded and looked down at me. "He says that you have film from the sheriff's camera, as well as a fragment of the projectile. Is that right?"

"Correct."

"All right. We need to get those to the lab," Hocker said. "Just as quickly as we can."

"The film is being processed into prints right now," I said. "And two of the deputies are working on the bullet fragments."

"What, you didn't send the film off somewhere, did you?"

I didn't bother to dignify the question with an answer, and Estelle must have seen the flush on my cheeks. "One of our staff is processing the film downstairs," she said.

"And the fragment analysis…they're doing the work here as well?"

"Yes," I said. Somehow, Hocker had made the word *here* sound as if it referred to the end of the earth, and that irritated the hell out of me—even more than the implication that we'd entrust evidence to MinutePhoto down at the mall, if we had a mall.

"I'll be glad to share with you what we have so far." Hocker frowned and I added, "What, we're going to have one of those ridiculous turf wars now? Where we all waste time arguing about whose case it is?"

Hocker twisted his head and looked sharply at me. I returned his gaze without further comment. After ten seconds or so, I saw the crow's-feet at the corner of his eyes deepen just a bit.

"No, we're not going to do that, Sheriff. The Federal Aviation Administration and the National Transportation Safety Board asked for our assistance. I wish that they'd made that request through your office initially, and I apologize that they didn't. You have to admit that it's a case that will draw considerable attention—a Canadian plane, a Canadian citizen at the controls, shot out of the sky not a stone's throw from the U.S.-Mexican border, killing both the pilot and a passenger, who just happens to be the county sheriff." He paused. "That's the story as it was passed on to me. Am I about right?"

"You're about right. Except that the incident has nothing to do with either the Canadian citizenship of the pilot, the Canadian registry of the aircraft, or with the proximity of the incident to the Mexican border."

Hocker raised an eyebrow. "You're sure?"

"No."

He relaxed and this time, the smile lit up his face. "Well, we can all hope that it doesn't." He stood up. "What about the bullet fragment?"

"We have one piece, about the size of—" I glanced around for something to make a comparison. I pointed at the little rectangular amber light on the front of my computer—"a little bigger than that light. There may be others."

"That's going to be a tough one," Hocker said.

I nodded. "I've assigned two deputies to work that up. When they exhaust their resources, and I imagine that will be fairly quickly, then we'll send the fragment to whatever lab is most appropriate. We may develop specific questions to ask that will help in the analysis."

"Do you know what kind of work the deputies are planning to do on the piece?"

"I would imagine that they'll take basic measurements, weigh it, that sort of thing. If the fragment includes marks from the rifling in the barrel, that may be useful. With a fragment that small, it's going to be hard to establish the caliber with any certainty. Establishing the make or model of weapon is going to be even more difficult. And photos will be taken, of course. If by some stroke of luck we should come up with

a suspect's firearm, we might be able to make a comparison—
if there are enough marks to go on." I smiled. "The deputies
won't ruin the evidence, Agent Hocker."

Hocker shook his head quickly. "I didn't mean to imply
that," he said. "I just want to make sure that the initial avenues of investigation are opened quickly."

"That's what we do around here," I said and leaned back.
"We open avenues." I glanced at Estelle, who had remained
silent and stood near the door. She regarded Hocker, her face
expressionless. I couldn't tell what was going on behind those
black eyes, and maybe that was just as well.

"And the photos?" Hocker asked.

"As the detective said, one of our personnel is in the darkroom right now. The film has been developed and she's working on a series of enlargements."

Hocker nodded. "Outstanding." He squared his shoulders
and tucked in his shirt. "Did you get a preliminary look?"

"Yes. Detective Reyes-Guzman has several of the initial
blowups, if you'd like to see them."

Hocker did, and after Estelle spread the photos out on my
desk, he spent several minutes looking at each in turn, with
Costace at his elbow.

"This windmill apparently interested the sheriff," I said,
tapping the photo of the block-house site. "There are two
ranchers whose land covers the crash site, the Boyds and the
Finnegans. This is on the Finnegans' property, about a mile
from the site."

"Bizarre," Hocker mused. He lined up the edges of two
prints. "And this little building here is just off to the side, a
few yards from the windmill?"

"Right."

"Prairie, fence, more prairie. A few head of cattle," Neil
Costace said.

"Actually, they're antelope," Estelle said. She managed to
make it sound like simply an interesting fact rather than a
correction.

Hocker didn't look up. "And what would the sheriff care
about antelope?" he asked. "They're all over the southwest."

"We don't know," I said.

He stood up and shook his head. "Huh." He shrugged and added, "Well, all this is interesting, but it doesn't tell us much. We agree on that?" He slid the photos back into the packet and handed them to Estelle, then picked up his leather folder. "The fact that one of the crash victims was the county sheriff is what interests me," he said. "If the shot wasn't just a random one, if it was intentional, then it's a case of an altogether greater dimension."

I nodded and said nothing. We had been down that road before, without any answers popping out of the sand.

"I've made some inquiries through the regular federal channels," he said. "In fact, I just got off the phone. We have only four names so far that are connected with this thing, and it made sense to me to run each one through the federal centers and see what we got."

"Holman, Camp, Boyd, and Finnegan," I said. "I would guess it's going to be slim pickings."

Hocker shrugged. "The day is yet young," he said and grinned. "But first I'd like to take a look at the aircraft and see what that tells us."

I couldn't imagine seeing much more than a neat hole through a piece of crumpled aluminum, but sifting through the remains of the Bonanza would give us all something to do. Maybe the others didn't, but I needed that. I was growing impatient, waiting for the slow wheels of forensic science to tell me something I couldn't already guess with equipment no more fancy than a good pair of bifocals.

TWENTY

AS WE ARRIVED AT Posadas Municipal Airport, Robert Torrez, Tom Pasquale, Vincent Buscema, and another FAA official whom I hadn't met were in the process of lifting a large portion of the right wing off a small flatbed truck.

The shield on the truck's door read "Posadas Electric," and I wondered briefly which of Torrez's relatives had donated the use of his vehicle. The sergeant was related to half the town and knew the other half.

I watched as Deputy Pasquale operated the forklift and for once, he drove the machine as if he had a Ming vase on the forks.

Inside the cavernous and cool hangar, I surveyed the litter. In the hours since dawn that Sunday, Vincent Buscema had been able to work miracles. The hangar floor looked as if someone were arranging a display of landfill art. As the wing settled to the cradle of two-by-fours that Buscema kicked under it, I walked around the back of the forklift, staying well clear when Pasquale threw the thing into reverse.

With no load, he spun the lift around in its own length and charged back outside to the apron, operating once more at his normal pace.

Buscema approached and shook hands with the two FBI agents. "We're making progress," he said.

"I would never have guessed that a small aircraft could make so many pieces," I said.

He nodded. "What we're going to do as we bring more and more down is to arrange everything we've got so it makes sense, nose to tail, wingtip to wingtip. That helps us understand what we've got."

I stepped over to the engine block. The propeller hub was still in place, but even my unpracticed eye could see the bend in the crankshaft and imagine the tremendous forces slammed against the hub and shaft as the prop hit the ground. "I've seen pictures where the plane was basically reassembled," I said, "actually put back together, patched together. They did it with that airliner that blew up back East didn't they?"

"Sure," Buscema said. "But we won't have to do that here. We're ninety-nine-percent sure of what happened. I mean, that engine you're looking at tells most of the story. It was turning at least cruise RPM when the blades hit the ground. Two of the blades were sheared off, and we've got the tips. The third blade looks like a pretzel.'' He nudged the engine with his toe. "There was nothing wrong with that engine when the plane hit the ground. You can bet on that.'' He put his hands on his hips and turned, surveying the collection.

"We could spend days and days trying to decide if there was a mechanical control failure of some kind, but I think that's going to be a waste of time, too. What you want,'' he said as Hocker bent down and examined a chunk of white-painted aluminum roughly the size of a large grocery bag, ''is to find a small hole that doesn't belong.''

"Or holes,'' Hocker said.

"Or holes, yes,'' Buscema pointed off to the left. "We're putting the fuselage right in here.''

"So show me the seats,'' I said. "If the fragment hit the pilot low in the back, it had to go through the seat first.''

"Exactly, and the hole is exactly where we thought it might be. Look.'' I grimaced as he stepped over and beckoned me to one of the brightly upholstered seats, now twisted and looking so out of place amid the scraps on the floor.

Hocker and Costace were quicker than I was, kneeling beside one of the seats as Buscema turned it slightly. A small piece of red survey flagging had been tied to part of the seat's framework.

"It's such a small cut that at first glance, it doesn't show,'' Buscema said. He slid his hand under the seat cover from the bottom and spread the fabric. "Entry,'' he said. "Of course that little cut in the fabric could have been caused at almost anytime by somebody careless with a ski pole, fishing rod''— he shrugged—"even with the latch of a briefcase, I suppose.'' He slid his hand out of the seat.

"But higher up on the front side, we've got a companion tear, a little bit larger.''

"A really steep angle,'' Estelle murmured.

"For sure,'' Buscema said. "The angle fits. There's blood on the seat, but that's consistent with the crash trauma.''

"The wound from a small, high-velocity fragment isn't going to cause much bleeding,'' Bob Torrez said, and Hocker glanced at him.

''All right,'' Hocker said. ''We've got holes in the pilot. We've got holes in the seat. Then it shouldn't be hard to find where the bullet pierced the belly of the plane, ripped up through the flooring, whatever that's made of, zipped through the carpet, then through the seat and into the pilot.''

''That's what we plan to do,'' Buscema said. ''The next truck down will have the majority of the fuselage's remaining pieces, including the major cabin structure.'' He glanced at his watch. ''I expect that within the hour. Sheriff, I really think that you'll have something solid to go on in just a short while.''

I nodded. ''What we need to do,'' I said, ''is to start the process of matching the fragment with other fragments. What are the odds that when you take that seat apart, you'll find more of the bullet?''

''Maybe,'' Hocker said. ''And maybe inside the cabin floor structure too, if the bullet hit a frame member and shattered.'' He turned to Estelle. ''There were no exit wounds on the body?''

''No, sir.''

''Any calculated guesses on the bullet caliber?''

''That's going to be a tough call,'' I said. ''Maybe when we see the first entry hole that it made in the plane, we can make a guess.''

''I'm guessing twenty-two caliber,'' Torrez said. ''Maybe twenty-five.''

''Is that just a hunch, or do you know something we don't?'' Costace asked.

''On the fragment that Mitchell and Abeyta are working up,'' Torrez said, ''there's a small portion of rifling marking. Just enough that it can be measured. It's real narrow, like you'd find on something of that caliber.''

''You're not talking twenty-two rimfire like in a kid's gun?'' Hocker asked.

''No. Two-twenty-three. The sort of bullet fired in any of the high-performance center-fire rifles. The M-16 is a two-twenty-three. So is the Mini-14. Or the twenty-two two-fifty. And a whole bunch more. And if it's twenty-five caliber, it opens up a whole world of possibilities—the twenty-five-ought-six, two-fifty-seven Roberts, and on and on.''

"And then there's the whole world of foreign cartridges, too," Costace added.

"Robert, let me ask you something," I said. "If you've got a good clear sample of the marks left by rifling, can that be compared to other samples?"

The sergeant grimaced. "Really tough," he said.

Hocker frowned. "The answer is yes, Sheriff. They can be compared under a good microscope. But you're not going to get the *points* of comparison that you're going to need in court. Not unless you're really, really lucky."

"But it gives us someplace to start," I said. "And that's what we need now."

A truck drove up to the hangar door and I looked outside to see the dark blue Dodge four-by-four with the "New Mexico Department of Game and Fish" decal on the door.

"Finally," I said.

TWENTY-ONE

DOUG POSEY appeared in the doorway and hesitated. He stood with his hands on his hips, surveying the collected remnants. He saw me and shook his head, a grimace on his face as he walked over. As tall as Bob Torrez's six-four, Posey was so thin that he looked as if he'd break in the middle in a stiff breeze.

I introduced him to the federal agents. "Officer Posey has been with the State Department of Game and Fish for four years," I said. "If we could steal him away from them, we would." Posey tried to smile and he tugged nervously at all

STEVEN F. HAVILL   125

the junk on his Sam Brown belt. He looked more like nineteen than the twenty-nine that he was.

"I sure was sorry to hear about the sheriff," he said. "God, look at this. The crash just tore it to bits, didn't it?" He bent down and touched one of the twisted propeller blades. "It's on the television, even."

"You know it's big when news from Posadas hits the airwaves," I said, and then reflected privately that all the publicity would have made Martin Holman nervous. He wouldn't have liked this at all—being the center of federal, state, and local attention. And sure as could be, now that the preliminary reports had leaked out, we'd be targeted by the news crews.

"They'll descend like vultures when they find out it was no accident," Neil Costace said. "I'm surprised they're not knocking on the door now."

"It wasn't an accident?" Posey looked up, startled.

"Looks like it wasn't, Doug," I said. "The pilot caught a bullet that we think was fired from the ground."

"No shit?"

I nodded. "Keep it under your hat for now, all right?"

"Sure. Frank Dayan was at the office when I stopped by. Gayle was giving him the official story, from what it sounded like."

"Which means she was giving him zilch," I said. I had nothing against the editor of the *Posadas Register*. In fact, there had been times when I'd orchestrated events—or at least news releases—so that they benefited the *Register*'s Wednesday/Friday publication days, giving them a local scoop over the big-city papers. But we needed some peace and quiet now.

"Look," I said and took Posey by the elbow.

"You want some privacy?" Hocker asked.

I waved a hand in dismissal. "No. In fact, you might be interested, too. Doug, our call logs show that Sheriff Holman was trying to get ahold of you yesterday. He tried several times."

"Yesterday?"

I frowned. "What the hell is today? Sunday? Not yesterday,

then. Friday. On Friday, he was trying to reach you. Did you get those messages?''

Posey nodded. ''I was stuck down in the eastern part of the state with a little operation we had going there. I got his message on my machine when I came in just a little while ago.''

''What did the sheriff want, do you know?''

Posey rested his hand on the clip pouches on the front of his belt. ''The crash wasn't an accident? You're sure of that?'' he asked, and he glanced across at Hocker and Costace. I liked the kid even more.

''No, it wasn't,'' I said. ''The firing of the bullet might have been. At this point, we don't know if the bullet that struck the pilot was fired intentionally or not. None of us know for sure which direction we should be going with all this, but we're trying to track down each loose end. There's the question of Martin's calls to you and we need to know where those lead, if anywhere. It's conceivable that the flight he was making was somehow related to what he wanted from you. We don't know.''

''Well,'' Posey said, ''about two weeks ago, he stopped me downtown as I was coming out of the bank. He asked me what I knew about the legalities of impounding wildlife. Game animals.''

''Impounding?''

Posey nodded. ''That's what the sheriff said. He told me that someone had asked him about it and that he didn't know what the regs were.'' Posey looked pained. ''We both had places we needed to go, and he told me that he'd get back to me on it with more specifics if there was a problem. I got busy with other things and didn't follow up on it. I guess he didn't either, until last week.''

''When you say 'impounding,' you mean fencing in wildlife so it can't roam outside of a given area?'' Estelle asked.

''Sure. Mostly it's done with fish. You dam up a waterway with a real restricted intake and overflow sluice so the fish can't go upstream or down.''

''I don't think we're talking fish,'' I said.

''I sure don't know what you'd impound around here,''

Posey said. "Antelope, I guess, maybe deer, although there's enough of them out on the open that I don't see what sense it'd make. Up in the northern part of the state, there have been a few ranchers who got into trouble restricting the movements of elk. The big-game ranches do that all the time. They manage herds, the whole bit—but they have the proper permits for it." He shrugged. "I just don't know. We didn't talk again after that, so I don't know what he was up to."

I looked at Estelle thoughtfully. "What do you think?"

"I just don't know either, sir."

"Let's go talk to this Boyd person," Hocker said. "See if he was out shooting at prairie dogs on Friday."

"You ready for it to go public?" Costace asked quickly.

Hocker shrugged. "Hell, why not? Maybe somebody'll call in a hot tip."

I beckoned to Estelle. "Come along," I said. "If you get a chance to talk to Maxine Boyd, go ahead. Find out what's eating her."

I turned and nodded at the FBI agents. "We were just out there at the ranch before you came to the office. The Boyds haven't had so much company in a long time. And they're going to be really pleased to see you folks."

Hocker caught the tone of my voice. "I bet," he said.

TWENTY-TWO

WHEN I TURNED AROUND and saw the dust plume as we turned south from Newton, I was glad that Estelle Reyes-Guzman was driving the lead vehicle. The two agents had elected to follow us, taking Costace's Suburban. The monstrous truck would have held the four of us plus luggage for a month.

"It's a back-seat thing," Estelle said with a hint of a grin.

"If they rode with us, one or both would end up sitting in back."

"Can't have that," I said. To avoid traffic, we drove the loop around Newton, guaranteeing that if the two agents weren't feeling lost before, they would be now. Neither Costace nor Hocker had visited the crash site, and we planned to go there afterward...not that there would be much left on the ground to see.

As we neared the Boyds' ranch, Estelle slowed, forcing the pace down to little more than an amble. I knew exactly what was going through her mind.

Two big four-by-fours, spiraling vapor trails of dust, sliding to a stop in the middle of someone's yard and then spewing out all kinds of strangers wearing dark glasses—it was enough to make anyone uneasy, especially folks whose list of monthly visitors rarely broke single digits. And especially well-armed folks who harbored an almost irrational distrust of things federal.

We idled into the Boyds' front yard. I could see Edwin over by one of the trucks, a one-ton GMC fitted with a flatbed and a large feed hopper. Johnny Boyd came out from behind the rear of the truck and watched our progress toward the house. When we pulled to a stop, he tossed his gloves onto the back of the truck bed and started toward us, head down, fingers of his right hand groping in his shirt pocket for the habitual conversational smoke.

The dogs started yapping, but at a word from Johnny, all but the shepherd retreated to the workshop behind the truck. The dog trotted along beside Boyd, tongue lolling, ears toward us.

Boyd grinned wearily and extended his hand. "Sheriff, you still out and at it, eh? I keep thinking of how nice a long afternoon nap would go right about now. Don't get too many nights like the last couple, that's for damn sure."

I shook hands and nodded. "That's about it. Johnny, these two gentlemen are with the Federal Bureau of Investigation. Walter Hocker from Oklahoma City, and the one who looks carsick is Neil Costace from the El Paso office."

He shook hands with each in turn and then touched the brim of his cap. "Detective," he said to Estelle. "Nice to see you again. It's been a couple of hours." Edwin remained by the truck, leaning against the front fender, weight off his bad knee.

"Two visits in one day, I don't guess this is a social call. What can we do for you?"

I took off my Stetson and ran a hand across the stubble of gray hair. "Well, we've got some things that sort of puzzle us and thought that maybe you might have some answers. Or some ideas."

Boyd sucked hard on his cigarette. "Do what I can. You know that. You want to talk in the house? No point in standing out here in the dust if we don't have to. Got cold beer. Hot coffee. The worst water you ever tasted. What's your pleasure?"

"Actually, a cup of hot coffee would be wonderful," Walter Hocker said. He'd been surveying the ranch setting, both hands shoved into his pockets, rotating at the waist as if his feet were cemented in place. "Water a problem out here? That's a good-sized windmill you've got there."

The contraption hadn't drawn my attention before, but the windmill *was* big, its blades spanning at least twelve feet, maybe sixteen, the pumping motor supported on a tower that must have been forty feet high.

"That well's three hundred and thirty feet deep," Johnny said.

"That's a fair lift," Hocker mused.

"You a farm boy?"

Hocker grinned at Boyd and tilted his head. "I've done my time. You ever been up on one of those rigs with a storm brewing?"

I looked over at the windmill's steel tower again and saw it for what it so easily could be—a massive lightning rod. I could picture the young Finnegan boy scampering up the steel ladder with the speed and coordination that only the young enjoy. And then...a flash and a thunderclap all in one as a couple million volts shot through the angle-iron structure. The boy would never have known what hit him.

"Nope," Boyd said. "Had a cousin killed on one, though. Over in eastern Kansas. And the neighbors here lost their boy that way. So it happens."

"What do you do when the wind doesn't blow?" Neil Costace asked. He had craned his head back to look up at the blur of blades.

"That don't happen much," the rancher said. "We got an electric auxiliary pump for those few times. But I don't guess you came in to talk about my windmill." He started toward the door and then turned to frown at me. "This about that picture you had earlier, Sheriff?"

"We haven't been out to the block-house site yet," I said, and that vague answer seemed to satisfy Boyd for the moment.

"Come on in," he said, and we followed him into the house. He led us to the kitchen and gestured at the white table in the center of the room. "Have a sit-down," he said. "Maxine!" he shouted, and added, "Excuse me a minute." We heard him off in another part of the house and in a moment, he returned with his wife.

"She'll get us fixed up," Boyd said. He quickly introduced Maxine to the two agents, calling them "these federal boys," and even before he'd finished, I heard the front door open and in due course, Edwin Boyd appeared, his face in a grimace and one hand reaching down toward his knee. He nodded at us and drifted off toward the easy chairs in the living room. He left no doubt in my mind about who was ranch boss.

"So," Boyd said and clasped his hands together in front of him. "What brings the Federal Bureau of Investigation out to these parts?" At the mention of the agency, Maxine murmured something and almost lost her hold on the coffee urn. She shook her head and poured water into the machine, then turned to find the coffee and a filter. She shot a glance first at me and then at Estelle, but otherwise, her face was impassive.

Estelle hadn't settled in a chair yet, and she took a step

over to Maxine Boyd, setting a light touch of the hand on the woman's shoulder. "Mrs. Boyd, would it be too much trouble to use your rest room?"

"Well, of course not," the woman said. "It's right around past the living room, that little doorway on the left. Let me show you."

She flipped the power switch on the coffeemaker, smiled warmly at the rest of us and said, "Give it about five minutes. Johnny, use the mugs in the cupboard over the sink." Johnny Boyd was already seated, well into the process of finding another smoke, one thin, long leg hooked over the other. I got the impression that he didn't fetch his own coffee cups on a regular basis.

Estelle and Maxine left the kitchen and I didn't waste anytime. "Johnny, a couple of things have all of us puzzled." He drew smoke and exhaled a thin blue jet. "In the past couple of days, have you or Edwin seen anyone around on your ranch property?"

"Strangers, you mean?"

"Anyone."

"Not since the satellite guy was out here last week. Damn dish doesn't work about half the time, and the other half, there's nothing worth watching." He smiled.

"No one Friday afternoon, when the plane went down?"

"Not that I know of. Of course"—he looked over at the coffeepot—"this is about six thousand acres we're talkin' about...so I guess that at one time or another, there could be a whole damn army over the hill and we wouldn't know it. But no, I didn't see anybody."

Hocker turned so that he was sitting sideways in the chair, his left arm hooked over the back. The fingers of his right hand drummed a nervous little tattoo on the tabletop. "Hear any gunshots Friday?"

"Excuse me?" Johnny Boyd said, and Hocker didn't reply immediately. He was gazing out the kitchen window at what appeared to me to be blank sky. Boyd got up and stepped to the cupboard. With one hand on the cupboard latch, he turned and asked, "Why would I hear gunshots?"

"Johnny," I said, "we've got some information that's pretty nasty." He took four mugs out of the cabinet and I waited until he'd lined them up on the counter. He was a patient man. He said nothing as he pulled the decanter out of the machine and filled each mug in turn.

"Take anything?"

I shook my head, and Hocker and Costace did the same.

"Edwin, you want a cup of coffee?" Johnny said loudly, and we heard a muddled, "No, no thanks," from the living room. Johnny started to fetch a fifth mug, but I stopped him.

"Detective Reyes-Guzman doesn't drink the stuff," I said.

"So, then," Johnny said, returning to his chair and his cigarette, "you were talkin' about nasty information."

"The pilot of that airplane was killed by a rifle bullet fired from the ground," I said.

Dead silence hung in the kitchen for the count of ten. Hocker turned his head and regarded Johnny Boyd impassively, and Neil Costace did the same, coffee mug cupped between two hands.

Finally, Boyd said quietly, "You don't say."

I nodded.

"You're sure?"

I nodded again. "A portion of the bullet was recovered during autopsy."

Boyd frowned. "You mean somebody shot a rifle and that bullet flew all the way up and hit that airplane? Hit the pilot?"

"So it would seem," I said.

He set his coffee mug down carefully and snubbed out his cigarette. "And you think it came from somewhere around here, or you wouldn't be out here right now." He regarded me, eyes unblinking. "Let me ask you something, Sheriff. When you and the detective were out here earlier today, did you know about this…" He paused and groped for the right words. "…this mystery bullet?"

"Yes."

"Why didn't you mention it then?" His tone was even and controlled, just above a whisper, but a little muscle ticked under his left eye.

"The information was still preliminary," I said, and knew how lame that sounded. The quirky thought drifted through my mind that this was exactly the sort of time for a little dissembling—the sort of thing Martin Holman had been damn good at when need called for it. "We didn't know what to think," I said.

Boyd lit another cigarette. "So tell me just how you come to figure the shot was fired from somewhere around here."

"Not from right here, Johnny. I didn't say that. But the plane was flying in a pattern—a roughly rectangular pattern—that extended east-west from about your property here over toward the Finnegans' property."

"And then it up and crashed," he said.

"Yes, it did. If the pilot had been shot, let's say when they were flying over the mesa, or over the landfill, or over something like that, then they wouldn't have flown all the way over here, circled, and then crashed."

"Bullet kill him right away, did it?"

"It looks that way. A fluke thing."

He frowned and took a tentative sip of his coffee. Mine remained untouched in front of me. "No one in this household," he said finally, "fired a gun at any airplane. Not yesterday, not ever." He set the mug down with a thump of finality. "You going to drive on over now and ask Dick Finnegan the same damn-fool question?"

"What question did we ask you?" Costace said quietly. "Just if you'd heard anything. We didn't ask if it was you who fired that shot."

Boyd flushed crimson and clenched his mouth shut so tight that his lips were two white lines. Hocker gestured toward the living room. I looked that way and realized that the agent could see the large gun cabinet from where he was sitting. "Mind if we take a look at your firearm collection?" he asked. The request was pleasant enough, conversational, but Johnny Boyd had heard enough.

He stood up and as if in slow motion, turned and set his coffee mug down on the counter by the sink. He looked out the window, eyes narrowed and jaw muscles so tight I could see them clench from across the room. His hands gripped the counter, and he turned without releasing his grip, looking at Hocker over his left shoulder.

"I guess what you can do is pack up and get off my property," he said. "You can get yourselves out of my home, and you can get yourselves off my land."

I heard quiet voices, and then Estelle appeared in the kitchen doorway. She stopped there, watching Boyd.

"Johnny—" I started to say, but he cut me off.

"There isn't a thing more we need to say to each other, Sheriff. Just pack up your friends and get on out."

Hocker sighed and pushed himself to his feet. "Mr. Boyd, you have to realize that in the course of an investigation like this one, we're forced to dig out answers wherever we can."

Boyd released his grip on the counter and turned around. "Well, you just go dig somewhere else. Can't say as I'm surprised. Took you two goddam years, but you managed."

"What's that supposed to mean?" Hocker asked.

"You just get," Boyd snarled ignoring the question. His face was flushed and his anger had set his jaw to quivering.

"You know as well as I do," Hocker said, "that if we have a bullet fragment, we'll be running some ballistic comparisons. That includes your firearms. I can get a warrant if I have to, but we'd prefer—"

"I don't give a good goddam what you prefer, Bucko," Johnny said. "The next time you want to come on this land and talk to me, you make sure you have that warrant. And if it isn't signed by Judge Hobart, then you better get it signed by him."

Hocker shrugged, still glacially calm, and started to cross the kitchen toward Estelle.

Neil Costace took a final sip of his coffee and grimaced. "I'd think that you'd want to do all you could to prove you—" and that was as far as he got. Boyd pushed himself away from the sink and took two steps, bringing himself nose to nose with the FBI agent. Out of the corner of my eye, I saw Hocker's left hand drift down toward the gun under his jacket.

"I don't have to prove a goddam thing," Boyd snapped.

"Neil," I said gently, "let's let these folks be." The two men stood as if frozen, Boyd glaring with white spots of anger on his cheeks, Neil Costace unflappable.

"Thanks for the coffee," Hocker said. "We'll be in touch." He slipped past Estelle, and I waited until Costace and Boyd had unlocked eyes and Costace left the kitchen.

"Johnny," I said, "we've got a murder on our hands. You know as well as I do that the investigation is not going away. Now, if you know something, you tell me." He didn't reply. "You hear me?" His only response was to pull another cigarette out of his pocket. The hand that held the lighter shook.

I turned to Estelle and motioned toward the front door. Johnny Boyd's voice stopped me. "I'll be talking to you later, Sheriff," he said. "Give me sometime to calm down, and then we'll see."

I knew that was the best I could hope for.

TWENTY-THREE

WALTER HOCKER agreed that he'd take a tour of the crash site with Vincent Buscema after the two had had a chance to talk in private. That was fine with me. It would keep them busy for a few more hours, and keep them off of Johnny Boyd's back.

I had a feeling that Boyd's reaction was as much to the federal authority as to anything else. I didn't know what he'd meant with the comment about it taking the agents two years to figure something out, and it hadn't been the time to push the point.

I hadn't told him about the cause of the crash when I'd had the opportunity, and now he had heard the message loud and clear that the federal agents, at least, included him in the pool of suspects. If he was innocent, and at that point I was sure he was, becoming the target of an investigation would be enough to send his blood pressure off the scale.

I couldn't imagine Johnny Boyd taking potshots at a passing airplane. Almost certainly he carried a rifle in at least one of his ranch trucks, and I had no doubt that he could drop a coyote in its tracks at a couple hundred yards. But firing at a pesky, circling airplane was another matter altogether.

As we drove away from the ranch, I turned to Estelle, whose only contribution to the conversation as we left the ranch house had been a quiet "Thank you" directed at Maxine Boyd. "So, what did she tell you?" I asked. "And that was nicely done, by the way."

"She's worried, sir," she said. She didn't look at me, but concentrated on the gravel road, her black eyebrows knitted.

"She has good reason to be, after that exchange," I said.

"No, not about that. She's really upset about trouble brewing between her husband and Richard Finnegan."

"Really? Trouble how?"

Estelle took a deep breath. "Apparently Richard Finnegan has a grazing allotment from the Forest Service for a piece of property on the back side of Cat Mesa. There's no more grass there than anywhere else, but there is a productive spring on the allotment. Finnegan wants to pipe the water over to one of his major stock tanks. Remember those rolls of black-plastic pipe that we saw by Finnegan's barn?"

"Sure. But that's got to be a hell of a distance. And pipe isn't cheap. So what's the argument?"

"Simple, as ever, sir. There's a corner of the Boyd ranch that's situated right in the way. If Finnegan can't run the pipe across Boyd's property, then it means going up an escarpment and out of the way over the east. A lot more distance, and going up the escarpment means that he couldn't use gravity flow. He'd have to pump."

I frowned. "And so...what's the argument? Are you saying that Johnny won't let Dick Finnegan run a few yards of black plastic across his property?"

"He will," Estelle said. "But he tried to cut a deal with

Finnegan to use some of the water in exchange for letting the pipe go across his land.''

"And Finnegan objected to that? Is he out of his mind?''

"Maybe. The last argument they had, and I guess from what Maxine was saying, it was right in the Boyds' front yard, was that Dick Finnegan maintained that he can't afford the extra pipe it would take to go around Boyd's property, or pay for a pump, and that there isn't enough water to serve both their needs. He's being held up, he contends.''

"Oh, for God's sake,'' I muttered. "What's the old saying out here—there are more friendships broken over access to water than anything else?''

"Except in a wet year,'' Estelle said. "Then it's over alcohol.''

"And this is what Maxine wanted to talk to you about?''

Estelle nodded. "She's afraid that the two of them will exchange more than words sometime. She said that her husband has a hot temper and so does Dick Finnegan.''

"No kidding,'' I said. "By the way, did she happen to say which stock tank Finnegan wanted to run the pipe to? Was it the one at the block house, by any chance?''

"She didn't know. And we didn't have long to talk. I did ask her, though, if she knew anything about someone up in this part of the county impounding wildlife.'' Estelle slowed for the Newton cattle guard and at the same time, glanced in the rearview mirror. The dark Suburban still followed us at a discreet distance.

"At first she didn't want to say anything, but I could tell she knew something about it. I told her that we really needed to know and that before the crash, the sheriff had been talking with Doug Posey...and that maybe that was why the sheriff was flying out over that area. Anyway, she said, 'Oh, that's another get-rich-quick scheme. It doesn't amount to anything.' But she wouldn't say whose scheme it was.''

"What did she mean by that, I wonder.''

"I don't know. I was going to ask, but then I heard the ruckus out in the kitchen.''

We rode in silence for a few minutes, watching the last of

Newton's sorry buildings slide by. We hit the pavement and heard a roar of engine, and then Costace passed us. Hocker lifted a hand in salute.

"You know," I said, watching the truck dwindle ahead of us, "Johnny Boyd said something to me yesterday, or maybe the day before, to the effect that if the federal agents got the chance, they could invent almost any case out of this scenario. We need to make certain we find the person who fired the shot, but I sure don't want a bunch of other lives destroyed in the process."

"Sir, if Johnny Boyd is running his own herd of antelope, then he might have reason to be edgy."

"I can't imagine that," I said. "Of course, I've been wrong before."

"The first thing I think we need to do is to find the blockhouse windmill," Estelle said. "It's on Finnegan's land. I suggest that we drive out there and get ourselves a tour. Sheriff Holman thought it was important enough that he took a photo from the air. Let's see if we can find out why."

An hour later, a flustered Charlotte Finnegan was trying to explain to us how to find the windmill in question. Her husband wasn't home, and at least one of the large rolls of black pipe had been taken. Mrs. Finnegan knew exactly where the government spring was, though—or so she said. If we followed her rambling directions, we would no doubt end up in Utah.

As we were preparing to leave her to her petunias, Estelle turned and asked, "Mrs. Finnegan, are there many antelope out here? Do you often see them?"

The woman frowned. "Now, sometimes," she said. "We used to have a herd of nearly fifty that would roam of an evening." She took a step forward and pointed. "You see that swale down past the fence? Well, they'd even come right in there." She turned and smiled. "The little ones, you know. They're so fetching. Just like little fractious goats."

"Fractious goats," I repeated and chuckled. "You say there used to be more of them than there are now?"

"Oh my, yes." She paused to ponder the numbers, brightened and added, "But they move so much, you know. It's so hard to tell. There must be some, because we still get the occasional hunter." She smiled. "Most of the time, they're lost too, especially if they're from the city."

Armed with one of the county maps that purported to show every road, trail, or cow path that had ever been worn into the Posadas prairie, and with Charlotte Finnegan's instructions to "just stay north of the rise there," we set out. Immediately behind one of the barns, we stopped for a barbed-wire gate and I held it open while Estelle drove the Bronco through. I managed to get it closed again without being bitten by the wire.

Away from any thoroughfare, the New Mexico prairie took on a marvelously textured beauty of lines, shadows, and patterns. I relaxed back in the seat, my right hand curled over the panic handle above the door, letting Estelle cope with the vague two-track.

"Tawny," I mused aloud. "Tawny and russet."

"Sir?"

"The colors out here. Tawny and russet." I heaved a sigh. "You know, Martin Holman never really felt at home out here. All the years he lived in Posadas, the one love he never cultivated was being able to just enjoy the quiet of the prairie."

"He preferred the solidity of asphalt," Estelle said, but there was no ring of condemnation in her tone.

"I think he felt a little threatened by the vastness of country when it wasn't neatly marked up into manageable chunks," I mused. I let go of the panic handle and let the bumps gently nestle me down into the seat. "And he liked to plan ahead." I cleared my throat. "You know, every once in a while he'd ride with me, and I know it used to drive him crazy when I'd turn off the headlights, open the windows, and just idle along, listening." I chuckled. "He was forever asking me what I was listening *for*." I turned and gazed out the window. "And I could never really give him an answer that he understood."

"You probably would have been just as uncomfortable and

out of place at one of his service-club luncheons,'' Estelle said, and I laughed.

"For sure. And on an occasion or two, I was.'' We fell silent for another dozen bumps or so and then I said, ''You know what colors you're going to have to get used to up in Minnesota?'' Estelle shot a glance at me and then looked heavenward.

"Yes, sir.'' And then, no doubt weary of hearing about it, she added, ''White and green.''

"That's it,'' I agreed. ''In the summer, it looks like green corduroy up there. Lumpy little hills, all roundy and green. And in the winter, white corduroy. Your mother is going to go crazy. Then the rest of you.''

"My mother is looking forward to the move, sir.''

"I know. You've said that before. It's hard to believe. From Mexico to Minnesota. Ouch.''

"Maybe after all these years without any water, she's ready to see some of it standing around.''

"Standing around is right,'' I said. ''You guys are going to end up buying a boat.''

"That sounds like fun, sir. Another year or two and *los niños* can learn to water-ski.''

"Don't enjoy the place too much,'' I muttered. ''And I'll get it.'' I opened the door as she slowed for another gate, this one little more than a tangle of barbed wire snarled between two posts. I found the end that would cooperate and swung the whole thing to one side.

Back in the truck, I picked up the map. ''If that's the rise that Charlotte was talking about, then the windmill is just beyond it.'' The road almost immediately forked, and I added, ''To the right.''

After another hundred yards, we idled up to the edge of a major arroyo. The two-track, in truly optimistic fashion, just plunged down one side, across two dozen feet of loose sand and then up the other side. The arroyo was at least twenty feet deep, and I could picture us stuck in the bottom while Dick Finnegan stood up on the rim and laughed.

"You might want to put it in four-wheel-drive," I said, but Estelle was already accelerating.

Even as we tipped forward for the trip down, she said, "I think it's plenty hard," meaning the beckoning arroyo bottom, where we would plunge up to our axles and churn to a helpless stop. She was right, of course. We thumped across the bottom, a sprinkling of sandy gravel over bedrock, and roared up the other side.

As soon as we were level again, I could see the windmill, still tiny in the distance. "Over there," I said.

I released my death grip on the panic bar and pulled the pile of photos out of the folder. I riffled through them until I found the block-house windmill shots, one of the house, the other of the windmill itself. I held them together, then looked over the top of the prints at the terrain ahead of us.

"This is it," I said. "If you park on that rise, we can walk over."

Outside the truck, the sun was hot. The breeze out of the west was just hard enough to make itself a nuisance, and I left my Stetson in the truck and pulled a Sheriff's Department cap down hard on my head.

One of the problems with being fat, old, and bifocaled is that uneven ground becomes a major challenge. Estelle strolled beside me, scanning the surrounding terrain, musing about this and that. I walked with my head down, planting my boots in the few flat spots between the bunchgrass and the cacti.

The two-track beside us had been beaten into a powdery, pockmarked trail by the cattle, but the tracks were not fresh. Several tire prints ran past the windmill, but none angled over to it. The two-track was an arterial to elsewhere, with the windmill abandoned for another time when the water table might recharge.

The windmill was stationary, its rudder locked over so that the motor wouldn't continue to drive the pump up and down. The galvanized-metal cattle tank, three feet high and a dozen feet across, had seen better days. Dark with rust from the times it had once held water, it was dented and far from level.

And it probably leaked like a sieve, too. At one time, the water had puddled on the east side of the windmill tower, and when the cattle had waded in, they'd stomped a quagmire that had compacted the earth six or seven inches lower than the surrounding dry prairie.

I walked up to the tank and rested my hands on the rim. It was stone-dry inside. "In the photo, it looked like there was some water in here," I said.

"Just the shadow of the tank rim," Estelle suggested.

To the north, the block house nestled in a grove of junipers and greasewood. It looked even smaller than it had in the aerial photo.

I tried to imagine Philip Camp's Bonanza flying overhead, coming in low and fast from the west. In order for Holman, seated on the right, to shoot the photo of the windmill, the flight path was just to the north, over the small rise behind the block house.

"So," I said, "we've got an old windmill and a dry stock tank." I turned and sat on the edge of the tank, arms crossed over my belly.

Estelle had the folder of photos, and she pulled out the one of the house. "Let's go see," she said.

"See what?" I muttered, but doggedly followed, determined to enjoy the tawny and russet colors of the dried vegetation, and now, the worn stones of the block house.

Maybe Martin Holman had become a fan of early southwestern ranch architecture. And then, to give him the credit that he'd been perfectly capable of earning in the past couple of years, perhaps he'd seen something here that wasn't immediately obvious to me.

TWENTY-FOUR

THE BLOCK HOUSE was ninety paces from the windmill, slightly uphill. Roughly rectangular in shape, it was situated against the slope of a small mesa, its length running almost north-south. One door, perhaps the only one, was on the south end, facing the windmill.

Every time I saw one of these remnants from the homestead era, I marveled at how much physical labor the people had invested in the vain hope that the land would bloom for them, that the cattle would run fat and sleek, that this hundred-sixty-acre gift from their benevolent government would offer the magic they sought.

I ambled up to the structure and put my hand gently on the wall, feeling the cool silence of the stones. Some of the blocks showed shaping marks where the builder, sitting in the hot sun, chisel in hand, had whacked off the rock spurs that prevented a good, solid fit.

The walls were surprisingly square, still vertical after years of every manner of assault that the fickle weather could hurl at them.

The roof beams had been of juniper, and fragments stuck out from the upper portion of the walls.

Estelle was moving slowly along the outside wall, head down, searching the ground, and while she did that, I went inside, slipping past a jumble of roof boards and beams that had crashed across the doorway.

No doubt hunters had used the house in years past, but there was no sign now of their fires. Over in one corner, a wooden crate with "California Oranges" stenciled on its side had been crushed by one of the rocks that had slipped from its position high up, just under one of the ceiling-beam sockets.

The place was home to pack rats, but not much else. I toed the dirt floor with my boot. The earth was powdery, churned up by cattle when they'd wandered inside before the roof had caved in.

A bit of metal caught my eye, and I stooped and picked up an empty cartridge casing. The brass was dull and lifeless, and the end where the bullet had been was crushed flat.

I wet my thumb and rubbed the base of the cartridge, then held it up to try to read the head stamp. After several attempts, I gave up.

"Sir?" Estelle said. Her voice was muffled behind the wall.

"Inside," I said.

"Can you come here for a minute?"

I picked my way out and walked around the side of the building. Estelle was standing near the wall with her back to it, facing east.

"Can you make this out?" I asked and handed her the casing.

She turned it this way and that, frowned, and read out loud, "Remington UMC, twenty-five thirty-five." She looked up and handed the casing back. "That's an old one. And it's been here a while."

I nodded. "What'd you find?"

She grimaced and looked at the wall beside her. "This is the north wall," she said. "Am I right?"

I glanced over my shoulder at the afternoon sun. "Sure enough," I said.

"Now, if this is north, that means that Sheriff Holman snapped the picture as they were flying west, and he tripped the shutter when the plane was actually a little way west of here." She stepped away from the wall and held an arm up. "About there."

"He was sitting on the right side of the aircraft, so that's right," I agreed. "He got the windmill, and then in the background, looking north, this structure. And so?"

Estelle opened the folder and took out the photo. "The sun is in the pilot's face," she said, holding up the photo. I tilted my head back so my bifocals would have a chance to bring the thing into focus. "The airplane is moving right along, and Martin takes the photo."

"Remember that the Bonanza is a low-wing aircraft," I said. "Unless they're in a steep bank, the wing's going to be in the way. So in order to take that photo, he's got to actually turn and shoot almost over his shoulder.'' I held up both hands, miming the photographer, and twisted to my right. ''He's shooting back and down.''

''That's right,'' Estelle said. ''Back and down. The east wall of the house is in the shade, and it casts a pretty good shadow away from it, to the east. Right here.'' She touched the photo with her little finger. ''There's no shadow on the west side.''

''Couldn't be,'' I said and looked at her quizzically. ''So what's your point?''

''What's this, then?''

''Where?''

''Here,'' and this time she slipped the pen out of her pocket and used it as a pointer. ''The shadows are hard and well-defined. I mean, look at the windmill's shadow, sir. You can count every cross brace. But what's this?''

I frowned. Turning the photo didn't help. ''Let me see,'' I said, and walked back to the northeast corner of the old house and stood facing east. If I stepped just a pace to the north, away from the building, the western mass of the structure didn't block the sun, and it became a soothing warmth on my back.

''And directly in front of you, sir, is your shadow.''

''That doesn't surprise me,'' I said.

''But look at the picture,'' she persisted. ''There is a shadow there. It's not perfectly definite because of the distance. But it is a shadow.''

''Sure enough,'' I said. The dark mark, little more than what would be left by a careless touch of a fine-line marker, stretched out from the northeast corner of the building, just about the same distance as my shadow was then doing.

''There's nothing here to cause a shadow, sir.''

I turned and studied her face, then looked at the photograph, then back at her. She waited for me to catch up, her black eyes excited.

''You're saying that someone was standing right here?'' I asked.

''I think so. We need to have Linda enlarge this section. If she can't do it, maybe the FBI labs can do something.''

"They can do anything," I said. "If the government can read license plates from satellite images, it certainly can enhance this. But wait." I stepped away from the house again and raised an arm. "The Bonanza is flying along, close to a hundred fifty miles an hour or so. I don't believe that Martin Holman could have seen someone standing behind this building."

"I don't believe so either, sir. But look at the angles." She raised her arm next to mine and swept it across the sky along the path that the airplane must have flown. "Whoever it is, he sees the plane and ducks behind the building here, out of sight. Now right there"—she stopped the swing of her arm— "is about where the airplane must have been when Martin took the photo."

"The wall hides the person from view, but his shadow extends out to the east. It'd be visible," I said.

"That's what I think."

I pursed my lips and studied the photo. "Mrs. Finnegan said that the plane was flying east-west tracks."

"That fits, sir."

"What a photo," I said. "But if Charlotte is correct, the aircraft was coming toward her when it reared up. If this is the shadow of a man, then either it's of the gunman or of someone who was really close to where the gunman was standing. He would have heard the gunshot clearly...if he didn't make it himself."

"It would make more sense to make the shot on a return trip, when the aircraft was heading east. Maybe on the next leg, they flew slightly north of this site. Whoever it was, he could see the plane coming and set himself up."

"Why?"

"We don't know that yet, sir."

"And we don't know for certain that this tiny black speck is a shadow, either. Not for sure."

"It's pretty clear, sir."

I leaned against the cool stones of the north wall and regarded the ground. "As rocky as this area is, we're not going to find prints."

"Are you up for a little stroll, sir?"

"Stroll? That sounds nasty. To where?"

She gestured up the slope. "I'd like to see what's up there. It's just enough of a rise that we'll see…" She stopped and shrugged. "Who knows what we'll see?" She opened the folder again and looked at the photo. "Nothing is centered in this," she said. "It's always possible that Martin was aiming at something else and just plain missed."

An unkind remark came to mind, the sort of thing I would have cheerfully voiced had Martin Holman been alive. I shook my head.

"That's easy to do," I said. "Let's stroll."

TWENTY-FIVE

AS THE CROW FLIES, or even as the lizard scuttles, the distance to the top of the little mesa behind the block house was nothing at all—perhaps fifty yards. But most of it was at a significant slope, far steeper than it appeared in the aerial photograph, where the tricks of the camera flattened features and distorted distances. By the time I worked my way to the top, ever mindful of my precarious balance on the rocky footing, I was puffing like an old steam engine.

Estelle stood waiting on the rim, a study in patience. She'd had plenty of time to catch her breath—if she'd lost it in the first place.

The rise gave us enough elevation that I could see the slope-backed bulge a couple of miles to the west against which the Bonanza had pulped itself. As I gazed at that spot, a dust trail caught my attention, and if I squinted hard enough, I could imagine that I could see the small, dark dot that kicked up the plume.

"It looks like a parking lot over there," Estelle said.

"I'll take your word for it," I replied.

"It's too bad someone wasn't standing right here when the

crash happened," she added. "They would have seen the whole thing." She moved her hand in an arc across the sky, finally sweeping down to point over at the crash site. She then thrust her hands in her pockets and just stood quietly, looking out across the prairie.

"Suppose that the person who was standing behind that building fired the shot," she said finally. "Suppose that's what happened. What would be the most logical way for him to drive out of here?"

I peered back down the slope at the block house. "Right from there," I said. "He'd drive out the same way that we came in and then hook up with County 9010. And then on out east to Forty-three. If that's where he was headed."

"Richard Finnegan would drive out that way to go back to his house. Johnny Boyd would have to turn west. And it's possible that they could have driven due south, up the back of Cat Mesa."

"Lots of choices," I said. "Too many. It leaves us with nothing, except one big, glaring fact."

"What's that?"

"If he wasn't familiar with the area, Estelle, he wouldn't have been here in the first place. He couldn't have known that the aircraft was coming over here. It's that simple."

"Assuming the shot wasn't accidental."

"Assuming that. And the simple logistics of it say that if the shot was fired from about here, then either the person left to the east, through Finnegan's, or west through Boyd's. That's about the choice. If he took that road"—I pointed toward the north-south track—"and headed south, toward the back side of Cat Mesa, he'd have to know the roads really well to pick his way out of there once he got into the trees."

Estelle nodded and pulled out the folder of photographs. "So far, we've identified two of these," she said. "The windmill, and the block house." She shuffled through the other pictures, frowning. "Before that truck gets here, I'd like to take a look at the fence line just north of us."

I turned, expecting her to be looking off into the distance. Instead, she was still sorting photos.

"What truck?" I said, scanning the prairie.

This time she looked up and pointed to the south. "If you follow the road down from the back of Cat Mesa, you'll see the dust. Right now he's about a finger's width below that dark belt of junipers, headed this way."

The binoculars were in the truck, of course, where they always did the most good. But I shaded my eyes with both hands and concentrated, and sure enough, eventually a tiny portion of the distant terrain moved. I saw the dust plume first, then the speck.

"You're right, Sharp Eyes," I said. "And what fence?"

Estelle held up a photo. "Linda marked this as the next photo on the roll. It's also the last photo that Martin Holman took. And I think this grove of trees"—she indicated a small blotch in the top right corner of the photo—"is right over there." She turned and looked north. A hundred yards away, a stand of junipers was bunched near a jumble of boulders that marked the north edge of the mesa on which we were standing. "There's a fence just over the crown of the hill."

"Just around the next corner," I said and grinned. "Lead on."

I had no doubt that we'd find the fence. If I'd learned nothing else working with Estelle Reyes-Guzman over the past decade, it was that she didn't make idle guesses. As we walked toward the junipers, she held the photo in front of her as if it were a witching rod.

"Just north of the rim," she said. We circled around the grove of stunted, withered old junipers. They were skirted with mountain mahogany, making a dense brush barrier. But sure enough, after we picked our way through a jumble of rocks, we found our progress blocked by a livestock fence.

Estelle stopped and turned this way and that until she was satisfied that she had the orientation of the photograph correct. "We are here," she announced, and used her pen as a pointer. "This fence goes east-west, and you can see quite a bit of it in this photo. Sheriff Holman snapped the shutter when the plane was still a bit west of here." She turned and looked along the fence. "He was shooting ahead of the wing, and the shadows say he was looking east."

"And if he'd swung the camera just a degree or two to his right, he'd have been able to see the top of the mesa, maybe even the back side of the block house."

Estelle pursed her lips and gazed at the barbed-wire fence. "If we assume that Martin took a photograph of exactly what he *meant* to, then he was interested in this fence. Or at least in something in this area."

The fence was not new, but it was well-maintained. The four strands of wire were tight, with two twist-'em wire stays spaced between each steel post. "This would be a boundary fence, I assume," I said. "There's nothing temporary about it. If it is, then the Boyd land is on the other side and this is Finnegan's. Or state property." I shrugged. "Or federal. Who the hell knows? Maybe it's just a section fence." I put a hand on the top of one of the posts and shook it. "And it must have been hell getting these posts in the ground up here," I said. "So what's the big deal, I wonder. Why this fence, why now?"

"I don't know, sir." She replaced the photos in the folder and looked back the way we'd come. "If that truck that we saw earlier was Richard Finnegan, he'll be just about to the windmill by now. Maybe he knows."

The rancher's dark blue Ford pickup was parked beside our county unit, and I could see the four-wheeler ATV in the back. As Estelle and I started down the rocky slope toward the block house, I scanned the area, looking for the rancher. It wasn't until we were a dozen yards from the back corner of the structure that I saw Richard Finnegan taking his ease in its shade, smoking a cigarette and leaning against the cold-stone east wall.

"Howdy," he said as we approached. "I saw your outfit and figured you must be up here somewheres."

"We took a short hike up to the top," I said. "Our daily constitutional."

"I bet," he said, but there was little humor in his voice.

His posture said that he'd done all the walking he wanted for one day. "Can I help you find something?"

"Is this your property, or do you lease it from the feds?" I asked, knowing damn well what the answer was.

"I own it," Finnegan said and took the cigarette out of his mouth. With deliberation, he curled his little finger around and nudged the ash off, watching the process as if it were the major fascination of the moment. And the tone of his reply added, "What do you want?" But he had the courtesy not to say it, even though I'd ignored his initial question and certainly given him cause to ask.

"Is that fence that runs east-west on the other side of the hill the property line between you and the Boyds?" I asked.

"Parts of it. On over to the west some."

"If we were to follow it off to the west, how far would it run?" Estelle asked, and Richard Finnegan eyed her for a moment. "I assume it has to join a north-south boundary eventually," she added.

Finnegan raised the hand with the cigarette and pointed with the butt. "Eventually it does," he said, and then he glanced at me as if he'd just realized he didn't sound overly helpful. "That fence runs down the back of this mesa, then maybe a quarter mile on." He bent his hand. "Jogs to the south, runs along over to his Black Grass Tank, then west and then south again." The crow's-feet around his eyes crinkled. "Runs all over the place." He took a deep draw on the cigarette and then ground it out on his boot heel. "Why the sudden interest in property lines, folks?"

"There's some evidence that Sheriff Holman was interested," I said. "We don't know why. And Black Grass Tank? What's that?" I asked.

Finnegan nodded. "One of Johnny's cattle tanks. Like this one." He indicated his windmill with a thrust of his jaw. "Only difference is he's got water there."

"And you don't here?"

"Nope. She ain't pumped for six, seven months now."

"And so you're planning to pipe water from the Forest Service spring, is that the plan?"

Finnegan glanced at me and his eyes narrowed. "That's the idea," he said.

"All the way up here?" I continued.

"Nope. No point in that. There's another tank a mile or so south. We'll pipe it there."

"That's expensive," I said.

"Sure enough is."

"Mr. Finnegan, is it true that there's some friction between Johnny Boyd and you over where you want to run that water line?" Estelle asked.

"We got us a few things to work out," he said. "Is that what the sheriff told you?"

"Did you have a chance to talk to him about this?" I asked. "To Sheriff Holman, that is."

"Never met the man," Finnegan said. He pushed himself away from the wall. "And what Johnny Boyd does, or what I do, ain't nobody's business but our own. But I don't guess, what with a plane crash that killed a couple people, that you're all that interested right now in what a couple of old ranchers do with a black-plastic water line." He grinned and found another cigarette.

"No, I guess we aren't," I said.

Finnegan's grin widened. "Let me walk with you on up there," he said, indicating the mesa. "Give you a tour. You can see most places from there. Maybe give you a chance to ask whatever it is that's eatin' at you." He stepped out of the shade and squinted up at the sky. "Hot day for spring," he said. "It's going to be a hot summer, for sure."

He set out up the hill, streaming smoke from his cigarette. Estelle touched my arm. "I'm going to get my camera," she said, starting toward the vehicles. "I'll catch up with you."

I nodded and hastened to join Finnegan.

"Quite a pretty young señorita," he said. "She's not coming with us?"

"She wants her camera," I said. "What for, I don't know." That was only partly true, of course. We plodded along, the two of us watching our feet as we picked our way through the loose rocks and around the cacti that studded the hillside.

I would have liked to claim that it was my eagle-eyed vision that did the trick, but it was simply the habit of watching the ground so I didn't trip and break my neck. Estelle had no trouble catching up with us. When she did, we were standing near a runty juniper, waiting for her about a third of the way up the mesa...less than fifty yards from the back of the block house.

I held up a hand so she wouldn't walk past me, then pointed at the ground. The rifle cartridge casing wasn't bright and shiny, but nevertheless, the contrast was stark against the earth.

TWENTY-SIX

RICHARD FINNEGAN bent down and damn near had the casing in his fingers before I could say, "Leave it." He straightened up and his face was an interesting study in the dawning of an idea.

"What's the matter? You startin' to think that someone took a shot at that airplane, is that what's goin' on?" he asked. Neither Estelle nor I replied, and Richard nodded. "It adds up, you being out here and all. Are you going to tell me what happened, or am I going to have to wait and read it in the paper?"

"We don't know what happened," I said. "We're following up on a few ideas, that's all." I put my hands on my knees and bent down, eyeing the casing. Estelle unscrewed the barrel of her ballpoint pen, removed the slender filler and slipped it inside the casing's mouth.

"Looks like a two-twenty-three," I said, and she nodded. She turned her back to the wind and held the casing to her nose for several seconds. "Recent?" I asked, and she grimaced, then shrugged.

"It's hard to tell," she said quietly.

"One of yours?" I asked Finnegan, and he looked at me with surprise.

"No," he said. "Last coyote I shot was over by the springs. And I sure as hell don't use one of those little things. That looks like something from one of those military jobs."

Estelle turned the casing this way and that, frowning at it, no doubt wishing it could talk. "It's clean," she said, "so it's been here since the last rain."

Finnegan laughed. "And that's been a while, young lady." Estelle only grinned.

"You want a bag?" I asked, but she was far ahead of me. She produced a plastic evidence bag from her back pocket, slipped the casing inside and marked the tag. Richard Finnegan watched her with interest. She jotted a note to herself on the bag's tag, then looked up at me. "I think it's important that we grid this area, sir. I want to mark where each casing fell. If the rifle was an autoloader, it will make a difference where the casings were ejected."

"Assuming there are others," I said, and surveyed the ground.

"There's one by your left foot, sir," Estelle said, "and another two behind Mr. Finnegan."

Finnegan jerked like he'd been goosed. He cranked around at the waist to look at the ground without moving his feet. He pointed and chuckled. "By God, sure enough. And there's another one over there." He pointed at a spot not three feet from my right foot, a spot obscured from Estelle's view by a large chunk of limestone. "What I'd give for a set of eyes like she's got," he said.

"Amen," I said, and then to Estelle, I added, "I'll go get my briefcase."

By the time we had finished, we had a collection of twelve .223 shell casings and a remarkably neat rendition on graph paper that marked where each had fallen and the distance between them. The pattern they formed on the ground was roughly fan-shaped.

I eyed the paper critically. "If a person stood in one place and fired all twelve rounds, then we would expect them to all group fairly close." Estelle was busy packing her camera after shooting an entire roll from every imaginable angle. "And if we draw a line that is roughly of the same length to each casing, then the point of origin is somewhere around here," I said, indicating a spot just off to my left. I held up my left hand and made throwing motions away from it with my right, trying to visualize the casings being spewed out of the rifle's ejection port.

"It's possible, sir," Estelle said in that exasperatingly non-committal tone that I had come to know so well.

Finnegan put his hands on his hips and regarded me. "So, you're sayin' that airplane was shot at? Actually shot down? Or what?"

"We're not sure yet, Richard," I said, and Finnegan wasn't so quick to accept my fabrication.

"What, you can't find holes in the airplane? If you ain't got holes, then you wouldn't know about its being shot at, now would you?"

I took a deep breath. "Yeah. We've got holes," I said. "At least one round struck the pilot and killed him. They went down so fast that the passenger—Sheriff Holman—didn't have time to react and try to save himself."

Finnegan just stared at me, and I stared back. Finally he dug out another cigarette and lit it. "Well, Jesus," he said. "Who'd do a thing like that?"

"Interesting question," I said. I hefted the bag with the twelve brass casings. "Maybe this will get us a little closer. And maybe not."

Despite our best search efforts, the side of the mesa produced nothing else of interest—no identifiable marks, no more casings, no handy piece of torn fabric, no lost wallet full of identification papers.

I realized the day was catching up with me, and I wasn't so eager to trek back up the mesa. Estelle didn't mention the need again, so we worked our way back down to the vehicles. On the way, she took several more photos of the block house and the area around it, particularly of the spot where we thought someone had been standing.

But the rough walls produced no convenient threads of fabric, and there were no readable footprints that I could see. Maybe Estelle had her own theories, since she expended a fair-sized film budget taking portraits of the ground, especially east of the structure.

One of Finnegan's blue heelers greeted us with rapid-fire yapping as we approached the trucks, but it didn't jump out of the back. The rancher's rig wasn't for show, that was for sure. The truck itself was battered and dented, the sort of scrubbing I could imagine it received every time Finnegan pulled to a stop and the livestock mobbed around, looking for the feed.

The ATV in the back, once bright red and ready to charge out of a television commercial, was equally battered and bent. It was crowded between various boxes of pipe fittings, oil cans, and other bits and pieces.

I put a foot on the back bumper and regarded the dog, which strained to the end of its light chain, bicolored eyes eager to figure out who I was.

"That's your rifle, I assume," I said, indicating the bolt-action inside the truck. It hung upside down from the window rack.

"Yep," Finnegan said. The rifle was as battered as everything else.

"May I see it?"

"Sure." He reached inside the Ford and slipped the rifle off the rack. I took it, surprised at its weight. The scope was worn but expensive, just like the rifle.

"I'd hate to lug this during a day of deer-hunting," I said.

He grunted. "So would I. Most of the time, it rides right there, in the truck."

I opened the bolt just far enough to see the extractors draw the long, brass body of the cartridge part way out of the chamber.

"Two-sixty-four Winchester mag," Finnegan said.

"Antitank," I grinned, and out of habit, I closed the bolt

while I held the trigger back, uncocking the rifle. I handed it back to him.

"Nah," he said and turned back toward the truck. With just a flick of his wrist, he pulled the bolt handle up and then thrust it down again, cocking the weapon. He hung the rifle back in the rack. "But it's hell on coyotes. I busted one last week at almost five hundred yards." He clapped his hands together. "Never knew what hit him."

"I can imagine," I said. I glanced around and saw that Estelle was standing at the opposite side of the pickup, putting her camera back in the bag.

"Well, you need anything else, you just let me know," Finnegan said.

"Expect some traffic the next few days," I said. "Other than that, I don't know what to tell you."

He nodded and hoisted himself into his pickup. The diesel started instantly, and he pulled away with a final lift of his hand in salute. The dog dashed back and forth on top of the toolbox, excited to be going back to work.

"So, what do you think?" I asked Estelle. She started the Bronco and levered it into gear.

"I want to see what Linda was able to piece together," she said. "And then we need to finish what we started earlier. We need to sort through Martin Holman's files. There're pieces missing, sir."

"Many, many," I agreed, and braced myself for the first cattle guard. "And I'd be interested to find out what our friends from the FBI spent their time doing. If anything."

"Oh, I'm sure they've been busy," Estelle said, and the tone of her voice brought my head around.

"We're not in competition here," I said.

"Of course not, sir."

TWENTY-SEVEN

THE BRONCO thumped over the last cattle guard, and Estelle steered onto County Road 43, taking us back to Posadas. We drove in silence for the first couple of miles.

During those infrequent moments when Martin Holman was feeling his administrative oats, he would gently jibe me about my habits—one of which was an aversion to the continual squawking and static of police radios. I routinely left them turned off...leaving the airwaves to the regular road deputies.

Cellular phones in each unit had been one of his solutions, and I suppose it made sense, unless an officer crashed into a tree while trying to punch in a number on one of those tiny pads.

I reached forward and turned on the two-way radio, keyed the mike and said, "Posadas, three-ten."

Gayle Sedillos was on the air, and from the tone of her voice, I couldn't have guessed the sort of afternoon that she had had with the federal contingent breathing down her neck.

"Three-ten, Posadas."

"We're ten-eight," I said. "Ten-nineteen."

She acknowledged without requesting elaboration, explanation, or ETA, as if it were a Sunday afternoon with blooming roses the only source of noise and excitement.

"What?" Estelle asked. She glanced my way and caught the grin on my face as I hung up the mike.

"Just passing thoughts," I said. "Remember when J.J. Murton worked for us? The Miracle?"

"Sure." She smiled but kindly refrained from comment.

"The man who actually asked, 'Do you know what your ten-four is?' over the air."

"I remember that."

"The Miracle was one of Holman's greater triumphs," I said. "I could never make either one of them understand that

STEVEN F. HAVILL 159

people other than the police listen to radio conversations.''

"You'll miss Gayle if she and Bobby end up moving away somewhere.''

"I'm hoping they don't,'' I said. "I'm hoping they stay right here and continue the endless Torrez-Sedillos dynasty. Between the two of them, they're related to half the county.''

"Nearer to two thirds,'' Estelle said. "And we've got company.'' She indicated the rearview mirror, and I turned around to see the dark Suburban coming up behind us. I recognized Neil Costace's blocky shape behind the wheel. The lights flashed, and Estelle slowed the Bronco and pulled off on the wide shoulder.

"Where did they come from?'' I asked.

"Parked in the turnoff to the boneyard,'' Estelle said, referring to Consolidated Mining's access road.

The Suburban slid in behind us, and when Walter Hocker stepped out, his face was grim. He stalked toward us, a manila folder in hand. I rolled down the window and waited. He appeared at the door and nodded at Estelle.

"What did you find out?'' he asked without preamble.

"About what?''

A brief flash of irritation crinkled his forehead and then he leaned on the doorsill like a rancher looking for conversation. "About anything at all, Sheriff.''

I could feel Estelle's gaze boring into my skull. No doubt she remembered my exact words as we'd left the windmill.

"We just chatted with Richard Finnegan,'' I said. "His wife is the one who saw the aircraft and heard the 'backfiring.''' Hocker nodded impatiently. "We went out there primarily because of this photograph.'' I turned, and Estelle snapped open her briefcase and handed me the folder. I handed the blowup of the block house to Hocker, pulled the pen out of my pocket and pointed. "That appears to be a shadow,'' I said. "We think it's of a person standing behind the building.''

Hocker pushed his dark glasses up onto his forehead and bent close, squinting at the photo. "Finnegan?''

"I don't know. He says not.''

"You believe him?''

"I don't know that either."

Hocker turned his head and looked off into the distance, then tapped the photo. "Where's the negative for this?"

"In our darkroom with our deputy," I said. "She's been working most of the day on this."

"And so what did you find out there?"

"No footprints. Nothing to indicate that someone was there. But the ground is rocky and it's harder to leave a trace than not. So I'm not surprised." I reached over and pulled the evidence bag of .223 casings out of the briefcase.

"And these. Twelve rounds."

"Son of a bitch," Hocker muttered. He handed the photo back to me and took the bag by the closure. By this time, Neil Costace had ambled his way over to join us, preferring the view on Estelle's side of the Bronco. "Two-twenty-three," Hocker said, and nodded toward Costace. "Show those to him. And the picture."

"The position of the casings is kind of interesting," I said. I pulled Estelle's briefcase across my lap like a desk and spread the field drawing she had prepared. "The location of the casings suggests a fan. If the rifle was anywhere near consistent in the way it ejects spent cases, the shooter would have been standing uphill from the block house. Thirty, forty yards or so."

Hocker shook his head. "There's no way to tell by that what direction the shots were fired from."

"That's true. I'm saying there's a suggestion there. Nothing more."

I watched Costace roll the casings this way and that. "South Korean," he said. "Some of that surplus stuff."

"You're sure there weren't more?" Hocker asked.

"Not that we found. And we swept the area thoroughly."

He pursed his lips and regarded Estelle. "You're very quiet," he said. "What's your take on all this?"

"Those cases weren't fired recently," she said. "They're reasonably clean, but you can see traces of dirt in the crease around the primer. They've been on the ground for a while."

"So they weren't involved with this shooting?"

Estelle shook her head. "I don't think so."

"Convenient location, then," Hocker said.

"Yes, sir."

He grinned. "You think someone put them there to frame Finnegan? That someone figured we'd find them and put two and two together for the wrong answer?"

"No, sir."

He looked surprised. "Why not?"

"Because if that were so, it would assume that the person who planted the cases knew what was on that film. It assumes that he would know we'd be out here, looking around in that very spot. It would assume that the person who fired the shot knew that the occupant in the airplane was taking photographs."

"A lot of assumptions," Costace said and handed the bag of casings back to her.

"Yes, sir."

"So, just a hunter firing half a clip at a coyote?" Hocker persisted.

"Who the hell knows?" I said.

"Well, it gives us something," Hocker said. "I want to see the rest of that film."

"Follow us on in," I said.

Hocker hesitated. "By the way, did Buscema get in touch with you?"

"Not in the last couple of hours."

"He's got a probable path for that bullet. They found the point of entry, to the right of centerline, just about where the belly of the aircraft starts to turn upward into the sides."

"On the right side," I repeated.

"The right. From there, it deflected off a structural member of some sort, fragmented, and at least one chunk found its way up through the back of the victim's seat."

"Did Buscema find any other pieces?"

Hocker shook his head. "Another fragment continued out the left side of the fuselage. He's got evidence of that, too." He paused. "Now, let me ask you something. How well do you know this Johnny Boyd character?"

I shrugged. "I've known him for twenty years. He doesn't have a record, if that's what you mean. He's a hard-working rancher. Good family. His son's a student at the state university. The only contact the department's had with Johnny Boyd over the years was a property-line dispute he had six or seven years ago when the Bureau of Land Management traded for a piece of property that adjoins his. That was resolved."

Hocker shot a glance at Costace, and I added, "Why?"

"Let me show you something. You might find it interesting." He slapped the door of the Bronco with the palm of his hand and trudged back toward his own vehicle.

TWENTY-EIGHT

THE MORE I READ, the more my stomach churned as if I'd been served some spoiled green chili. And maybe not for any reason that Walter Hocker would understand.

I held up a photocopy of a handwritten letter dated in 1997. The penmanship was confident and brusque, written with a black felt-tip pen. It was addressed to the Secretary of the Interior of the United States. I skimmed it quickly and then returned to the beginning.

"Sirs," the letter began, and I read it aloud. *"It has come to my attention that an agency of your department is considering purchase or fair-value exchange for some 6800 acres located in Posadas County, for the purpose of establishing either a national park or a national monument.*

"The land in question is to include the entirety of what is known locally as the Martinez Tubes, and extends north beyond the southwestern boundaries of the Circle JEB Ranch, property owned entirely by my family and myself."

I stopped and glanced up at Estelle. "You remember that?" I asked. "They were thinking of making a park out of the lava tubes.'' She nodded. ''Nothing ever came of it,'' I added for Hocker's benefit, although I was sure he was well aware of that.

The letter got to the point in blunt terms that left no room for misunderstanding:

"The Circle JEB Ranch operation has no interest in entering into any sort of negotiations with the federal government, now or ever, for either land exchange or outright sale. It is also our understanding that the land may be acquired through condemnation proceedings. Be advised," and I paused for breath, *"that any action by the federal government, or any other government, to secure lands owned by the Circle JEB Ranch will be met with appropriate response."*

''Huh,'' I said. ''And then it's signed, *'Sincerely yours, John Patrick Boyd.'*'' I placed the letter back in the folder, wondering if Johnny Boyd had the slightest inkling about the extended life of his handwritten message.

''All right,'' I said. ''There's that. The letter makes perfect sense, and I remember the circumstances. For a while, there was talk of all kinds of development off the west end of Cat Mesa. A big national monument that would draw some tourist dollars to the area. And I remember that it hinged in large measure on being able to acquire the land—including a large chunk of the Boyds' ranch.'' I looked at the letter again. ''We even had a congressman or two down here at one time. And then the whole affair went away quietly when it became clear that the lava tubes were short, shallow, and boring—nothing at all like the big ones up by Grants, or certainly not like the limestone caverns over at Carlsbad. Not park material, one congressman said.''

I leaned back and gazed at Hocker, whose face was expressionless. ''So tell me, Walter, how does it happen that a letter from a small-time rancher to a federal land-management agency attracts the attention of the FBI?''

''I suppose someone in the Department of the Interior thought that the letter constituted enough of a threat that they forwarded a copy to us for our files. Just to have it on record.''

''A threat?'' I said. ''It reads more like a promise. And

there's no suggestion of violence, either. Just as easily, he could have been promising appropriate litigation. Or a 'Letters to the Editor' campaign."

"He could have been," Hocker agreed.

I frowned. "I don't understand, then. Since when do things like legitimate letters between citizens and a federal agency become part of a law-enforcement record? Am I being naive?"

"If you want my opinion," Hocker said, sounding very much as if his opinion wasn't worth much, "it's the words *'met with appropriate response.'*" He reached down, slid the letter to one side and tapped a report that bore the letterhead of the Department of the Treasury's Bureau of Alcohol, Tobacco, and Firearms.

"And now we've got the BATF," I said, puzzled. I scanned the report. "And this is routine?" I asked, holding my hands out. I looked up at Estelle and beckoned her closer so she could read the evidence for herself.

"It's the law, to my understanding, that if someone buys more than a single handgun during any one day's purchase, the multiple transaction must be reported by the firearm's dealer to the BATF. Isn't that right?" Hocker didn't reply, and I handed the stapled records to Estelle. She scanned down the columns.

"I think it's during any five-day period, sir," Estelle said. "This is a moderate arsenal," she murmured. "And much of it purchased within a year or two of that letter."

"You see what I'm saying?" Hocker asked.

I leaned back. "No, Walter, I don't. Even if Johnny Boyd's got a paranoid streak a mile wide, there's not a thing that's illegal about buying a whole railroad car full of arms, as long as each weapon is purchased legally."

"Depends what they're used for," Hocker said.

"That's a different issue," I snapped. "I said that ownership of the firearms is not illegal. Or even improper. The man fancies hardware. He can afford it, apparently. So what?"

Hocker leaned hard against the door. He clasped his hands

together, both forearms on the windowsill. "Keep going, Sheriff."

The next several documents covered other purchases John Patrick Boyd had made within the past eighteen months. This time the transactions were far from routine and required additional registration, or Class 3 fees, as fully automatic weapons: a Browning Automatic Rifle, caliber .30-06; a Schmeisser, caliber .9mm; and a Thompson A-11, caliber .45ACP. I stopped reading and looked up at Hocker.

"See what I mean?" he said.

"What baffles me is that Johnny Boyd came by these weapons, and the federal paperwork, perfectly legally, Walter. And the last purchase was made within the year. What, you think that suddenly he whips one of them out and starts shooting at airplanes?"

Hocker grinned and looked across at Costace. "Sheriff, let me ask you something. We've got a plane brought down by a bullet. Maybe stray, maybe well and truly aimed. That airplane is hit, the pilot is killed, the plane crashes in the backyard of a man who at one time thought he was being threatened by the feds...who thought he had received at least enough of a threat to warrant writing letters.

"And after he writes the letters, he spends what had to have been a hell of a bankroll on firearms purchases, including at least three fully automatic weapons. Ammunition isn't recorded, so we don't know anything about that." He leaned toward me and lowered his voice even more. "Now don't you think that's reason enough to at least talk to the man?"

He reached in and picked up the folder and shook it gently. "I don't know if you're a fan of profiles or not," he said softly.

I interrupted him before he could go any farther. "No, no, Agent Hocker. We don't believe in any modern law-enforcement methods around here at all. Just men on horseback."

He stopped and smiled again, and shook his head patiently. "That's not what I mean, Sheriff. What I meant was, if we were to design a profile of someone who would deliberately fire a high-powered rifle, or a machine gun, at a low-flying aircraft, an aircraft that is obviously circling his property—and, if you figure in the weather, must be doing so for a fairly important reason—then Johnny Boyd fits that profile. He's on record.'' He shook the folder again.

When I didn't respond immediately, Hocker tucked the folder under his arm and stood back from the door. "There are at least ten handguns on this list," he said. "Each one of those falls under the Brady Bill guidelines, so one of your department was charged with doing a background check."

"And I'm sure one was done. We have one deputy who routinely handles all those, at least until we go to the instant check system. Then it will be the FBI's headache."

"Which deputy?"

"Sergeant Mitchell. If there'd been anything squirrelly, he'd have caught it."

Hocker took a deep breath and tapped the Bronco's door with the corner of the folder. "How well do you know Mr. Boyd?"

"Fairly well," I said. "And I've been in this business long enough to know that people aren't always what they seem. The Boyds stick to themselves. They have a son away at college. I was in their home earlier today, as were you. I saw a variety of weapons in a living-room cabinet. You saw the same cabinet, but didn't have a chance to do an inventory. But I'll tell you this…there was nothing in the cabinet anything like any of this. Nothing like what's on that list. Let me see it again," I added, and held out my hand.

"You know him fairly well, but you didn't know that he buys machine guns?"

"Nope," I said. "I didn't know that. There are probably things you do that I don't know about, either." I opened the folder and scanned the list of weapons. "An interesting collection. All military." I counted quickly. "Eight of them."

"You're assuming the bullet was from a rifle, and I agree. But any of these handguns takes ammunition that may be loaded with jacketed bullets. And at two hundred or so yards, a jacketed bullet from a high-performance handgun will easily punch a hole through the aluminum skin of an airplane.''

"And then fragment and scatter?" I asked. "I don't think so. And if you're talking about a deliberate shot, you're dreaming. Not at that distance, not at a moving target. Not with something that has a four-or five-inch barrel. And besides, none of these are 'high-performance' handguns, Walter. A forty-five automatic or a nine-millimeter is hardly high-performance." I held up the list of weapons. "I want a copy of this."

"Help yourself," Hocker said. "In fact, take it with you. Everything in that folder is a copy."

"Here's the deal," I said. "It makes perfect sense to talk to Johnny Boyd. The one condition is that I want to go with you when you do. You saw earlier what kind of a temper the man has. And he's entitled to that temper, up to a point. If he's guilty of something, I want him nailed every bit as much as you do. Martin Holman was a friend of mine. But if Boyd is innocent, I don't want him to run the gauntlet through holy hell.''

"I appreciate that," Hocker said. "But I want my ducks in a row. I want to talk to Sergeant Mitchell first. And I want to talk to the dealer where the weapons were purchased, too. And I want to see all of the photos.''

"That's easily done.''

Hocker nodded and stood up. "When?''

"Now's fine," I said. "Mitchell's on duty. We were headed back to the office anyway. Follow us on in.''

Hocker turned to go, then stopped. "Do you happen to know where Boyd does his banking?''

"No, Walter. I don't.''

Hocker nodded and followed Neil Costace back to their vehicle. I watched them go in the rearview mirror.

"Sir?" Estelle said, seeing the expression on my face.

I shook my head wearily. "You know what my trouble is?''

"I think I can guess, sir.''

I looked across at her. "My trouble is that I can't bring myself to believe that Johnny Boyd would do something so stupid. I want those guys"—I nodded toward the rearview mirror—"to flush out some worthless, foreign terrorist who's hiding in a barn somewhere, not one of my neighbors."

Estelle pulled the Bronco into gear. "Johnny Boyd's got a barn, sir. And I don't think Posadas is a hotbed of terrorists."

"You're starting to think he's involved somehow? Boyd, that is?"

She shook her head quickly. "I'm not saying that at all, sir. I don't know what to think. But I tell you what would help. We all need to sit down around the conference table and put our various puzzle pieces together. That's what you always drummed into my head. And now's as good a time as any, before someone does something we'll all regret."

TWENTY-NINE

I SUPPOSE WALTER HOCKER would have been happier if some grizzled veteran had emerged from the basement darkroom, perhaps wearing an eyeshade, perhaps muttering an acerbic, cynical reply to every comment. I don't think that he was prepared for Linda Real.

Linda was excited, and an excited Linda bubbled. She nodded rapidly as Estelle told her what we needed to see, her excited, lopsided grin getting wider and wider. When she was introduced to the two FBI agents, she barked a quick, unimpressed, "Hi," as if they were merely in the way, and turned to Estelle and me.

"You won't believe what I found, sir," she said.

"I'm waiting," I said. "Let's use the table in the conference room."

"When Sergeant Mitchell arrives, do you want me to send him right in?" Gayle Sedillos asked, and I nodded.

"She been working for you long?" Neil Costace asked as

he followed me into the new conference room—one of Martin Holman's pride and joys. The fancy maple-veneer table was twelve feet long. The black fake-leather chairs were almost comfortable. Costace glanced after Linda's departing figure.

"Linda? About thirty-six hours, give or take," I said. "We tend to lose track of time around here."

Costace barked a staccato laugh and glanced at Hocker. "She's got all the negatives from the sheriff's camera?"

"She's got one roll," I said. "That's all there was. Just the one in the camera itself. A single twenty-exposure roll."

"She processed it here?" Hocker asked.

"Yes."

"Color?"

"No. Black and white."

"Is that what you usually use? Black and white?"

"It depends," I said. "Most of the time, yes. We can do our own processing, and we've found over the years that color didn't add much. Her husband"—I nodded at Estelle—"does most of the medical photography for us in color. Bruises don't look like much in black and white."

"I'm aware of all that," Hocker said impatiently.

"And now that Officer Real is with us, if we can afford a color lab in next year's budget, we'll get it. One step at a time."

In less than two minutes, Linda Real returned with a hefty manila folder.

"Let me lay all these out in the order they appear on the negative," she said, and like a card dealer, she snapped out a set of sixteen eight-by-ten photos. I was delighted that she was taking complete control of the show-and-tell, not waiting to be prompted, not deferring to authority.

That done, she pointed at the photos that corresponded to the film's negative numbers one, two, five, six, eleven, and twelve. "These are blurred because the camera was jarred." She swirled a finger over number five. "Everything is uniformly blurred, but it's the kind of blur you get from motion, not from being out of focus."

She moved over to number thirteen. "This is the windmill

picture, and Estelle already has a copy of it. Number fourteen is a line of fencing, or what appears to be a line of fencing, and a bunch of open grassland. There's a hint of a road, or path, here in the left corner.'' She paused for breath and tapped the next picture. ''Number fifteen is a photo of a small stone building. Estelle also has that one. And then number sixteen is another shot of fence and pasture, with a grove of trees. You also have that. And it's the last photo on the roll.''

She straightened up and looked at me. ''Then what I did was to blow up each readable negative into four quadrants. That seemed a logical next step...sort of a survey process.'' She started to slide number three up and out of the way, but Hocker held up a hand.

''By 'last photo on the roll,' what do you mean?''

Linda glanced at him, her crooked left eyebrow dancing just a bit. ''The last one,'' she said. ''The last photo that the sheriff took.''

''No exposures followed that one?''

Linda frowned, no doubt thinking that Hocker was simple. ''The last time his camera blinked,'' she said and smiled. ''The end of the negative is clear, unexposed film. There were no more exposures after this one.''

Hocker nodded, satisfied. Linda waited for a couple of pulse beats, and when it was clear that Hocker was finished, she reached out and placed four eight-by-ten enlargements underneath the third photo.

''Huh,'' Hocker muttered. I stood beside him, leaning over the table. Estelle and Costace went around to the other side.

''Right,'' Linda said in response to Hocker's grunt. ''I don't see much there, either. It looks like the top of Cat Mesa, if I had to guess. All trees, one stretch of roadway just visible in the center. Now, number four is looking off to the north, from somewhere over the top of the mesa.'' She placed the four quadrant enlargements underneath the photo.

''In this enlargement, you can see what might be ranch buildings way off in the distance to the north.''

''Boyd's ranch,'' I said. ''I recognize the way the buildings are grouped.''

"Okay," she said and plunged on. "Photos seven, eight, nine, and ten are all of the same area, sir. I don't know where it is, or what it is, but apparently Sheriff Holman was taking a picture of this fence line." She touched one of the photos. "There's a characteristic spot where three fence lines meet, and another spot that looks like it could once have been a small pond. No vegetation of any sort. It appears in each one of the four photos."

"Huh," Hocker said.

"What's interesting is that in each of the photos, no matter what the angle was between the airplane and the ground, the intersection of the three fences is in the center. That's where he was aiming the camera."

"Fence fetish," Costace chuckled as he watched Linda placing her sets of four quadrant enlargements under each master photo. "So where is that spot, anyway? I mean, what's there, exactly?"

"I don't know," I said, and felt a bit foolish saying so.

"If the sheriff thought enough of that spot to make sure he had it recorded on film, then maybe someone should find out where it is," Hocker said blandly.

"Now that we have the photos, we can do that," I said. "Sergeant Torrez knows this country as well as anyone. Make sure he gets those pictures," I said to Linda. "I suspect he'll find the place for us within the hour." Hocker nodded, satisfied.

"And here's the windmill. Nothing unusual. But here"— Linda paused and beamed at me—"is that little stone house." This time, with loving care, she placed the four enlargements below the original eight-by-ten, pausing after each one. When she was finished, she said, "And this is what I wanted you to see." The eraser on her pencil touched the northeast corner of the building. "See that?"

"The shadow of someone standing beside the building," I said, and Linda beamed even wider. What I really wanted to do was to give her a paternal hug, but there were federal agents in the room, and who the hell knew what federal guidelines there might be to cover such unprofessional behavior.

"That's what I think. The sheriff was using pretty fine-grained film," Linda said, "and it enlarges well. So I blew it up some more." She pulled another eight-by-ten out of the folder, this one showing just the corner of the building. Although the resolution wasn't able to sustain much quality, my imagination could actually make my bifocaled eyes believe that I was looking at the shadow of a human being.

"Sharp eyes," Hocker said.

"Estelle—" I began to say, and checked myself. I had been about to say that Estelle had already started chasing that shadow and that we'd already discussed it with the two agents. But Linda didn't need to be deflated just then. "Estelle, what do you think? Is that what we're looking at?" I asked.

"Clearly the shadow of a person," she said.

"We need to have this digitally enhanced," Costace said, and his tone of voice said plainly that he thought the photo should have been on the express plane to Washington—or wherever their enhancing gadgets were.

To my surprise, Hocker shook his head, but Linda beat him to the punch. "You can't enhance a shadow, sir," she said, and I laughed out loud.

"She's right on that count," Hocker added. "You've got a shape, and that's it. That's all it ever was...a shadow. Nothing to enhance." He took a deep breath. "All right. There's a person standing there. And that's where you went today?" I nodded. "But you already told us that you didn't find any footprints or anything else beside that building."

"That's also true," I said, and realized that Linda was looking sideways at me, frowning.

"But a few dozen feet uphill, you found a dozen rifle shell casings. Then the next step is pretty simple," he said, and broke off as the door opened. Sergeant Eddie Mitchell entered the room, closing the door behind himself.

He stepped up to the table, scanned the photos and nodded. "This is what was in the camera?"

"Yep," I said. "This is the most interesting one." I indicated the shadow picture, and Mitchell bent over the table until he was a foot away from the photo.

"A person standing by the back corner," he said. "That's Finnegan's property. Did you ask him if that was him? Was he standing there?"

"He says that he was in town when the plane went down."

"That will be easy enough to check."

"Set Tom Pasquale on that. He'll enjoy doing something other than hiking through sand and picking up scrap aluminum," I said. "And Agent Hocker has some questions for you about Johnny Boyd's guns."

Mitchell looked across at Hocker, and in the silence between my remark and the time it took Hocker to realize that Mitchell had said all he planned to without a direct question, Linda Real started scooping up photos.

"I'll take these back," she said, but I held up a hand.

"Wait a bit. Don't be in a hurry." She started to move away from the table, as if she didn't really belong in our company. "Relax," I said. "We may have more questions."

"Sergeant Mitchell," Walter Hocker said, "BATF records show that Johnny Boyd purchased a significant number of military-type weapons in the past year or so, including a number of handguns, long guns, and even several fully automatic weapons. You did the Brady check on the handguns?"

"Yes, sir."

"Is that a fairly thorough check, Sergeant?"

Mitchell frowned. "It's as thorough as is necessary to determine that the BATF's guidelines are being followed."

"Meaning?"

"Meaning we check to determine if the person has a record. Any felony convictions. Any convictions for spousal abuse. Any mental illness adjudication. Routine things like that."

"How long does that normally take?"

Mitchell's gaze was unblinking. "Are you investigating the way this department does background checks for firearm sales, or is there something specific you need to know?" His tone was calm, almost glacial. He was leaning one hip against the heavy table, his arms relaxed at his sides. Hocker wasn't ready for Mitchell's reply and flushed crimson.

"Just answer the goddam question," he snapped.

"I beg your pardon, sir?" Mitchell's tone was wonderfully civil, about the way a rattlesnake is when it first twitches its tail, unsure if there's a threat or not.

To his credit, Hocker read the signals right the first time. "How long does the check normally take, Sergeant?"

"The 'normal' time for a background investigation varies with the person who is being investigated, sir."

"And for Boyd?"

"His file hasn't changed since his first purchase when the Brady policy went into effect. If I had received paperwork a couple of days ago for a handgun purchase by Johnny Boyd, I would have just signed it off. It would have taken a few seconds."

"That's it? A few seconds?"

Mitchell nodded. "His file hasn't changed any since the last time, so there's no point in wasting time. His or mine."

"You said if you had received it before the crash. What about now?"

"Well, sir, obviously I would want an ongoing investigation involving the Boyds, however tangential, to be resolved before I took any action."

"Commendable," Hocker muttered.

"I'm not sure what it is that you want me to say," Mitchell said.

Hocker grimaced and glanced at Neil Costace as if to say, "Why didn't you warn me about these people?"

"What I want is to find out what weapon fired those casings," Hocker said. "Then I want a match with that bullet fragment. You said that you were working on the fragments?"

"I said he was," I said quickly. "What did you find out, Eddie?"

"The fragment is too small for any clear measurements. We're going to need help from these folks on that. It's beyond any instruments we have here."

"Any thoughts, though? Any gut feelings?"

"Bob thinks that it's twenty-two caliber. I think it could be anything up to thirty."

"But it could be two-twenty-three," Costace said. "Like the shell casings."

"It could be, sir. It could also be from a hundred other weapons."

"If there's even a trace of the rifling the lab can make a comparison," Hocker said.

"The problem is that there are a lot of rifles like that in the county," Mitchell said. "There's a Mini-14 out in each one of our county units, as a matter of fact. I know that Johnny and his son have at least one. Lots of ranchers do. If you want casings from Boyd's, I'm sure all you have to do is ask him."

"We're going to need a warrant for that," Costace said.

"Or just go out to his range and pick 'em up. You don't need a warrant for that. It's almost within the bounds of the crash site, anyway."

"Range?"

Mitchell nodded. "He's got a place where he's set up a small range. Just a couple of target supports, some silhouettes, things like that."

"You'll show us where that is?"

"Yes, sir. It's not far from the crash site, actually."

"Could a bullet have gone astray from there, do you think?"

"No. You'll see why when we get there. It's deep in a narrow arroyo. In order for a bullet to fly out of there, it'd have to be fired up in the air intentionally."

"Did Boyd ever tell you why he was buying these guns?"

The deputy shook his head. "He's not required to have a reason, sir."

"But you weren't curious?"

"No, sir. What he spends his money on is his business."

Hocker grimaced again, and this time, he shot an annoyed look at me, as if it were my fault that my deputies listened to me when I lectured them on procedure. "Well," he said, "let's find out why he bought all those guns. Who's the dealer that he uses? In a town this size, there can't be too many...and anything he got mail-order has to go through a dealer as well.''

"The dealer for every transaction on that list is George Payton.'' Mitchell glanced at the wall clock. "This time on a Sunday afternoon, he'll be home in front of the television watching wrestling, if you want to talk with him.''

Hocker nodded. "Good. Maybe he can shed some light on the ammunition sales, too. I want to take that casing with me. And then, while we're at it, let's run out to Boyd's private shooting range and pick up some of that brass you were talking about. Maybe we can tie together a whole bunch of loose ends.''

"Estelle and I will be here, ripping the sheriff's files apart,'' I said, and I reached out a hand to make contact with Mitchell's shoulder. He had been headed toward the door, but stopped in his tracks and fixed his calm blue eyes on me. "When you're out there, remember Johnny Boyd's temper, Eddie,'' I said. "That's his property, so tread lightly.'' The two FBI agents had already gone out the door, and I nodded after them and added, "And make sure that they do the same. Keep your radio on.''

THIRTY

MARTIN HOLMAN had never hinted to me that he was the least bit interested in branching out on his own into criminal investigation. He'd never hinted to me that one of his passionate goals was to lead an important investigation—or any investigation, for that matter. I had considered ourselves lucky if we kept him from ruining evidence on those rare occasions when he had shown up at a crime scene. Thankfully, that hadn't happened too often.

His turf, his expertise, had been administration—dealing with county government, other agencies, the forward march of technology, grant-writing, budget concerns—and especially the press. Over the past decade, Posadas had suffered its share of high-profile cases, the sort that attract big-city television cameras. Each time, Martin Holman had been an effective buffer. He was the elected official who represented the department when we needed an official "face." Now I knew that I had only a matter of hours before providing that "face" was going to be my own personal headache—unless I could pawn the duty off on someone else.

With Martin Holman, my status had been simple, and perfectly suited to my liking. As undersheriff, I had been given supervisory status over all of the deputies and their law-enforcement activities. I had little or no interest in civil work, and so I had delegated the department's civil matters to Sergeant Howard Bishop. The pace of civil work suited him just fine.

When it came to criminal investigations, Martin Holman had learned long ago to adopt a hands-off policy. He hadn't interfered with my work, or attempted to supervise me—that being a losing battle anyway. It had taken him several years to accept Estelle Reyes-Guzman as more than just a pretty face.

He had sometimes offered suggestions and ideas—not all of them bad, either. On a few occasions—thankfully, very few—he had spent sometime by himself in a marked patrol unit cruising the county, and those times always made me nervous. Gayle Sedillos had standing orders to call me whenever Martin Holman suffered an attack of lawmanitis and took it upon himself to go patrolling.

How Martin Holman had been elected to the county's top law-enforcement position three times running was one of those political marvels that happened routinely in the southwest. But at least he had been no speedtrap-loving redneck, and if any county could win the "Be Kind To Tourists" award, it should have been Posadas—if only more tourists had chosen to stop.

Thus it was with considerable surprise that toward the back of the second file drawer from the top in the unit to the right of his desk, I stumbled upon a file division whose ear was clearly marked in the sheriff's neat, almost architectural block printing. "Pending cases."

"What pending cases?" I said and pulled out the entire section. We all had our own active files, kept separate from the main department collection until the cases were resolved one way or another. With some careful thought, I probably could have listed the important cases that each one of the deputies was working on at any given moment. We didn't hide work, and we didn't keep our favorites to ourselves.

But, judging by the contents of the folder, it appeared that Martin Holman had been doing exactly that.

Estelle looked over my shoulder and lifted up the corners of the manila folders. "He's got three separate files here," she mused. I handed the bundle to her and she opened the first file, turned, and spread it out on the desk. "Well, now." She pressed the covers of the folder open flat against the desk and leaned on them while she looked at the pages inside, as if the covers were controlled by heavy springs, ready to snap the thing closed.

"So what is it?"

"A complaint filed against County Commissioner Sam Carter by one of his employees."

"You're kidding. Which one?"

"Taffy Hines."

"You're kidding again. Taffy?" An image of the stout, middle-aged cashier flashed through my mind. I could picture her where I'd seen her just hours before, bent over the inventory books at the register of Sam Carter's supermarket.

Estelle nodded and held up a tape cassette in one hand and a deposition in the other. "Alleging telephone solicitation. She says here that she recorded Carter on three separate occasions. She calls them 'obscene telephone calls soliciting sexual favors.'"

"What's the date?"

"April nineteen is when she made the signed statement to the sheriff."

I groaned. "I don't want to hear it. I don't know why it surprises me when I find out things like that." I held out my hand. "Let me see that damn file." I took the folder and scanned the deposition. "And Sam Carter, of all people. He's got to be as old as I am. What a jerk. Why didn't he just proposition her in the store when no one was around to listen?"

"I can see why the sheriff had this filed away in here," Estelle said without trying to answer my question.

"Sure. With Carter being a county legislator, I'm not surprised that Martin was procrastinating." I looked at the tape cassette, then dropped it back in the folder in disgust. "Wonderful," I said. "Maybe if I ignore this, it will go away."

"I'm sure," Estelle said. She reached out for the folder. "Let me talk to Taffy and then to Mr. Carter."

I shook my head. "With less than a week to go before you pack it in, I don't think you want to get involved in a mess like this."

Estelle almost smiled. "I think Taffy will drop the complaint, and I think Sam Carter won't ever call her again," she said.

I looked closely at her, then grinned. "Can I be there when you talk with Carter? I'm beginning to understand why he was concerned that you might be appointed sheriff." She laughed and I gestured at the folders. "What's the other stuff? I'm not sure I want to know."

Estelle turned the second folder right side up and opened it. She frowned and read for several seconds. "It's paperwork from Sheriff Burkhalter requesting an evaluation on Eddie Mitchell."

"I'll make sure Burkhalter gets something. Someday. What's the third?"

Estelle opened the last folder, glanced at the cover page, and grinned.

"What?"

"You don't want to know, sir."

"Yes, I do. What is it?"

Estelle smiled up at me and handed me the folder so I could read it for myself. "It's a list of people he wanted to be sure to invite to your retirement party, sir. It looks like he was still in the process of adding to it. Probably when he remembered a name, he'd add it to the list."

"A party?"

"September thirtieth at the Don Juan de Oñate, in the Conquistador Room. Seven p.m."

"He never told me about that. Let me see this thing."

"Of course he didn't, sir. Evidently it was supposed to be a surprise." I caught the wistful note in her voice and glanced up at her.

"There're a lot of people here."

"Yes, sir."

"Including you and Francis." She nodded and I closed the folder. "You were going to come all the way down from Minnesota?" She nodded again and I added, "That would be silly." The telephone on the desk buzzed and blinked, and with a sigh, I dropped the three folders on the desk.

I picked up the phone and slumped down in Holman's chair. "Gastner."

"George Payton on line one, sir," Gayle Sedillos said, and the phone clicked.

"Thanks," I said and punched the button. "George? This is Bill. What's up?"

"Hey there," George Payton said. We'd been friends for two decades, and we were both at that stage where we figured the other would die first. "I've got company."

"I know you do," I said.

"This is sure a sorry, sorry business," he said and coughed. "How come you didn't come over with these two feds?"

I chuckled. "Estelle and I are sorting through the wreckage of Martin Holman's office paperwork, George. I couldn't breakaway."

"Sorry, sorry thing. But Eddie's all right."

"Yes, he is," I said, assuming he was referring to Sergeant Mitchell. "What can I do for you?"

"Look…" He hesitated. "The law says that I have to make all the federal paperwork involving firearm sales available to law enforcement if so asked, correct?"

"That's correct, George."

"There's nothing on the yellow forty-forty seventy-three form that asks *why* a customer is purchasing a firearm. Did you know that?"

"I guess I knew that." I heard some conversation in the background and could picture Agent Walter Hocker standing there patiently, arms folded over his chest.

"If a bona fide law-enforcement officer asks me what my knowledge is of a customer's purpose in purchasing any weapon—or any product at all, for that matter, even a goddam chain saw—am I required to tell him?"

"If there's evidence of a crime, and if what you know is germane, and if it's not self-incriminating, then yes—either now or later, and later, it may be in front of a Grand Jury," I said. "But understand that we've got a significant criminal offense here. We need all the help we can get."

"What's the offense?"

"Evidence indicates that Martin Holman was murdered."

Dead silence followed. "Nobody told me that," Payton said finally. "Johnny Boyd did that?"

"We don't know who did it."

"I thought Martin was killed in a plane crash."

"He was."

"Then you're not making sense."

"George, we've known each other for a long time, isn't that true?"

"Sure enough, we have."

"Will you trust me on this one, then?"

"Do I have a choice?"

"Sure."

Payton chuckled dryly. "Sure I do. So you want me to tell these gents anything they want to know?"

"That's just about it. And by the way, while I'm talking to you…did Johnny Boyd ever actually tell you why he bought all that hardware?"

"Well, of course he did."

"Then tell the agents, George. It's as simple as this: what Johnny Boyd did with his various weapons purchases, and I mean all the details, may well end up as the stuff of a Grand Jury session. Whether he's innocent or not."

"Sorry, sorry state of affairs."

"I couldn't agree with you more. By the way, do you have any South Korean two-twenty-three ammo in stock?"

"Sure."

"The agents are going to ask you that. Do me a favor and give them a few samples, will you?"

"I can do that. What, did someone shoot Holman, or what?"

"Someone shot the plane and the pilot, George."

"Good God."

"Yep. Just tell the feds what they need to know. And keep it confidential for the time being, all right?"

Payton agreed, and I hung up. "I don't know why he felt the need to call me," I said.

"Because you're an old, trusted friend, sir," Estelle replied. "Remember Johnny Boyd saying to have Judge Hobart sign the warrant? Same thing."

I sighed. "I suppose." I looked up at her. "Can I go to Michigan with you?"

"Minnesota, sir. And that'd be neat."

I grinned, picked up the three file folders again and handed them to Estelle. "That'd be neat," I repeated. "And this shit is *not* neat. A complaint of solicitation by one of the county fathers, a threat to hire away one of my dwindling supply of best officers, and a goddam party that Marty Holman will never get to attend." I relaxed back in Holman's chair and watched Estelle shuffle the files into order. A deep weariness was finally beginning to catch up with me. I rested my head back against the chair.

"I'd like to know what the actual trajectory of that bullet was," Estelle said, and she sounded as if she were talking just to try to keep me awake. "What the path was through the airframe. And then, if we can coax Charlotte Finnegan to focus a little, she might remember just where the plane was when she heard the backfiring. That might give us a closer idea of where the shot came from.''

"Within a county or two," I said. "Buscema will be down at the hangar, I imagine."

"Unless he took time out to eat or sleep."

I looked at Estelle in mock surprise. "Now who does that?"

THIRTY-ONE

WE REFUELED hurriedly at the Don Juan, and I could have lingered over the wonderful green-chili burritos and fresh coffee for the rest of the evening. But I was anxious to find out what Vincent Buscema had determined as he sifted his pile of junk, and Estelle needed to stop by her home on Twelfth Street for a moment to reassure her family that she hadn't abandoned them.

I waited in the Bronco. Her husband's Isuzu Trooper was parked in the driveway, and ten minutes later when she came back out, she wasn't smiling.

"Francis finished the autopsy," she said as she closed the car door. "At least all that they could do here." She looked across at me, and I could see that there was something else.

"And?"

"Nothing beyond the gunshot wound that would contribute to the crash. There's still quite a bit of lab follow-up that they want to do. But that's going to take several days."

That answer didn't explain the expression on her face, so I repeated, "And?"

"And Martin Holman had multiple myeloma."

I heard and understood perfectly well what Estelle had said, but my reaction was to say, "He what?"

"Multiple myeloma. It's a bone cancer."

"I know what it is," I said, mystified. "Francis told you that?" She nodded. "At what stage was it?"

"If he'd felt ill enough to be seeing a physician, it wasn't anyone in town, sir. It was a surprise to both Alan Perrone and Francis."

"How did they discover that? It's not a cancer that you'd see, like a big tumor or something, is it?"

"Francis said that the protein levels in the blood test tipped off Alan. They had done a preliminary screening in the lab here at the hospital. And then they did a series of X rays of bone samples, and I suppose that confirmed whatever it is that they look for."

"Christ."

"Do you suppose he knew, sir?"

"I don't think so. Martin was something of a hypochondriac, so if he'd been under medical treatment for cancer, he would have found a way to say something. And with as much time as I've spent in the hospital for various wonderful things, I think he would have mentioned it to me. I don't think he'd keep it to himself."

"Francis said that the average prognosis is two or three years after diagnosis."

"I think he would have wanted those years," I said. "And Janice didn't know, or she would have said something to us earlier, when we were over at the house."

"Francis said he was going over there this evening," Estelle said. "He thinks that Janice ought to know."

"Of course she should," I said, and at the same time, felt a selfish wash of relief that someone more talented than I at breaking news of that nature was taking the initiative. I saw a small head appear in the living-room window of the house. A hand lifted and offered a sober wave.

"Are the kids okay?" I asked, returning the greeting. It seemed weeks, not the short day or two it had been, since my two godchildren had used me as a target for their energies.

Estelle nodded. "Francisco asked me if Erma was going to Minnesota with us."

I grinned. "And what did you say?"

"I said she can if she wants to."

"How does she get along with your mother?"

"Mama calls her *hija*," Estelle said.

"And that's what she calls you too, so I guess it's settled," I said. "All you have to do is break the news to Erma." I shrugged and gestured forward. "Let's go find Buscema and get some details."

By the time we arrived at the airport, it was dark, with the wind still fitful out of the west. Buscema's team had done an amazing job of assembling the wreckage, but it looked like a caricature of its former self. Everything was in generally the right place, give or take a foot. The resulting jumble resembled an airplane as it might appear if six blind ladies had tried to make a patchwork picture quilt.

A folding table had been set up off to one side, and five very weary men sat around it, eating from an enormous tub of fried chicken. The size of the mess told me that others had come and gone, leaving just the bones picked clean behind.

Vince Buscema looked up as Estelle and I came through the door. He waved at us and shouted, "Pull up a chair!"

"We ate, thanks," I said and stopped at the end of the table. Tom Pasquale had a plate in front of him with a pile of chicken bones ten drumsticks high. The others were working hard to catch up. "What did you find out?"

Buscema gestured toward a second table on the opposite wall, near the front of the shattered fuselage. "Lookee here," he said and got up, a chicken breast still in hand and a smear of grease on his chin. We followed him over to the table.

Three large schematic drawings of the airplane were taped to the table, one that included both left-and right-side views, another including top and bottom, and the third showing front and rear. Over the top, Buscema had laid a transparent plastic sheet. The black marker lines clearly told the story.

"In order to enter through the outer skin here"—he tapped the circled X on the bottom view of the fuselage just ahead of the wing's trailing edge—"and then exit here"—he pointed at a second X on the left side of the aircraft, approximately a foot above the left wing root, just behind the vertical line of the pilot's-side window frame—"and send a fragment into the pilot, we're talking about a trajectory that would be approximated by this back line."

"Shooting steeply upward," I said. "Just a few degrees off of vertical."

"The old duck shot," Buscema said grimly. "Almost over the blind." He tapped the paper again. "The bullet fragmented against one of the frame members and secondarily against a portion of the seat framework."

"Did you find any other pieces of the bullet?"

"We're not going to be that lucky."

"And no evidence of other shots? No other holes anywhere that don't belong?" He shook his head. "What are the odds of intentionally making a shot like that?"

"Depends on the marksman, of course," Buscema said. "But if the plane was flying low, it was a pretty big target."

"But moving fast," I said.

I sensed someone standing right at my elbow, and I turned to see Bob Torrez. The sergeant smelled of sweat and fried chicken.

"How hard would it be?" I asked him. Torrez spent every hunting season in the field, and I couldn't recall when he'd ever come close to running out of venison, elk, or antelope steaks. He hunted duck and geese along the Rio Grande bosque and chased quail all over New Mexico and a few prized, secret spots in Arizona.

"I mean, I suppose it doesn't matter," I said, "because the shot was, in fact, successfully made. But what are the odds?"

Torrez shrugged. "Who's got a calculator?" Buscema reached into his shirt pocket and pulled out one of those little things that looks like a case for carrying business cards. He handed it to Torrez. "If we use a hundred and fifty miles an hour for the plane, that means that..." Torrez punched the tiny buttons with the eraser of his pencil "...that it covers two hundred and twenty feet each second, give or take."

"Give or take," I said, amused.

"Right," Torrez said. "A good average to use for a rifle

bullet's velocity is about twenty-seven hundred feet per second.'' He punched more keys. ''So it takes the bullet a third of a second to fly nine hundred feet, or three hundred yards.''

''And in that third of a second, how far does the plane travel?''

He shrugged. ''A third of two hundred and twenty feet. About seventy-three feet.''

''Or about three times the aircraft's length, if his math is right,'' Buscema added.

''And that's if you're trying to lead the target for a single shot,'' Torrez said. ''If someone were firing an automatic weapon, it'd be simpler to just put up a string of bullets and let the plane fly into one or two of them.''

''Huh,'' I said, and shoved my hands in my pockets. ''I certainly don't doubt that the math is right. But I think it's just goddam dumb bad luck.''

''The Boyds shoot a lot,'' Torrez said. ''Or at least the boy does. They've got that little range a few hundred yards off the main county road into their place. I drew Eddie a map so he could take the agents out there without getting lost. I think he's been there only once or twice before.''

''And they should be back in a few minutes,'' I said, looking at my watch. I glanced at Estelle, who was leaning on the table gazing at the aircraft diagrams. ''What are you thinking?''

She didn't look up, but her frown deepened a bit more. ''We've been trying to come up with a reason for all this,'' she mused. ''I'm thinking it may be staring us in the face.''

''Meaning what?''

Estelle straightened up, still looking at the schematic. ''If we assume that the shot wasn't just a freak accident, if we assume that it was actually fired at the aircraft with the intent of hitting it, what makes the most sense?''

''That whoever fired the shot knew who was in the airplane, and that whoever was in the plane posed a threat of some kind,'' Buscema said. He hooked a chair with his toe and pulled it over, sitting down so he could rest his arms on the back.

"And unless Martin Holman broadcast to the community beforehand that he was going to be making an aerial survey of that area, who could have known it was him?" Estelle continued.

"No one," I said flatly. "Everything points to its being a sudden whim…an opportunity of the moment."

"Right. So that means that whoever fired the shot saw this aircraft and made some assumptions."

"The way it was flying made its intent pretty obvious," Buscema said. "An organized back-and-forth track, fairly low-level."

"And the big question is, so what?" I said.

"Seeing something on the ground was the threat," Estelle said. "It had to be." She reached out and tapped the schematic. "And it's an aircraft that locals wouldn't recognize, unless they'd been down at the airport during the past week. And"—she tapped it again—"look at the registration."

I took a step closer. "There isn't anything on the diagram," I said, but Estelle was already turning away from the table.

"No, but over there—" She pointed at the remains of the Bonanza's aft fuselage. The large black lettering, torn and bent, was still clear.

"Gulf Victor Mary Alpha," I said. "With a hyphen between the Gulf and the Victor."

Estelle nodded. "And even someone without any particular knowledge of airplanes would see a registration number on the rear of an aircraft and assume that it was, in fact, the registration."

"And so?" I asked.

"Sir, I think that whoever fired the shot saw the one thing that was unique about this aircraft—the large lettering on the fuselage—and made an assumption about who was in the plane. He saw letters, maybe inaccurately, and made an assumption that the aircraft posed a threat to him."

"It would be easy to think the V was an N—that would make part of the registration NM, or New Mexico," Buscema said. "And if Detective Guzman is correct, the assumption might have been that the aircraft was an official one. A state plane.''

"And maybe the G represented 'Game,'" Tom Pasquale said. "And the A for 'Agency.'"

Despite the edge on everyone's nerves, I laughed. "Let's not get carried away," I said. "Maybe, maybe not. At least it gives us something to think about.''

I dragged the cellular phone out of my pocket and punched the auto-dial button for the sheriff's office. Ernie Wheeler answered.

"Ernie, have Sergeant Mitchell and the federal agents returned yet?''

"That's negative, sir."

I glanced at my watch again and saw that it was pushing seven-thirty. "Have they called in?''

"No, sir. Do you want me to try to raise them? I don't think the radio repeater carries into some of that area, and Eddie might not have taken the phone from his unit.''

"Do that," I said and punched off. "They've been out there long enough," I said to Estelle. "If they've collected rifle shell casings, the first thing you want to do is a preliminary firing-pin imprint comparison. You can do that with the stereoscope in Francis's lab. First that, and then extractor marks, just in front of the rim." Estelle nodded, far more expert with a microscope than I.

"That will give us an idea," I continued. "In the meantime, Bob, I want you to come with me. We're going to have a little chat with Mr. Boyd and Mr. Finnegan.'' Estelle frowned, but she didn't say anything. I stepped over to the wreckage and eyed the torn aluminum. "Vince, I want to take this with me," I said and tried to lift the section of fuselage with the most legible registration. "You got a metal shears with you? The skin's about torn loose anyway. Just this small section. None of the framework behind it.''

"What are you going to do with that?" Buscema asked.

"A little target-recognition contest," I said.

THIRTY-TWO

THE INSTANT that Sergeant Robert Torrez switched on the ignition of his unit, the radio barked into life, catching dispatcher Ernie Wheeler in mid-sentence.

"...seven, PCS. Try channel two."

A few seconds of silence followed, and I reached forward and turned the volume up slightly. By then, we were headed out of the airport parking lot onto State 78.

"Three-oh-seven, PCS. Do you copy?"

Static followed, and I keyed our mike. "PCS, three-ten is ten-eight."

"Three-ten, PCS, ten-four. Did you copy a transmission from three-oh-seven?"

"Three-ten, negative."

My telephone chirped and I dug it out of the jumble of papers between the seats. "Gastner."

"Sir, Mrs. Boyd just called." Linda Real's tone was clipped and businesslike, but the words came so rapid-fire that I had a hard time keeping up. "I've still got her on line one. Apparently her husband received a telephone call—she doesn't know from who—and then he left the house on the run. Mrs. Boyd said he was really angry. And he took a gun with him."

"Linda." I said, "slow down. Boyd left the house with a weapon after receiving a telephone call? Is that what his wife is saying?"

"That's right, sir."

I swore under my breath. "And she didn't know who called?"

"No, sir."

"Ask her again."

I heard mumbling in the background, and about a minute

later, Linda came back on the line. "She has no idea. She said that her husband listened and that she heard him cuss a couple of times. And then he said, 'Thanks a lot,' and hung up."

"Is Johnny's brother home? Edwin?"

"Just a minute, sir."

I could picture Linda with a telephone against each ear. I watched the highway in front of us as the white lines and the double yellows blended into a high-speed blur.

"Sir, she said Edwin's not home. He went into town earlier."

"Probably to the goddam bar," I muttered. Edwin liked the sauce anyway, and a hurting knee would encourage him even more.

"Yes, sir," Linda said without a trace of surprise in her voice. "Ernie has been trying to raise Sergeant Mitchell on the radio, but apparently they're in a dead spot. And he hasn't responded to the phone. Ernie said for me to contact you while he kept on trying the radio."

I only half heard Linda's explanation as my mind raced ahead. Bob Torrez had come to the same conclusion I did, because he accelerated hard. "Linda, tell Mrs. Boyd to stay in the house and to stay off the telephone. We're going to head up that way. And, Linda?"

"Sir?"

"I don't want any other traffic getting in our way. Tell Ernie that. Everyone stays put until they hear from me. While you're there, give me the Finnegans' phone number. Ernie knows it by heart."

She did so, and before I dialed, I took a second to tighten my shoulder harness, hoping that Torrez remembered that the intersection of State 78 and County 43 involved a right-angle turn.

While I tried to fit my fat finger on the tiny buttons of the damn phone, I glanced at Torrez. "I wouldn't put it past old George Payton to have called Johnny," I said. "Maybe he figures it's the least he could do for him."

Charlotte Finnegan answered the phone on the second ring.

Her "Hello" sounded like the whimper a child might make peeking around a door into a darkened room.

"Mrs. Finnegan, this is Sheriff Gastner. Let me talk with your husband, please."

"This is Sheriff Gastner?"

"Yes, ma'am. Is Richard there?"

"We don't have a very good connection," she said reprovingly. "I can barely understand you."

"Mrs. Finnegan, this is Sheriff Gastner." I slowed down and exaggerated the enunciation as if she could read my lips across the phone lines. "I need to talk with your husband." I braced my feet against the firewall as I saw the signs announcing the intersection with the county road.

Even as we squawled around the corner and emerged wheels-side-down heading northbound on 43, I heard Mrs. Finnegan say, "Richard went into Posadas, Sheriff."

"He's in town?"

She laughed apologetically. "I was rearranging the pantry and discovered I was out of canning lids."

That stopped me short. I frowned and braced my free hand against the dashboard as we blasted up a series of tortuous ess curves below Consolidated Mining's access road. "You were what?"

"I was out of canning lids. I know it's early, but I find that if I don't do things just when I think of them, why, when I need something, it's not there. Now Richard came in earlier and mentioned that he needed several rolls of duck tape for morning. You know he's working on that pipeline. And so as long as he needed that, I just added to the list." She sounded most pleased with herself. "I believe the Day-Night market on Grande has both the tape and the canning supplies."

"Thanks, Mrs. Finnegan. When he comes back, tell him I called. Good night." She sounded like she'd have liked to settle into an all-evening confab, but I cut her off.

"Huh," I said to myself and dialed dispatch. "Ernie," I said, "have Tom Mears or whoever is available swing by the Day-Night store. Ask Peggy—I think she's the one who works there at night—if Richard Finnegan stopped in sometime this evening to buy a few things.''

"That's it, sir?"

"That's it." I switched off and for a few minutes, watched the darkness slide by. "Canning lids," I said to no one in particular. "He went into town to buy canning lids. Canning lids in springtime."

"Canning late snow peas," Torrez said, but he didn't crack a smile. We roared up the steep section of twisting macadam that passed Consolidated Mining, and a few moments later as we crested the hill above the reservoir, I tried the radio again. But either Mitchell had his radio turned off or he was in one of the many areas in the county where the signal couldn't reach one of the repeater towers on the west end of Cat Mesa or across the county to the peak of San Cristobál.

"PCS, three-oh-three is ten-eight."

Deputy Pasquale hadn't had anymore sleep than any of the rest of us, but he was in his element. He couldn't even say routine numbers without sounding eager.

"He'd be a good one to have at our backsides," I said and keyed the mike. "Three-oh-three, work your way up County Forty-three to the intersection with the ranch road. Wait on the pavement."

"Ten-four."

"Make sure you wait on the pavement," I repeated, and Pasquale acknowledged. In another couple of minutes, we reached the turnoff, now so well-used by the airplane salvage team that the dusty tire marks of vehicles turning onto the highway from the dirt road had left a pronounced arc on the dark asphalt.

"Kill the lights," I said, but Torrez's hand was already moving toward the switch. The moon wasn't up, and Torrez tapped the little toggle switch down low by the emergency-brake release. The tiny bulb mounted on the back side of the bumper, what he affectionately called his "perpetrator light," cast just enough glow that he could see the edge of the road in his peripheral vision.

I buzzed down my window, straining to see ahead. We had

3.8 miles before we reached the first intersection, the two-track that wound off to the south, up the back side of Cat Mesa to where Dick Finnegan was fiddling with his spring and his piping. I wasn't sure exactly what reference Torrez was using to keep the Bronco on the road, but he kept the speed moderate, looking off into the distance as if he could actually see where we were going.

The smell of dry sage was strong as the night air wafted by my face. I realized I was straining to hear more than to see. We reached the intersection, and Torrez stopped and switched off the engine. Both of us sat holding our breath, listening. Not enough wind stirred to rustle the few stalks of bunchgrass that hadn't been trimmed by cattle.

For a full minute, we sat listening, and then I could hear a car coming up 43 east of us. By the way it was being flogged, I knew that it was Pasquale. Why he hadn't chosen a career driving the NASCAR circuit, I didn't know, but every once in a while, his prowess—or recklessness—behind the wheel came in handy.

I twisted around in the seat and saw the headlights in the distance sweep an arc across the prairie as he turned into the dirt road without putting the high-slung vehicle on its roof in the ditch.

I picked up the mike. "Stay right at that intersection, Tom," I said. He keyed twice to acknowledge. "No one comes in or out this road until you hear from me."

"Three-oh-three, ten-four."

Torrez started the Bronco and we idled ahead, still listening. Another 2.2 miles brought us to a main intersection, this one a well-worn two-track to the north, and I knew it led to the block house windmill.

"Do you know where this shooting area is?" I asked.

Torrez nodded. "It's on the same route as we took to the crash site, except there's a fork up a ways, and instead of bearing left up onto the flat, we stay to the right. It'll kinda snake around and then it ends up in a little box canyon. Boyd's got one of his corrals there, too."

"Then as the crow flies, it's not far from the Boyds' house."

"Maybe two thousand yards," Torrez offered.

"And about three miles if you have to drive it." I leaned forward, staring into the darkness. The prairie was spooky, dark shapes looming up out of the darkness to slide by as we passed. The crunch of the tires on the gravel was inordinately loud, a sound that the silence of the prairie amplified to broadcast our presence for hundreds of yards.

"How far are we?" I asked.

"A mile or so," Torrez said.

"All right. Let's—" and I damn near choked on the words as the gunshots pealed out over the prairie. They came in rapid sequence, first three and then two more, so fast that the sounds were gone before the next heartbeat. I slammed forward against the harness as the Bronco jarred to a halt. We both held our breath, listening.

"Lights," I said. "Let's make some noise."

Torrez pulled on the lights, and the sand and cholla and creosote bushes sprang into stark life, softened here and there by the remains of bunchgrass.

"And I want them to know it's us," I said and reached down and threw the little toggle switch that turned on the light bar on top of the Bronco. "Even if he's just shooting at coyotes."

Bob Torrez's reply to that wishful thinking was to trigger the electric release for the shotgun that rode in the center vertical rack. I pulled the weapon out and set the butt on the floor between my feet.

I was a fair enough shot if the sun was just right and the ground under my feet was level, if the target was stapled into position downrange and the wind wasn't blowing, if I had remembered the correct pair of glasses.

Not one of those conditions was in play just then, so a shotgun filled with five rounds of double-ought buck was a comfort. But what made my skin crawl was considering where those five, quickly fired rounds had gone.

"No one shot back," I said aloud. Torrez didn't answer.

THIRTY-THREE

WE REACHED the fork in the two-track where one path led steeply up a graveled grade, beaten smooth by the constant traffic to and from the crash site.

The right-hand fork angled away sharply, following the bottom of what at one time had been a fair-sized arroyo. The sides steepened, dotted here and there with stumpy growth and cacti. The trail surface was packed gravel. In a heavy rain, the place would be a certain trap as run off from a thousand acres of bunchgrass prairie funneled down the limestone rocks and collected.

Torrez reached out and turned the handle of the spotlight, but we didn't need it. The confines of the arroyo focused the glare of the headlights, and the winking of the red and blue lights on top of the Bronco bounced off the rocks and sand in surrealistic patterns.

"The area that Boyd uses for a backstop is just around the next bend or so," Torrez said quietly. The Bronco's back tires spun in the loose sand and we lunged this way and that against the ruts in the arroyo bottom. As the engine labored, Torrez reached out and tapped the four-wheel-drive button on the dash.

We rounded the corner in a spray of gravel and damn near crashed into Johnny Boyd's pickup truck, parked squarely in the middle of the tracks. With no time to stop and a violent wrench of the wheel, Torrez took the high ground. We slid sideways and I heard a loud bang as the left rear hit something far more solid than sand. We jolted to a stop crosswise in the arroyo, squarely in front of Boyd's truck, its headlights silhouetting us in grand style.

"Not good," Torrez muttered, and I damn near hit my head

on the dash as he slammed the truck into reverse and the
Bronco shot backward. He spun the wheel and turned on the
spotlight at the same time, so that three powerful lights illuminated the scene ahead of us.

Hocker's Suburban looked huge and black in the harsh
light. Sergeant Mitchell's unit was parked beside it.

Twenty yards in front of us, frozen in place by the drama
of our charging, sliding entrance, stood Johnny Boyd. He held
what looked like a short, black weapon. Off to the right were
three other figures—two looking as if they were in a passionate embrace, and a third sitting awkwardly in the rough gravel.

"What the hell is this?" I said and grabbed for the door
handle.

Bob Torrez was far faster, far more agile, than I. In the
time it took me to open the door and work both myself and
the shotgun out of the Bronco, he was braced against the
driver's-side door, handgun steady against the Bronco's windshield post.

"Put down the weapon, Johnny," he bellowed. I hefted the
shotgun, and in the awkward, harsh light, I could see that
Boyd was turned with the muzzle of the weapon facing away
from us. He didn't move.

"Eddie, are you all right?" I shouted.

By then, I could make out who was who, and evidently
Mitchell wasn't about to break his embrace with Neil Costace.
The two of them were plastered against the front fender of
Mitchell's vehicle, with the FBI agent bent backward until his
head was touching the windshield wiper.

"We're just fine," I heard him say matter-of-factly. "Tell
that asshole to put down the rifle."

I pumped the shotgun, the mechanical racking loud and
deadly on that soft night air. "Johnny, do as he says."

"I'm not going to put this in the dirt," he said, and for an
instant, I couldn't believe what I'd heard.

"You what?"

"I said I'm not putting this weapon down in the dirt. Tell
those two clumsy morons to stand off, and we'll see."

The tone of his voice saved his life. I couldn't guess what

the circumstances were that had led to this strange tableau, but Eddie Mitchell was busy restraining one of the agents, not the rancher. On top of that, Mitchell's back was turned to Boyd.

"Bring that weapon over here." I snapped out the order just loud enough for him to comfortably hear me. "Put it on the hood of the vehicle."

Boyd thought about that for a minute, then turned his head toward Mitchell and Costace. "Have you got ahold of him?"

"We're fine," Mitchell said.

And then, for the first time, I heard Neil Costace's voice, almost conversational. "Goddam it, all right," he said, as if he'd just lost a long-standing argument.

"Don't get itchy," Boyd muttered, and he held the weapon by its fore end over his head with one hand and walked toward us. I lowered the barrel of the shotgun, but Torrez's weapon never wavered. The rancher reached our unit and slowly lowered the rifle and laid it on the hood.

"Back off," I said, and he did so, standing easily ten feet away, hands on his hips. Torrez moved quickly and secured the rifle. It was one of those small rifles patterned after the larger military M-14, identical to those mounted in each one of our department vehicles. He popped the clip and racked the bolt back in one swift motion. A live round clattered against the hood of the truck and slid off into the gravel.

"Put that thing in the truck," I said. "Now, what the hell is going on here?"

"Why don't you ask those stupid sons a bitches?" Boyd muttered and at the same time, he fished a cigarette out of his shirt pocket.

Eddie Mitchell took a step backward, and Neil Costace shook himself as if his joints were all out of place. He held out his hands, fingers spread and palms toward the deputy, then he knelt beside Walter Hocker. The only portion of the conversation I could hear was the cursing.

I stepped around the door and approached Boyd. He stretched out his arms, wrist to wrist, in the voluntary "cuff me" position.

Torrez started to oblige, but I waved him off. In the gleam of the lights, I could see the brassy glint of live rounds still in the assault rifle's clip. If Johnny Boyd had wanted to clean house, he could have done so long before this.

"Stay here," I told him, and trudged across the gravel toward the other men.

Walter Hocker was on the ground, his right leg stretched out in front of him, the other twisted under his rump. He was leaning on his left elbow, trying to cradle his right arm. His eyes were partly closed, and as I approached, he opened them and grimaced at me.

"What happened to you?" I asked. There was no blood pumping out onto the sand, so he obviously hadn't been shot. But his right wrist wasn't going in the direction it was supposed to.

"Ohhhh," he said, a long heartfelt exhalation of breath that was part groan, part general commentary on the state of things.

"Sir," Sergeant Mitchell said, "this all needs some explaining."

"I can see that. Why don't you give him a hand up?"

"Nah," Hocker said immediately and leaned over even farther as if to protect himself from further assault.

"Bob," I shouted over my shoulder, "call an ambulance." I knelt down, holding the shotgun's butt in the sand. Hocker was biting his lip, his eyes now closed.

"Mr. Boyd fired off a string of rounds," Mitchell said. "We weren't expecting it. Agent Hocker jumped back and tripped. I think he broke his leg. I heard it pop."

"My hip," Hocker said through clenched teeth. "It's my hip, goddam it."

I reached out a hand and touched Hocker's right hand. He flinched backward. "That's broken," I said. "Even I can see that. How did it happen?"

"I kicked him," Mitchell said.

I looked up sharply, first at him and then at Costace. With a grunt, I pushed myself to my feet and stepped over so that I was practically nose to nose with Eddie Mitchell.

"Suppose that I didn't have to pry this out of you one sentence at a time. Tell me what the hell happened."

"Mr. Boyd fired a string of shots that startled us. He fired into the bank over there." Mitchell pointed off to his right. "Agent Hocker startled, twisted, and fell backward and in the process, broke his hip. When that happened, I was the only person actually facing Mr. Boyd. I knew that he had not fired at us, but apparently Agent Hocker thought that he had. Apparently Agent Hocker thought that he had been hit, and apparently Agent Costace thought the same thing. Agent Hocker drew his service automatic and was about to return fire. I was sure that at such short distance, he would hit Mr. Boyd. I didn't have time for anything else, so I lashed out with my foot. The toe of my boot struck Agent Hocker's wrist and knocked the weapon out of his hand."

Mitchell took a breath. "Apparently, in the heat of things, Agent Costace mistakenly thought that both Boyd and myself were assaulting Agent Hocker and himself. He was in the process of drawing his own weapon when I tackled him. We struggled and I was able to successfully pin Agent Costace against the side of the Bronco." Mitchell stopped again and a faint grin twitched the corners of his mouth. "And then you and Sergeant Torrez arrived." He paused again. "And that's what happened, sir."

I suppressed the urge to break out in laughter only because Hocker was still on the ground, his breath coming in little seething gasps between clenched teeth.

"Just apparently wonderful," I said and looked across at Neil Costace. I'd known him for a long time and could read from the expression on his face that there was no point in asking for his version of the events.

"Let me find Walt's handgun," he said instead.

I stalked over to Boyd and glared at him. He drew on the cigarette, not the least bit impressed. "And what was the point of firing that weapon?"

"And what was the point of them being out here in the middle of the night snooping around my private property?"

"Johnny…" I started to say, but I was so angry that the words just sputtered into silence.

The rancher shrugged and gestured toward his pickup truck. "They were all excited about finding samples of my brass. So I told 'em I had some in the truck, if that's what they wanted. I guess they thought I meant empties. I'd brought the little two-twenty-three from the house." He nodded at the weapon that Torrez had taken. "So I took the rifle out of the gun rack and fired off a few rounds." He shrugged again. "I guess they weren't ready for that. If they want the gun, you've got it."

"You guess," I said. "You're damn lucky you weren't killed."

"So are they," Boyd said evenly. "If your deputy hadn't been here, there's no telling which way this might have gone."

I pumped the shell out of the shotgun and put the weapon back in the vehicle. "The ambulance is en route," Torrez said, and I nodded.

"Let's see if we can make Hocker anymore comfortable while we wait," I said.

I could hear a siren far in the distance, but it would take the softly sprung ambulance a while to reach us—and I didn't envy Hocker his ride back into town. Costace had retrieved Hocker's gun, and he stood beside the vehicle with it in his hand, looking disgusted.

"Did you find the brass you wanted?" I asked and Costace nodded.

"I showed Mr. Boyd one of the samples that you collected over at the windmill. He said it was probably his. He says the last time they were out here shooting the two-twenty-three was during his son's spring break from college."

"And he doesn't know how the casings got there, does he?" I said.

"No, he doesn't."

THIRTY-FOUR

JOHNNY BOYD didn't move an inch from his spot by the hood of the Bronco. He leaned against the vehicle patiently, and the only sign of nerves was his lighting of one cigarette after another. We made Walter Hocker as comfortable as anyone with a fractured hip and wrist could be, and in due course, the ambulance winked its way into the narrow canyon.

When it left, I took Eddie Mitchell by the elbow. "Well, that's that," I said. "Let's have us a little conference over at my unit." Neil Costace fell in step with Bob Torrez, and I let them go ahead, my hand still on Mitchell's arm. I pulled him to a stop.

"I'm proud of you, you know," I said quietly. "I'm not sure you had to kick quite so hard, but that was quick thinking."

"Thank you, sir."

"We could have had a real tragedy."

Mitchell nodded and looked uncomfortable.

I grinned. "You think you're going to get this kind of excitement working for Burkhalter?" A ghost of surprise flicked across Mitchell's face. "He's content, by the way, to wait until this whole mess is wrapped up before you sign on with him."

"That's good, sir."

"For us, it is. I'm hoping you'll reconsider, of course. But I'll understand if you don't." I patted his arm once more. "I want to show you something."

We joined the others, and Johnny Boyd lit his tenth cigarette.

"Now that we've had our fun for the evening, there're two things I want to ask you, Johnny," I said as I walked around to the passenger door of the Bronco. I reached inside and pulled out the tangled piece of aluminum that included the letters of the Bonanza's registration. I held it so that the headlights caught it. "What do you suppose this is?"

Boyd reached out and took the crumpled metal in both hands, turning it this way and that. "From the airplane, isn't it?"

"Yes."

He tapped the aluminum. "Registration letters. What else am I looking at?"

"That's what I'm asking you."

He frowned, the smoke from the cigarette curling up into his eyes. He cocked his head and studied the metal. "That's all I see."

"Those letters mean anything to you?"

He looked up at me askance. "No. Should they?"

"Nothing at all?"

This time he removed the cigarette and turned a bit so that more light bounced off the white metal. "Well, I guess I could tell that this airplane wasn't United States registry. We use numbers. Canada, Britain, some of the others use all letters like this. And you said Holman's brother-in-law was from Canada, so I guess I'm not surprised."

"How do you happen to know that?"

"Know what, Sheriff?"

"That many foreign aircraft carry only lettering. No numbers."

Johnny Boyd laughed shortly. "When my son was growing up, we had so damn many model airplanes hanging from the ceiling and parked from every flat surface that his mother about had a conniption every time he'd bring home another one. That and buying one flying magazine after another. A man's bound to learn a little something from all that."

"So if you'd seen this aircraft flying low overhead, your first reaction would be what?"

"Just what do you want to know, Sheriff?"

"I want to know what your first reaction would be."

"I'd wonder how the hell some Canuck got himself lost in New Mexico." He drew deeply on his cigarette. "And if I

saw him crash into a mountain, I'd call you and let you sort
it all out."

"You wouldn't think it might be a state aircraft?"

"Why would I think that?"

"Unusual lettering?"

"It's not unusual, Sheriff. It's Canadian."

"But you didn't know that until after the fact."

Boyd took the cigarette out of his mouth and carefully
ground it out on his boot heel, then reached for another. Patiently, as if he were issuing a critical set of instructions, he
said, "Sheriff, do you remember a month ago when the gov-
ernor stopped in Posadas? He and the highway commissioner
flew into the Posadas airport. You remember that? Then they
went to some luncheon?"

"I remember. Sheriff Holman attended. I didn't."

"That was a state plane that brought them. You want to
know the registration? I was driving up the highway when
they took off, and I watched 'em because it's kind of a pretty
airplane. A jetprop Commander. And the registration is right
on the tail."

"And you remember it?"

"One-four-four NM." He lit the cigarette and inhaled
deeply. "With the N that they carry coming first. N-one-four-
four New Mexico. Don't take my word. Hell, no one else
does. Check it out. N-one-four-four New Mexico."

I put the torn piece of aluminum back in the Bronco. The
other officers stood by silently, waiting for some cue from
me. "Johnny," I said, "did George Payton call you tonight?"

As if the word "call" was a prompt, the phone on the front
seat chirped. Torrez reached in a long arm and answered it.
He listened for a moment, then said, "No. Everyone else is
just fine. Tell her that he'll be home in a few minutes. The
sheriff is talking to him just now."

He switched off and tossed the phone back on the seat.
"Your wife called the office," he said to Boyd. "She heard
shots and was worried."

Boyd nodded and turned his attention back to me. "Yes,
George called me."

"Did he tell you that federal agents had been at his shop inquiring about your firearms collection?"

"Yes."

"He called me first, to ask if he should cooperate," I said. "I told him that he should."

"What's your point?"

"Did he tell you that they were planning to come out here?"

"Yes."

"And so you decided to meet them, with a loaded assault rifle in your truck."

"There's always a loaded rifle in that truck, Sheriff. One kind or another, it doesn't matter. And if you're asking about the weapons, I figure any man with an ounce of education ought to be able to look at a list of firearms and put two and two together."

"Meaning what?"

"Did you look at the list?"

"I've got it right here in the truck."

"Well, get it. Let me shed some light."

I did so, and he spread the paper out on the hood. "Hold the flashlight here," he said. "Now look. Look at these handguns and you tell me what you see."

"Several types and calibers of semiautomatic handguns." I adjusted my glasses and reread the list. And that's when it struck me like a mallet between the eyes. "Walther P thirty-eight and nine-millimeter Luger. Those are German. Colt 1911 forty-five. That's ours. Tokarev for the Russians, Nambu for the Japanese. Beretta, Astra" My voice trailed off.

"Probably doesn't surprise you that my son's a history major, does it?"

"And I assume that the fully automatic weapons follow the same pattern? That's a hell of a collection."

"It will be. What he wants is a collection of all the major light arms that were issued to soldiers during the major conflicts of the twentieth century."

"That's ambitious."

"Damn near impossible, but he's got a start. I told him that if that's the kind of collection he wanted to make, he'd best get at it. Some of that material is going to be pretty dear in a few years. Or illegal. I admit, I found out that it's easy to get caught up in all this." He laughed, the first real humor I'd heard from him in days. "I even put off buying a new pickup truck this year. That's how bad it gets."

"And your wife hasn't divorced you yet," I said.

Boyd looked puzzled. "He's her son too. That's how we look at it. I just didn't expect this kind of trouble, that's all."

"One last thing," I said and opened my briefcase to find the photographs I'd brought along. I found the one of the intersecting fence lines and handed it to Boyd. "Where's this spot?"

He looked hard at the photo and then squatted down in front of the Bronco so that the headlights gave him daytime.

"Huh," he said and turned the picture over. "That's got to be over by what we call William's Tank. There used to be a windmill there years ago, but it went dry, hell, back in the seventies. Dick Finnegan took it out and put it over near his trailer."

"So this is on Finnegan's property?"

Boyd nodded. "Yeah. I recognize this fence line now. And this here is where he thought about digging a new dirt tank. He borrowed my little dozer for a day or two, then gave up. Said there wasn't any bottom to the gravel."

"So if I wanted to get there, how would I do it?"

Boyd stood up. "Just take this road back toward the highway. When you hit the trail that heads down south into the back of the mesa—where he's working on that spring—you go about a mile on that. This is off to the west there a little bit. There's what's left of a two-track that will take you over that way." He looked at the photo again. "Why this?"

"I don't know," I said, and then took a calculated risk. "Martin Holman took that photo on the day of the crash."

A slow smile spread across Johnny Boyd's face, but he just shook his head and handed the photo back to me.

"You don't want to tell me?" I asked.

He looked sideways at me as he drew on his cigarette, assessing just what I might be thinking.

"It's just a fence," he said.

THIRTY-FIVE

"IF THAT'S THE CASE, how about a guided tour?" I asked.

Johnny Boyd looked off into the night sky and blew smoke at the stars. "Oh, I think I'll pass on that, Sheriff. That's Dick Finnegan's property, and whatever those fellas in the airplane were interested in, that's their business, and maybe his. Sure as hell ain't mine. Matter of fact, what makes sense to me right now is to go home and get a good night's sleep. You ever do that?"

"Not often," I said. "But you have the right idea. We wouldn't have much chance of finding the place in the dark anyway. Even at the best of times, one windmill looks just like another to me."

Bob Torrez started to say something but thought better of it. I knew what was running through his mind, and probably Eddie Mitchell's too. Most of the time, darkness was a powerful ally for us. Either one of them could find the most remote nook and cranny of Posadas County at anytime of day or night.

"We all could use some sleep," I added. I heard the faint jingle of brass and saw that Torrez held several casings. "The FBI is going to want to run some ballistics tests, you know that," I said, and Boyd nodded. He didn't look at Neil Costace, and the FBI agent seemed perfectly content at the moment to let me either run the show or hang myself.

"You want to keep the rifle until such time, you can," Boyd said, dead serious in his belief that we were just asking nicely if we could run ballistics tests on his weapon...as if it were a special favor between old friends.

He evidently saw the expression on my face, and shrugged. "That was a damn-fool thing I did," he said. "I know that. I just lost my goddam temper." He pushed himself away from the truck and started toward his own. "The feds can do all the testing they like if it'll satisfy 'em. And if they think they need to look at the other weapons, most of them are stored in a safety deposit box at Ranchers' Trust in Posadas. If they want to examine 'em, I'll fetch 'em out of there."

"We'll see," I said. We watched him climb into his truck without further comment, and he backed out far enough that he could turn around.

The taillights of his pickup disappeared in the distance. Bob Torrez started to say something, but I held up a hand. "Wait a minute," I said, and the four of us stood there, grouped around the Bronco, letting the silence of the prairie return. I frowned and half closed my eyes as I listened to the sound of Johnny Boyd's truck retreat. I kept my hands poised in the air like a choral director's.

"He didn't turn toward his house," Eddie Mitchell said a moment later.

"Nope, he didn't," I said and reached for the mike on the dash of the Bronco.

"Three-oh-three, three-ten on channel three."

"Three-oh-three," Tom Pasquale snapped in instant reply. He must have been sitting there by the highway, mike in hand.

"Three-oh-three, Johnny Boyd is driving a blue Ford pickup truck. He's turned your way. If he shows up, make yourself scarce, and when he hits the pavement, keep an eye on him. I want to know where he's headed."

"Ten-four. You want him stopped?"

"That's negative. I do not want him stopped. I want to know where he's headed." I glanced at Torrez and Mitchell. They both were grinning. "Do I speak French or something?" I muttered.

"Watching isn't as much fun as stopping," Mitchell said wryly.

"That's what scares me," I said. "I want you to give Tommy some backup. I don't know what Boyd plans. Maybe he's just taking the long way home. Maybe he's going to do a little fence-hunting himself. If he does go on out to the main road, keep Tommy back, way back. We just want information right now, that's all. And if he turns off before he reaches the highway, just go on by, the way he'd expect you to do. We'll be on channel three if you need to talk to us. We'll be right behind him."

Mitchell nodded without comment and turned on his heel. We could hear the crunch of his boots on the gravel and for a moment, I just listened, getting my thoughts in order.

"You know where that fence line is?" I asked Torrez.

"I think I can find it with no trouble, sir."

"Then let's go. Neil, you game?"

"Sure," he said. "If you're not too tired." He said it with good humor.

I laughed. "I'm comatose. But you and Bob are driving, so I can kick back and sleep. In fact, I like the seats in that rig of yours. I'll ride with you." I turned to Torrez. "Lead the way."

Neil Costace and I settled into the federal agent's Suburban, and for a fleeting moment, I had the impulse to recline the seat and irritate Costace with my sonorous snoring. But he didn't give me a chance.

"So, what's perking in that nonstop mind of yours, Buddha?" he asked.

I looked at him in surprise. "Buddha?"

Costace pulled the truck into gear and we followed Torrez's Bronco out of the arroyo. Between bounces and wrenching of the steering wheel, he said, "That's what Hocker calls you."

"Buddha."

He nodded. "Don't ask me why," he added. "And let me give you a piece of advice. Don't wrestle with Mitchell."

"Are you all right?"

"Nothing a chiropractor can't fix, given time," Costace said and shook his head.

"Was Eddie's version pretty close to the way you saw it?"

"Not pretty close, Bill," Costace said. "The embarrassing thing is that he was *exactly* right. Thirty-five years' experience between the two of us, and now this."

"These things happen sometimes," I said, moving Neil Costace another couple of rungs up my ladder of estimation.

"All I could think was that Johnny Boyd was shooting at us. And when Hocker went down, I knew he was. My first thought when Mitchell kicked the gun away was that he was in on something with Boyd…that the two of them were working together. If that's not enough to make a man feel goddam simple, I don't know what is." He looked soberly over at me.

"These things happen," I said again for want of anything better.

"Your sergeant had his eye on Boyd. Hocker and I obviously didn't." Costace shook his head again. "Jesus," he said. "And so what are you thinking? It's obviously not about going to some dark corner somewhere and actually getting some sleep."

"Two things," I said. "First of all, it's ten minutes to eleven, and Johnny Boyd isn't going where he said he was going."

"Okay. I had that thought too. But there's an endless list of perfectly innocent possibilities."

"If you're an incurable optimist," I said. "Remember our little set-to in the Boyd kitchen earlier? You remember that temper of his?"

Costace nodded. "He does love his federal government, that's for sure."

"Well, all right. And tonight he lets his temper go again and takes the risk of firing off a handful of rounds? In the dark? In the glare of headlights that spook everyone? With three armed law officers standing right there? But now, all of a sudden, he's perfectly willing to acquiesce? To let federal agents rummage through his safe deposit boxes? To be Mr. Nice Guy? I don't think so."

"Maybe it's exactly like he said. He realizes what a stupid thing that was to do. If we wanted to be real sons of bitches, I guess we could come up with twenty or thirty things to charge him with. I'd hate to bring any of them into court except in front of a drunk judge, but they'd sure be enough to hold him in jail for a day or two. Boyd's got to know that, smart as he is. He's trying to mend fences.''

"Neil, come on. He could have just kept his mouth shut and been about as far ahead.''

"You think there's something else, then?''

"I don't know.''

"That's not the answer I wanted to hear, Sheriff,'' Costace said.

Torrez's vehicle was kicking up plenty of dust, and I hefted my handheld radio. "Give him plenty of room, Robert,'' I said, and the lead vehicle slowed. Occasionally, when the swell of the prairie was just right, I caught a glimpse of the taillights on Boyd's truck, and then, considerably farther back, Mitchell's unit.

"He's headed right for the main road,'' Mitchell said quietly.

"Don't ride him,'' I said into the radio. "Three-oh-three, you copy?''

"Three-oh-three, ten-four.''

Costace swerved to avoid a rock outcropping that was wearing its patient way up through the tire tracks. "So he's not going to the magic fence,'' he said. "I wonder what the hell he's doing.''

"Wait a couple of minutes and I'll make a guess,'' I said.

Our two vehicles ambled across the prairie, letting the distance between us and Mitchell's unit widen as he followed Johnny Boyd toward the highway.

In a moment, Torrez's brake lights flashed, and then he turned onto a two-track off to the right. We had driven no more than a hundred yards before the radio came in again.

"Three-ten, three-oh-three. Sir, he's hit the pavement and is heading in toward town.''

"Just follow,'' I said, and then added off the air, "Shit.''

"You thought he might be headed up to the Finnegans?'' Costace asked.

"That was the most obvious possibility,'' I said.

"And the others?"

"Buddha doesn't know," I said.

THIRTY-SIX

WE SAW THE BRAKE LIGHTS of Torrez's vehicle flash, bright and harsh in the darkness. We'd been idling along with our headlights off, depending on Torrez not to lead us into the middle of an earthen stock tank somewhere. After ten minutes, our eyes had adjusted so that the two-track we were following was a mere trace.

The beam from Torrez's perpetrator light was just a bushel-basket-sized yellow ghost moving along the side of the trail.

We stopped, and I could make out Torrez's large form outside the truck. Suddenly a ray of light stabbed out, illuminating a fence line.

"Gate," I said to Costace, but no doubt he was capable of figuring that out for himself. It took a moment for Torrez to wrestle the barbed-wire gate back across the road so we could pass. He did so, got back in his Bronco and drove through for two car lengths. We followed, and as we pulled to a stop, he closed the gate behind us.

He paused at Costace's elbow. "About a quarter mile or so," he said, then added, "I think."

I had cranked my head around and was looking back at the fence, the wires a faint gleam in the starlight.

"Shine your light over at the fence, Bob," I said. He did so and I grunted. "Sheep fencing," I said, seeing the rectangular, four-by-six-inch openings in the wire. "And four strands of barbed wire."

"He's got it on the gate, too," Torrez said. "Makes it a bear to pull open."

"Huh," I said. "Finnegan raises sheep?"

"Never knew him to," Torrez said. "Good antelope fence, though."

"Why would he bother trying to keep antelope off his range?" Costace asked.

"Maybe not off," Torrez said. "Maybe in." He didn't elaborate, but returned to his vehicle. We had driven no more than five hundred yards when his brake lights flashed again, and then the spotlight on the windshield post burst out across the prairie.

"Well, look at that," Costace murmured. The antelope herd was off to the left, most of it bedded down in the bunchgrass, but a few of the animals were standing and looking toward us, curious. Torrez swept the beam across the herd. One of the large bucks took two steps and stopped, its head turned away from us, the flashy white hairs on its butt grabbing the light and warning the rest of the herd. The spotlight died and the image vanished, replaced by uniform black. For a moment, all I could see was the tiny red light on the top of my handheld radio.

"That's a fair-sized herd," Costace said. "Fifty, maybe?"

"At least," I said.

"Amazing animals," Costace said. "With all the traffic back and forth out here, I'm surprised we haven't seen more of them."

"We're a ways from the main road," I said.

"You ever watched them run? My God, they're fast. We watched a couple of 'em when we drove over here yesterday…whatever day it was. Just two of them, not a herd like that one. They angled away from us, right over the hill. Must have been hitting thirty-five or forty miles an hour." He shook his head. "I don't think a little four-foot-high sheep fence would matter to them. They could jump that without breaking stride."

"I'll be damned," I said to myself, and then chuckled.

"Now what?"

I lifted the small radio. "Bob, stop for a minute," I said, keeping my voice soft. He did so without hitting the brakes, letting the unit roll to a halt. As we crunched up behind him, I asked Costace, "Does your dome light work?"

"'Course it works," Costace said, and I could see the motion of his hand toward the light switch.

"No, no, leave it off," I said quickly. "You need to fix that." And then to the radio, I said, "Bob, come back here a minute, will you?" By then, my eyes had adjusted enough to see the shape of his vehicle swell as the door opened.

In a moment, his large form materialized beside the Suburban. "His lights sure as hell don't work," Costace said.

"That's the whole point," I replied. "You need to be able to open your door without advertising the fact to the entire world." I leaned over and looked past the agent. "Robert, tell me what you know about antelope."

"Sir?"

"You hunt every year, don't you?"

"Yes."

"Where's your favorite spot?"

Torrez paused, and I wondered for a moment if he was reluctant to give up personal secrets. "I usually go down on my cousin's place. Down by Regal."

"That's Aurelio Baca's ranch?"

"Yes, sir."

"He runs cattle?"

"Santa Gertrudis," Torrez said. "And lots of antelope."

"Aurelio uses barbed-wire fencing?"

"Sure." Torrez leaned on Costace's windowsill, and I could tell from the change in the tone of his voice that he'd tuned in to the same wavelength. "He runs barbless wire on the bottom strand, though, so the antelope can come and go. One clean strand doesn't make any difference to the cattle, but it makes it easy for the antelope to scoot through."

"Cut to the chase," Costace said impatiently. "What are you guys telling me?"

"That fence we just crossed is designed to keep antelope in," I said.

"How can it? It's not high enough."

"Antelope don't jump fences," Torrez said.

"What do you mean, they don't jump fences? 'Course they do. There's fences all over this country."

"They duck through...or under," I said. "They don't jump."

"I don't believe that," Costace said. "Fast as they are?"

"Fast has nothing to do with it. Remember when you watched them running yesterday?" I asked. "Remember what they looked like? A nice flat sprint, back flat like a horse's. Not like deer. Deer bounce and leap, sometimes even doing that ridiculous gait where they go on all hooves at once, stiff-legged like some goddam four-legged pogo stick. Deer and elk jump. Antelope scoot."

An entire row of pieces fell together for Neil Costace at that moment. "The only reason I can imagine to bother containing game animals is to make them easy to hunt. This is Finnegan's land?"

"Yes."

"So if he's herding antelope, maybe someone complained. That would explain Martin Holman's wanting to put questions to the Department of Game and Fish. And it might explain why Martin Holman wanted to see the area from the air. He could wander around here forever on the ground and not see what he needed to see."

"Photos," I said. "Lots of pictures of fencing."

"None of which show the wire close enough to make it obvious," Costace said.

"No, but no one ever said that Martin Holman was a brilliant investigator. His intentions were on track, though."

"Are there any antelope in those pictures? If we blow them up enough, maybe we'll see something. You have a couple of the photos with you, don't you?"

"Yes. But let's find that intersection before we blow our night vision all to pieces. If we're right...if that's what Holman was after, and if he saw the antelope from the air, I'm sure he'd try for a picture. Maybe it's there, now that we know what we're looking for."

"And if Finnegan saw that airplane fly over, he might spook," Costace said.

"He might if he saw the registration numbers and thought they were on an official airplane," Torrez said.

I realized I had a fair crop of goose bumps on my arm. "Let's find out," I said.

THIRTY-SEVEN

BY THE TIME we reached the next gate, we had ghosted our way through three more herds of antelope—and one small group of thin, uninterested cattle. This time Torrez didn't stop at the gate, but swung to the right, driving along the fence line, the hummocks of close-cropped bunchgrass jarring his vehicle this way and that.

We followed. I noticed that whoever had strung the fence had done a workmanlike job. The four barbed-wire strands were tight and uniform, and the sheep fencing was taut and smooth, its top wire laced to the barbed-wire strand behind it.

"He knows where he's going?" Costace asked as we jounced over a hummock of rotting vegetation that had once been a yucca. The flower's hard stalk cracked under our tires.

"I certainly hope so," I replied.

Costace grunted something that told me he wasn't too happy with my answer. "If he's been out here before, didn't he see the wire?"

"You'd have to ask him," I said. "I'm not sure he's actually been in this particular spot."

"He said he knew where the corner was."

I laughed. "I think he looked at the map, Neil. Sergeant Torrez is one of those rare people for whom a topographical map holds no mysteries. And in this part of the country, most fences follow section lines—or at some point, connect to them. It's all very logical, most of the time."

"I know all that. And in ten minutes—no, make that two—

I'd be so goddam lost I'd have to sit and wait for the sun to
come up to figure out east from anything else." We jounced
over another hummock and Costace added, "You people have
forgotten what the hell headlights are for."

"They make you go blind before your time," I said, then
held up a hand that Costace probably couldn't see anyway.
"Hold it."

Torrez had stopped, and I could make out the looming
structure that blocked his path. He walked quickly back to us
and leaned down. "This is it."

I picked up the radio. "Three-oh-three on channel three."

Silence followed. "Three-oh-seven, do you copy?" When
Mitchell didn't answer, I dropped the handheld on the seat.
"Out of range. Robert, give them a try from your unit on the
main frequency. I want to know where they are."

The blast of light when we opened the doors made me
flinch. As I got out of the Suburban, I took along my heavy
flashlight and the folder that included the photo of the fence
corner.

"Mitchell says that he's just on the outskirts of town. Boyd
stopped at the American Legion Hall on Pershing. Pasquale
is parked behind the hospital down the street, with a clear
view of his truck. Boyd's been inside now for about three
minutes."

"Good. Let's see what we've got here." The walking was
mercifully easy. The ground had been beaten flat overtime by
the countless hooves of cattle. The windmill tower loomed in
front of us, rising thirty feet above the abandoned well.

"This didn't show in the photo," Costace said.

"Nope." I held the folder against my leg and fished out
the print. "If we're in the right spot, this tower is just out of
the picture—by no more than a dozen or so feet." I handed
the photo to Costace and stepped away, flashing my light up
the tower. The mechanical head of the mill had been removed,
as had the steel stock tank at the bottom, and the sucker rods
that would have hung down in the middle. Only the old
weather-scarred wood of the tower remained.

The ground was slightly dished on the north side of the

tower, where the tank probably had been at one time, and where Boyd said Finnegan had thought briefly about digging a dirt tank. I swept the light in an arc. "Nothing," I muttered. The beam reached out to the corner of the fence, and sure enough, another fence took off to the north, this one a four-strand barbed-wire line without the sheep fencing.

I walked over to it, fifty yards of dusty, hoof-rumpled dirt. At each step, the aroma of prairie sod and old manure wafted up. Costace followed, sweeping his flashlight this way and that.

"So we've got a three-way corner here," he said, and put a hand on top of one of the steel posts, rocking it. "So what?"

"This is the northwest corner of the antelope enclosure," Torrez said. "That's what it looks like to me."

I turned the flashlight on the eight-by-ten photo. "And this is the corner in the picture. Holman didn't catch the windmill tower in it. Maybe he intended to, maybe he didn't." I slapped the print against my thigh in frustration. "Goddam it, why the hell didn't he tell us what the hell he was doing?"

"The sheriff, you mean?" Costace asked.

"Yes, the sheriff. It's almost like he was trying to make this big coup...lay all the pieces out in front of us when he had it all figured out. Do it all by himself."

"That may have been exactly what he was doing," Costace said gently. "Ego's a wonderful thing," he added. "Reyes-Guzman is leaving. You said that Sergeant Mitchell has a standing job offer. This guy here"—he reached out and touched Bob Torrez on the elbow—"is getting himself married off, or so I'm told, and who the hell knows where he'll end up? And you're rumored to be retiring. You think it's unusual that Martin Holman felt just a little bit pressured, Bill? What was the last major case he worked by himself? Or even led the way?"

"None," I said.

"Well, there you are, then. It doesn't take a rocket scientist or a psychiatrist to figure out Martin Holman's motivation. The brainstorm hit him that he could get aerial photos—and that's a pretty good idea in itself. The chance came up when his brother-in-law arrived for a visit. Martin just ran out of luck."

"All this goddam tragedy for a handful of goddam mangy antelope," I said. "Somebody told him that there were impounded antelope somewhere around here. He could have just asked where the antelope were and then driven out to the Finnegans and asked, 'Are you impounding wildlife on your property?' If the man said no, then he could have driven out here with Bob Torrez or any of the other deputies and taken a million photos from the ground and—"

Costace interrupted my diatribe with a wave of his flashlight. "Bill...that's what you would have done. And in retrospect, that's what Holman should have done, or just turned the complaint over to the Game and Fish folks—and there's some evidence that he might have been trying to do that. But the opportunity came along to fly over the site. That's not so unreasonable. I don't guess he thought about the possibility of being shot down."

"There's still a problem," Torrez said calmly. "The antelope are over in this area. The aircraft was two miles north of here when it was hit."

I shrugged. "There are a couple of ways to explain that," I said. The cellular phone in the Bronco rang shrilly before I had a chance to proffer even one explanation. It continued to ring while Bob Torrez jogged the considerable distance back to the truck.

"Whoever fired the shot could have watched the plane making passes and just gotten nervous. When it passed overhead, he let fly."

"He, meaning Richard Finnegan," Neil Costace said.

"Odds are good," I replied.

"Sir!" Torrez shouted from the vehicle, and I turned. He waved his flashlight urgently. By the time I reached the Bronco, Torrez had already turned the unit around and was waiting with his foot on the brake pedal, passenger door open.

My first thought as I approached the truck was, "What the hell has Pasquale done now?"

"They've got a man down at the Pierpoint," Torrez said

as I slid into the seat. He pulled the Bronco into gear, and Neil Costace just managed to sidestep the door.

"Now what the hell—" I started to say.

"Richard Finnegan got himself stabbed," Torrez barked, and Neil Costace turned with an oath and sprinted toward his own vehicle. "Follow us on down."

I yanked my shoulder harness around me and snapped the buckle, pulling the belt very, very tight. The Pierpoint Bar and Grill was in downtown Posadas, twenty winding miles away.

In a handful of half-airborne seconds, we reached the gate and Torrez slid the Bronco to a stop, leaping out the door before I could even find my seatbelt buckle. He tore open the gate, sprinted back to the truck and we shot through, leaving the range etiquette of gate closure to the Federal Bureau of Investigation.

THIRTY-EIGHT

As WE CHARGED DOWN the hill that night, I didn't have much time for reflection, and I certainly didn't want to distract Robert Torrez with conversation. The county road into town was twisting, gravel-strewn on the corners, and populated with dim-witted deer and skunks, and an occasional drunk who strayed out from town.

The Bronco handled about as well as any truck, and it didn't take much imagination to picture us somersaulting down the mesa face in a pile of smoking, groaning metal.

We shot past the old quarry and I keyed the mike.

"Three-oh-three, three-ten. Ten-twenty."

If he was where he was supposed to be, I knew exactly what Tommy Pasquale was doing when he heard my call for his location. With a homicide just two blocks away, he was chafing at the bit. For the second time that night, he was being asked to sit off on the sidelines while something interesting was happening just out of sight. As he heard my voice, I could picture his hand flashing up to the gearshift of his patrol car, ready to pull it into drive, and his foot poised, ready to mash the accelerator to the floor.

"Three-oh-three is on Pershing at the Legion Hall," Pasquale said, and I could hear the tension in his voice. He had the discipline not to add, "Just where Sergeant Mitchell told me to be."

"Three-oh-three, ten-four." I knew there was no rear exit that Boyd could slip out of to return to his vehicle. If he left the building, Pasquale would see him. "Stay on him," I said, "and let me know the instant he moves." And when Pasquale responded with an audible twinge of impatience, I could picture his hand slipping off the gear lever.

"Three-ten, three-oh-seven. ETA?"

I could hear excited voices in the background, and Eddie Mitchell's tone was brusque.

"Three-ten is just passing Consolidated. About six minutes out," I said.

By the time we roared into the village, down Grande Avenue, past Pershing Park and across Bustos, the main east-west village street, I could see a fair collection of winking red lights up ahead, a couple belonging to one of the village units.

The Pierpoint Bar and Grill was a narrow, dark little building that shared the South 100 block of Grande Avenue with the *Posadas Register*'s modern, metal-sided and uninteresting plant. Tucked well off the sidewalk, its parking lot fronted Rincon Street, a dead-end lane that snaked back behind the newspaper building.

Torrez braked hard, skirted a group of spectators and turned into Rincon, damn near rear-ending Chief Eduardo Martinez's bargelike Oldsmobile. The old car was parked with its massive butt out in the street as if Eduardo had been too flustered to know what to do with it.

I caught a glimpse of Eddie Mitchell and Tom Mears at the far east end of the narrow parking lot, standing beside Richard

Finnegan's pickup truck. One of the part-timers who made up the three-man village department was unwinding a yellow tape. There were too many pairs of legs in the way to be able to see anything else.

It didn't surprise me that Richard Finnegan was a patron of the Pierpoint. Many local ranchers were—their pickup trucks filled the small parking lot at any given hour, the patient dogs that were their constant companions standing in the back of the trucks or lying on the toolbox, waiting with lolling tongues marking time.

Chief Martinez waddled over toward me as soon as he saw me disembark from the Bronco. I always got the impression that crime surprised Eduardo…that he thought of it as something that eventually would just go away if only we had enough nice parades and summer festivals in Pershing Park.

I readily admitted that we treated his department as if it didn't exist most of the time…which, in point of fact, it didn't, since a combination of what Posadas could pay a certified officer, and what little area there was to patrol within the village limits, resulted in an officer turnover rate that approached the monthly.

"What the hell happened, Chief?" I said. With the portable radio in one hand and a flashlight in the other, Bob Torrez strode past me, making a beeline for the village officer, who was doing his best to keep the spectators back. I saw a look of relief on Eduardo's face when he glanced over and saw Torrez's approach.

"They found him in the parking lot, right next to his truck," Martinez said. He put his hands on his hips. "Richard Finnegan, from up north of town? You know him, I guess."

"Of course."

"He's got a knife stuck in him. Dead as a fish, man."

I glanced over toward the corner of the parking lot and caught a glimpse of the body near the back bumper of the truck. Mitchell and Mears were in discussion, and I saw Mitchell point off toward the street.

"I think he got in a fight with somebody. I'm not sure who just yet," the chief said.

"A fight in the bar?"

"I guess it started there," Eduardo said. "Then I guess they came outside somehow."

The absurd image of that in Martinez's report skirted through my mind. They went outside somehow. I shook my head, trying to focus. "Who'd you talk to?"

"Well…" Martinez pointed off to his left, toward the side door of the Pierpoint, where a group of nervous patrons had gathered "…Lonnie Prior says he saw Mr. Finnegan leave the bar."

I patted Eduardo on the elbow and strode over to Prior. He was a short, wiry man who didn't do much of anything other than make a concentrated effort to turn his pension from the U.S. Post Office into liquid good times.

I beckoned him off to the side and he grudgingly complied, keeping his eyes on the action across the lot. "Lonnie, tell me what you saw."

"Well, shit," Lonnie Prior said. "Not much, you know."

One of the Posadas Emergency Services ambulances screamed to a stop on Grande, lights pulsing. At the same time, Estelle Reyes-Guzman's unmarked unit slipped up to the curb.

"Whatever that 'not much' is, I need to hear it," I snapped, and Prior took a step backward as if I'd slapped him.

"I saw Finnegan inside, that's all," he said.

"At the bar or at a table?"

"The bar."

"Where were you?"

"At the pool table in the back."

"How'd you happen to notice him?"

Prior looked nervous. "Well, he was there when I come in, you know. You know. All the regulars, and stuff. He was just one of them sittin' at the bar."

"Did you speak to him?"

"No. Nodded, maybe. Just like to all the others."

"And then?"

Prior might have been thinking hard, or he might have been

concentrating on Estelle's lithe figure approaching from the street.

"And then?" I prompted.

"He left sometime," Prior said. "I glanced up and saw him go out the door."

"With anyone?"

"Now that—" He stopped as Estelle walked up to me.

"Richard Finnegan," I said to her. "He walked into someone's knife. I haven't been over there."

She nodded and didn't pursue the vague "someone's knife." Instead, she walked back out onto Rincon Street and circled around the crowd of people to reach the scene.

"Did you see him talking with anyone? Arguing? Anything like that?"

"Nothing that drew my attention," Prior said finally.

"You didn't see him leave in company with anyone?"

He shook his head. "But I was occupied," he added.

"Who was sitting nearest him at the bar when you came in? Do you remember?"

Prior took a deep breath and looked off into the distance. "Let's see. Alex Taylor is workin' the bar." He turned and looked at the others who had drifted toward the yellow ribbon like flies to flypaper. "Stubby Moore, over there. Emilio Garcia. His brother there too. Juan. Jim Burdick and his wife. They were all kinda there, but I don't recall who was sitting where."

"Thanks. Don't go anywhere," I said. I strode over to Jim Burdick, who was standing near the back bumper of one of the patrons' vehicles, an arm protectively around his wife Peggy's plump shoulders.

He still smelled faintly of automotive grease and his face was pale. He didn't release his hold on his wife when he turned to greet me.

"Jim, who was Finnegan with tonight?" I said without preamble.

"He come in alone, as far as I know," Burdick said.

"Did you talk with him?"

"I was going to. He's ordered a rear axle seal for that truck of his, and I was about to tell him it come in today. But then he up and left, just all of a sudden."

"Had he been talking to anyone?"

"No, not that I remember."

"He looked like he wanted to say something to that rancher," Burdick's wife said.

"What rancher, Peggy?"

She looked up at her husband. "Who was that? Sitting at the table by the window? Remember? He was all by himself and when we came in, you kind of waved at him?"

"At the table?" Burdick said, puzzled.

"Right by the window."

"Oh. That was Ed Boyd. But he left."

"And then so did Mr. Finnegan," Peggy Burdick said. "I remember, because I heard Mr. Finnegan mutter something. I couldn't hear what it was. But I remember that he'd ordered a drink, and he left before Alex could get it to him. He tossed a couple bucks on the bar and just left."

"Edwin Boyd was here?" I glared hard at Burdick.

"Yeah," he said helpfully. "But he left."

"I bet he did," I muttered and spun around, only to crash into Neil Costace. I pointed across the lot at Estelle Reyes-Guzman's figure as we both regained our balance. "Go get her," I said. "Meet me at her unit right there."

I slipped into Estelle's sedan and grabbed the mike.

"Three-oh-three, three-ten."

"Three-oh-three."

"Tom, has there been any vehicular traffic past you in the last few minutes? Going northbound on Forty-three?"

"That's negative, three-ten."

"All right. I want you to go inside the Legion Hall and find Johnny Boyd. Tell him that I need to talk with him right now. We'll be there in less than a minute."

"Ten-four."

Neil Costace and Estelle appeared at the car door, and I pushed myself out.

"Edwin Boyd," I said and for the first time, saw a look of surprise on Estelle Reyes-Guzman's face.

THIRTY-NINE

"WHAT'S JOHNNY BOYD doing here?" Costace asked as we turned left at the end of Pershing Park and headed toward the American Legion Hall half a block ahead.

"He's angry," I said. "That's my best guess. Instead of going home and stewing, and facing questions from Maxine, he came down to the Legion Hall to cool off." I glanced around at Costace in the back seat. "And no doubt he's telling some wonderful tall tales about what happened tonight."

"They don't have to be too tall," Costace murmured. "And his brother is at one bar, he's at another. It's odd that they're not drinking buddies."

"Evidently they're not," I said. "Each to his own."

Tom Pasquale had pulled his patrol car up so that he was parked nose to nose with Boyd's truck, and in the wash of light cast by the sodium vapor light, I could see the young deputy standing beside Boyd. As we approached, a bright glow marked the end of Johnny Boyd's cigarette. Estelle braked hard and pulled to a stop.

"Now what the hell is going on?" Boyd asked as we got out. A scant three blocks' distance and a handful of trees in Pershing Park separated us from a view of the Pierpoint, and the winking emergency lights were clearly visible.

"Johnny," I said, and reached out a hand to take the rancher by the shoulder. "Where did Edwin go tonight when he left the house?"

"Why?" The answer came out automatically, a standard response to questions that Johnny Boyd considered no one's business but his own. And then he glanced to the south, toward the congregation of flashing lights. I saw the expression on his face change as he put two and two together. "What's happened?"

"Richard Finnegan is dead, Johnny."

He looked at me quickly. "What do you mean?"

"I mean just that. He's dead. I don't know the details, except that he was stabbed to death outside of the Pierpoint Bar and Grill just a little while ago."

He took an involuntary step backward, and when he reached for the cigarette in his mouth, he fumbled it and it fell to the sidewalk in a cascade of sparks. Tom Pasquale was standing beside him and evidently thought the man had lost his balance. He reached out a hand to take Johnny by the elbow, and the rancher reacted as if he'd brushed against an electric fence.

"Now wait a minute," he said. "I've been inside the Legion Hall ever since I drove into town."

"Johnny—" I started to say.

"No." He held up both hands and took another step backward. "I know what all of you think, or you wouldn't have been snooping around my property earlier. But this is just plain crazy. I didn't have anything to do with Richard Finnegan getting himself killed."

"Johnny, stop it," I snapped. "I'm not the least bit interested in what you've been doing since you came to town." That wasn't altogether true, of course, but it served the purpose. Boyd's eyes narrowed and he glanced first at Neil Costace and then at Estelle. "We have reason to believe that Edwin was involved somehow," I said, and Johnny's head snapped back around.

"*What?*"

"At least one of the patrons saw your brother at the Pierpoint. Edwin was there, sitting by himself. Richard Finnegan came in, and witnesses say that shortly after Finnegan entered the bar, your brother got up and left. And then so did Richard Finnegan. And now Finnegan is dead."

"Oh, Jesus," Boyd moaned.

"Johnny, we need to know—" But that's as far as I got. Boyd smacked his forehead as if he'd been struck by a vicious migraine, reeled past me, found his balance and dashed to his truck. Tommy Pasquale found his feet before anyone else, but by the time he caught up with Boyd, the rancher was already in the truck and slamming the door.

The electric locks of the fancy rig banged shut before the deputy could grab the door handle, and then the engine sprang to life. Johnny Boyd jerked the vehicle into reverse, trying for some space between his truck and the front of the patrol car. As he did so, I could see Pasquale's right hand snake down, reaching for the holstered automatic on his hip.

"No!" I bellowed. "Let him go, Tom!" The pistol was out, the momentum of the draw bringing the weapon up so that the muzzle stared Johnny Boyd full in the face, only a single piece of safety glass between the two. "Tom!" I roared again, lunging toward him. "Hold your fire! Let him go!"

Boyd jerked the gear lever into drive, wrenched the wheel, and the big truck roared out into the street.

"Now listen," I snapped, and held out a hand toward Pasquale. "Put that thing away." He holstered the automatic and I grabbed him with one hand and Neil Costace with the other as if they were two recalcitrant urchins.

"Here's what I want you to do. If he goes north past the mine—that's if he takes the usual route in to his ranch, I want you to follow him, red lights off. Don't push him. He's not thinking straight, and I don't want him shoved into some arroyo, or you either. Just stay well behind. Estelle and I are going to take the state road, the long way around through Newton. Maybe Edwin went that way. It's smoother, for one thing. If Johnny goes that way too, just let him go. You continue up the hill. Go in the front way."

"You don't want us to take him into custody?" Pasquale asked, and even though it was his "I'm just checking to make sure" tone of voice, I damn near lost my temper. I had taken two or three steps toward Estelle's car, and I whirled around, hands on my hips.

"You don't get close to him," I snapped. "You do exactly what I told you to do. You stay behind him and don't spook him. Keep your eyes open and use your head."

"Yes, sir."

I glanced at Costace. "Ride with him," I said, and if he didn't nod eager agreement, at least he didn't say no, nor did he take time to point out to me that he wasn't one of my deputies. "Now let's get on with it."

Estelle was already behind the wheel of her unmarked car when I slid into the seat. Johnny Boyd had a one-minute head start, and considering the way he was flogging his pickup, that was enough to keep him out of sight until we'd cleared the village and hit the two-mile straightaway on County Road 43 that led due north toward the intersection with State 78, at the foot of the mesa just below the landfill entrance.

We covered those two miles in a blur, and as we approached the intersection, I saw a pair of taillights heading up the hill, just entering the first set of switchbacks below the mine. Judging by their rate of speed, they belonged to Boyd.

"We see him," Costace's voice said over the radio. Estelle moved into the left lane, giving Pasquale room to pass as we slowed for the turn onto the state highway. He did so, flogging the Bronco until its V-8 screamed.

State Highway 78 cut across the western half of Posadas County diagonally, exiting the county at the northwest corner. About the only road in the county that was straight for any appreciable distance, that night it was devoid of traffic. Estelle was tense, both hands on the wheel, the pencil beam from the spotlight lancing out far ahead, searching for the glint of startled eyes in the road.

We flashed by the airport, the final set of lights before the darkness of the prairie turned our headlights into a white tunnel.

"If Edwin went this way, he's got about a fourteen- or fifteen-minute head start, and that means no matter how fast you go, you won't catch him before he reaches the ranch, unless he's puttering along at thirty miles an hour."

"Even with his old truck, he'll do better than that," Estelle said.

Eighteen miles out of Posadas, a single set of taillights popped into view. Well before I could judge that they were

small, low, and close-set, Estelle had drifted the car into the
left lane. I reached down and flipped the switch by the radio
console that activated the grille wiggle-waggles, and the little
Subaru station wagon jumped to the right like a kicked puppy.

"They won't be drowsy for a few minutes," I muttered as
we blasted past. I turned the red lights off. For the rest of the
run to the Newton intersection, Estelle kept the car ballistic,
the speedometer registering well over a hundred miles an
hour.

And even as we awakened the sleepy little hamlet with our
passing, it was clear to me that Edwin Boyd hadn't nursed
his old truck along. As we turned onto the dirt road south-
bound from Newton, not a trace of dust hung in the air from
his passing.

I glanced at the clock on the dashboard. It would have been
almost impossible for Johnny Boyd to beat us to the ranch
coming in from the county road to the east. That meant, with
just a bit of luck, that we'd reach the ranch before he did, or
before the two officers on his tail did. That was the only
comforting thought just then.

FORTY

WE SLID INTO the Boyds' front yard, and the billows of dust
drifted off like great ghosts, illuminated by the single arc light.

A figure materialized on the front step and before I could
make out who it was, Estelle said, "Maxine." The woman
bustled across toward us, and I pulled myself out of the car.
I could hear the roar of vehicle engines in the distance.

"Maxine," I said, and she surprised me by catching me by
both arms as if she wanted to be sure I would stay rooted in
place. "Where's Edwin?" I asked. "Did he come here?"

"Not five minutes ago," she wailed, and then the words

came out in a flood. "He's so upset, and he wouldn't tell me what was wrong, just that he was in awful trouble somehow, something about Dick Finnegan being killed in town. And then he left. I've been trying and trying to get ahold of Johnny, but I don't know where he is. And then I thought I should call Charlotte Finnegan...but I just couldn't. Not until I knew for sure. I was just on the telephone with your office when I saw you drive in. Oh, Sheriff..."

"Where did Edwin go, do you know?" Estelle asked, her voice warm and gentle.

Maxine shook her head. "He just kept saying, 'They'll be along soon. They'll be along.' He didn't say who. And when I tried to make sense out of what he was saying, he just said, 'I've killed Dick Finnegan. They'll be along directly. They know where I'll be.' What does all this mean, Sheriff?"

I didn't try to shake loose from her grip, but I turned my head as Johnny Boyd's pickup truck rounded the corner below the barn. "Which way did Edwin go, Maxine?"

"Oh, thank God he's back," she said, ignoring my question.

The pickup truck came in much too fast and slid to a stop in a shower of stones, narrowly missing the rear end of the patrol car and stopping within a hairsbreadth of the back wall of the house.

"Edwin was here, not more than five minutes ago," I shouted as Johnny Boyd sprang from his truck. The rancher stopped as if I'd struck him. "He's left already, so he must have passed you. He didn't head out to the north."

"He ain't done that, or the law that's behind me, either." Even as he said that, the department Bronco idled into the yard with an astonishing display of self-restraint on its driver's part. Pasquale pulled up so that his vehicle was almost touching Boyd's back bumper. In order to leave, the rancher would have to either move the county vehicle or take the back bedroom off the ranch house.

Johnny strode toward me. "Maxine, where is he?" he snapped.

"Johnny, he wouldn't tell me where he was going. He

drove out just the way you came in. He said you all would know where he is. That's all I know. That's really all I know. That's all he said. He was in such a state."

"He drove right out there?" Boyd said in disbelief, looking at the east driveway.

"Right out there," she said. "Not five minutes ago."

"And he didn't come back?" She shook her head. "Well, what the hell..." Boyd said. He swept off his hat and ran a hand through his hair. "He ain't gone far, then. And how the hell would we know where he was headed?"

"Estelle, turn off the car," I said, and then shouted at Pasquale to do the same. "Now be still a minute." One of the dogs in the house was yapping, and I heard the quiet thump of the door as Neil Costace got out of the Bronco. After that, the silence fell heavily. We all listened hard, and finally could hear it—the distant sound of an engine, laboring in low gear.

"Now that's got to be—" Johnny started to say, and I held up a hand sharply. For another few seconds, the sound continued, but it was impossible to sense the direction from which it was coming. The sound floated this way and that across the prairie, and then abruptly ceased. "That's over by the juniper drag," Boyd said. "South of here." He started back toward his truck.

"Johnny, wait," I said. "What's he doing?"

"Now how would I know that?" the rancher retorted without turning. He thumped a hand on the front fender of Pasquale's Bronco. "You going to move that, sonny, or do you want me to drive through you?"

"Hold it," I snapped. "Goddam it, just hold on. It doesn't make sense for any of us to run into this blind. Your wife just told me that Edwin admitted killing a man and that he's spooked. You don't go charging after him."

Johnny turned and took several steps toward Maxine. "He told you *what?*"

Maxine reached out a hand to her husband. "Johnny, what's happening? Edwin said he killed Dick Finnegan. That's all he would say. And that you all would know where he'd be. Then he just drove off."

A second engine note drifted to us then, the deep, guttural sound of a heavy diesel. "What's that?" I asked.

Boyd listened, his brows knit. "That's the dozer, Sheriff."

"A bulldozer?"

He nodded.

"If that's Edwin, what the hell is he doing?"

"There's a pasture south of here where we've been chaining down juniper the past few days. Nobody'd be down there but him or me, so that's got to be Edwin." The diesel roar increased, and I could hear an occasional metallic clank of the tracks.

"Goddam," Johnny Boyd muttered. "You can see some of that juniper where we're workin' from over behind the barn." We followed him around the black hulk of the long, low three-sided structure, past the enormous framework of the windmill tower. I didn't have my flashlight and walked like a flat-footed old drunk, trying to keep my balance.

"There," Boyd said from some point in the darkness ahead of me. His ranch yard might have been second nature to him in the dark, but to me, it was a featureless black box. I looked in the general direction of where "there" might be and saw a faint wash of lights.

"That's the dozer," Boyd said. "I don't know what the hell he's doing. Or where the hell he's going. That isn't where we've been working. He's headin' off to the south and east."

"William's Tank," Estelle said quietly, and she turned and made for the car.

FORTY-ONE

"RIDE WITH US," I said to Johnny Boyd, and he hesitated. Maybe he was wondering what Estelle knew and he didn't. If that was the case, he had company. But she had already reached the vehicle, and I knew better than to stand there and demand explanations from her. "Look," I said, "your brother's in deep trouble. There are some things I need to know before there's any kind of confrontation, and I think you can help."

"You need to get some backup out here," Neil Costace snapped, and I looked at him in surprise as he continued, "You've got some crazy man loose on a bulldozer. He's already killed one man, and there's no telling what he'll do next."

Boyd half turned in angry response, and I grabbed him by the arm. "Listen, Johnny." I jerked his arm hard, pulling him toward me. I lowered my voice. "Enough's enough. If we're going to help your brother through this, then you've got to tell me what you know. Goddam it, trust me just this once. Ride with us."

"We'll go on ahead and cut him off," Costace said, and his words were in that "Let's lynch him, boys" tone that riled the crowds in old western films into action.

"The hell you will," I said, and the ludicrous image of our new county Bronco being crushed like an aluminum can by the bulldozer ran through my mind. That was all the prompting Johnny Boyd needed.

"Let's go," he said, and pulled loose from my grip.

"Get in front," I said after him, and as the lanky rancher slid into the front passenger seat and yanked the door closed, I turned on Neil Costace.

Before I could get two words out, he held up a hand and in the dim light, I could see a half grin. "That's one that's safe," he said. "We'll follow you on out—wherever it is that you're going."

"Thanks," I said. As I walked to the car, I saw Maxine Boyd standing alone, hands held in front of her as if in prayer. I detoured over to her and wrapped her in a bear hug. "Stay near the phone," I said. "I'll do what I can."

She murmured something, and I gave her a final squeeze and then walked to the car. I'd forgotten how difficult it was to contort into the back seat, but I managed.

I knew we didn't have much time, and I leaned forward, Boyd's left ear just inches away. "Did you know where Edwin was going this evening?"

For several seconds, he didn't say anything, and when the nod came, it was just the faintest of movements, just a little tick of the head. "Jesus H. Christ," he murmured. I wasn't sure if he was responding to our launching over the cattle guard behind the barn or to my question. He half turned in the seat, using one hand against the dashboard to brace himself, with his left arm hooked over the seat back.

"He said he was going to get something for his knee. Every now and then, he likes to wrap himself around a glass, and the Pierpoint...that's his favorite watering hole over in Posadas. Now what?"

"He and Finnegan had an argument about something. We're not sure about what, and we certainly don't know who provoked it. The other deputies are down there now, and they'll take statements from everyone who saw anything. Right now, we don't know what the hell happened."

"Yeah," Boyd said distantly. "Well, I can guess what happened."

When he didn't elaborate, I pulled myself forward on the seat, practically talking right in his ear. I could smell the cloying aroma of beer and cigarette smoke. Estelle drove almost sedately, which was fine with me. I didn't relish being tossed through the roof. And it didn't take hell-bent-for-leather to beat a bulldozer.

"I want your help," I said. "I don't want him hurt, or anyone else hurt either. And neither do you. But he's the only one with all the answers."

Boyd took his time lighting a cigarette, the smoke curling up and out the side window.

"Johnny," I went on, "when I told you that it looked like your brother and Finnegan had an argument, you didn't seem surprised. You want to tell me about it?"

"It won't be the first time," he said and pushed himself back in the seat, wedging himself against the door. "My brother and Dick Finnegan haven't seen eye to eye on a lot

of things over the years." He sighed. "I don't know what it
is, 'cause my brother is about the gentlest man on the planet.
He minds his own business and just asks that the rest of the
world do the same."

"Did he and Finnegan argue over something recently?"

"The damn antelope," Boyd said, and he shut his mouth
tight after those three words and turned to watch the road as
Estelle negotiated a turn where the ruts had been cut deep into
the prairie. She bridged the deepest portions, keeping the big
sedan's undercarriage out of the dirt. The lights of the dashboard were just enough to outline Boyd's features, and by the
set of his jaw, I could only guess at the struggle he was having.

"Finnegan was impounding antelope," I said. "We know
that. We were out there just a little while ago. We saw the
sections of sheep fencing. We went all the way over to the
corner, by the abandoned well. That's the one you called Wil-
liams Tank."

"Well, then," Boyd said, and let it go at that, as if we
knew all there was to know.

"I don't understand, though," I pressed. "Sheep fencing
isn't cheap. Where's the profit in a handful of antelope? I'd
think you could sell a good steer for more money than you'd
get for some critter about the size of a big German shepherd."

"First off, it ain't no 'handful,' Sheriff. Dick's workin' on
a pretty good herd. Hell, I counted thirty-four once, in just
one clan. And it isn't selling the animals for meat that it's all
about." Boyd fell silent again.

"Then what's it for? Hunters?"

"That's right."

"There's money in that?"

Johnny Boyd snorted. "You're kidding. Hell, some of the
city boys will pay a thousand bucks a pop for a chance at an
antelope with a good set of horns. Guaranteed success. A nice,
private little hunt. Dick's got about a section of land fenced
in like what you saw, both to the south by the old windmill
and another area north. You remember where that old stone
house is?"

"Sure."

"Up north of that." Boyd crushed the remains of the cigarette out and dug another from his pocket.

"So he sells hunts," I said.

Boyd nodded. "That's where the money is. Ten hunts at a thousand bucks each will pay for a lot of ranching. Tax free, interest free. Anytime of year that it's convenient. My brother doesn't think much of that," Boyd said.

"Finnegan gets hunters from out of town, then?"

"Well, sure. Folks that don't know better. See, he's got this deal with some fella in Santa Fe. As a matter of fact, if I got it right, the guy is Finnegan's former brother-in-law...or some squirrelly thing like that. Dick was boasting about it to me once, acting real coy, you know. He was pretty proud of himself. Anyway, this guy is in the business."

"What business?"

"Travel, hunting. All that sort of stuff. There's some big-game ranches up that way, legitimate ones. Rich folks come out and spend a week getting wined and dined and go home with a trophy elk or ram. Dick was hinting that every once in a while, his brother-in-law would send some hunters down this way for a quick trophy buck."

"It's hard to believe anyone in his right mind would pay that much," I said.

Boyd laughed, a short, hacking chuckle. "They'll pay even more for less, Sheriff," he said. "Fifteen hundred or two thousand is petty cash to some folks. And the way things are going, open-country hunting is getting harder and harder. There's less and less private land every year, and a good many landowners and ranchers don't want hunters on the property...myself included. And the kicker is, Dick never cared much one way or another what season it was. Nobody was the wiser, so why inconvenience the payin' customer by restricting him to one of the state's seasons?"

"And Edwin doesn't approve of all this? Of what Finnegan was doing?"

"He don't think much of it. Neither do I, for that matter,

but what Dick Finnegan does on his land is his business, long as it don't get in my way."

"You never tipped off the Game and Fish Department?"

"Nope. The thought crossed my mind once or twice. Guess I should have. But this is the way I figure it. The judge would hand a stiff fine on old Dick, and maybe he could pay it, and maybe he couldn't. They might even stick him in jail for six months and leave old crazy Charlotte out there all by her lonesome. Maybe, maybe not. But then after a time, he'd be out of jail, and I'd still have him for a neighbor, still meet him now and then on some back road. Don't get me wrong. I'm not afraid of too much, but I don't need that. It's his business, and I let it go at that."

"Johnny, did Dick Finnegan shoot at that airplane?"

This time he didn't hesitate, didn't turn coy. "I don't know, Sheriff," he said and added, "If I knew, I'd tell you. He could have, and he could have hit it, too. I've seen him drop a coyote at five hundred yards, just resting the rifle over the hood of the truck. And that's no small trick. But I don't know."

"Do you suppose Edwin knows?" Estelle asked. Her voice was quiet and husky, but it startled both Johnny Boyd and me.

"I don't see how he could," Johnny said. "He's so goddam lame he can't do much more than hobble. And at the time that shooting happened, he wasn't even in the county."

"That's what he told us," I said.

"If that's what he said, then that's what's true," Johnny said vehemently. "My brother don't waste a whole lot of words, but one thing he don't do is lie."

"He hasn't said anything recently that was out of the ordinary about Finnegan? They weren't arguing about anything?"

"If they were, he didn't tell me anything about it."

I watched as we turned south on the narrow lane that would lead us to the first gate that marked Finnegan's zoo. "When was the last time you talked with him?" I asked.

"With Dick? Oh, we cross paths regular. We both use the same road, you know."

"When was the last time you talked to him?"

"I saw him the day before yesterday."

"That was before the crash?"

"Yes. That morning. We met at the intersection of the county road."

"He say anything?"

"He said he was still thinking about running the pipe across that little spur of land I own. But he wasn't sure of how much water there'd be."

"And that was it?"

"And that was it. I told him that whatever he decided was fine with me. Just that if he was going to run pipe across my land, I could use some of the water a time or two."

"It would have cost him quite a bit to go around, wouldn't it?"

"Sure. Some." He chuckled that dry, hacking laugh again. "Half an antelope, maybe."

"What did Edwin think about that?"

"Not much. He was pissed at Finnegan for borrowing our dozer to try digging his goddam pond and then turning around and being so goddam tight about the pipe deal. He stewed about that some. I figured it was just one of those things, you know. One of those things that gets sideways. To this day, I don't know why Dick wanted to bother trying another pond. This country is mostly gravel. There's no dirt tank in the county that will hold water unless you line it. Plastic or bentonite. But it's his business. I told Edwin to just let it ride. Hell, it didn't cost us anything except a couple gallons of diesel."

We pulled to an abrupt halt, our headlights illuminating the wire gate. In all the frenzy earlier, Tom Pasquale had actually paused long enough to make sure it was closed and the herd of evidence secured. Boyd didn't seem in much of a hurry as he loosened the wire closure.

"What do you think?" I said to Estelle. "You're the only

one of us who seems to have an idea of where Edwin's headed.''

She drove through the gate, pulling far enough ahead that the second vehicle could follow.

''I don't think Dick Finnegan was much interested in ponds,'' she said.

FORTY-TWO

ESTELLE PULLED the patrol car close to the fence and stopped with the headlights off. She opened the windows and killed the engine. Sand, gravel, and bunchgrass crunched as the Bronco pulled in behind us and halted. Pasquale switched it off, and for a few seconds, the five of us sat in the darkness.

''Be kind of funny if he was going the other way,'' Johnny Boyd said in a half whisper.

''He'd be easy to track,'' I replied, and the rancher hacked what could have been a chuckle.

''I got to thank you,'' he said after a moment. I didn't see any cause to be thanked, so I didn't reply. ''You don't exactly go chargin' in on things, do you?''

''We try not to,'' I said. ''You get as old and clumsy as I am, you learn to watch where you put your feet.''

''I can see that the kid behind us gets a little squirrelly now and then.''

''Yes, he does. As you say, he's young. But Deputy Pasquale is a fast study. And he's got a veteran riding with him.''

Boyd coughed again. ''Costace? That's his name?'' I nodded. ''He seemed eager enough to ride on over here with the cavalry before you reined him in.''

''He got you in the car, didn't he?'' I said, and Boyd chewed on that for a moment. The thinking would do him good.

"And what are you going to do when Edwin gets here with that dozer? If this is where he's headed?" he asked.

"I plan to get out of this car, walk up to him and ask him what the hell happened. And maybe while I'm at it, I'll ask him why the first thing he did was jump on a goddam Cat and drive it a mile or two in the dark." Estelle stirred as if she wanted to say something, but then thought better of it.

"He's going to be arrested?"

"That depends on what he tells me."

"Odds are good, though, aren't they?"

"Yes, they are."

"You'll let me be here?" I had never heard Johnny Boyd's voice so small.

"I'm counting on it, Johnny."

He fell silent.

"There it is," Estelle said and pointed. Sure enough, off in the darkness to the west a couple of hundred yards, two bright lances of light appeared as the dozer clanked its way around a small outcropping that thrust up sharp limestone in the machine's path.

"Let's go find out," I said and started the process of hauling my tired self out of the car. Before I had pulled myself upright, I realized that Deputy Pasquale was holding the door open for me.

"How are we going to stop that thing?" Pasquale asked, and I saw that he was holding a pump shotgun.

"Before you do anything else, put that back in the unit," I said. He hesitated. "You piece all this together in your mind and you'll understand why I'm asking you to do that," I said gently.

Neil Costace stood in front of the Bronco, watching the approach of the ponderous machine, his hands thrust in his pockets. "Any man with even half his marbles doesn't choose a bulldozer as an escape vehicle, Tom. The man wants to show us something," he said.

Edwin Boyd drove the machine straight toward our position, until the only thing between him and Dick Finnegan's property was the tightly strung fence. The machine never slowed. The blade caught a fence post squarely. Standing a hundred yards away, I could hear the groan and twang of the wire.

With enough tension stretching them over the sharp edges of the dozer's blade, the barbed-wire strands finally parted and snapped away, their ends curling and snaking, lashing the dirt and tangling in the scant vegetation. The gridded sheep fencing was tougher, and it wrenched loose from the posts and followed on either side of the machine as it clanked across the flat toward the windmill.

Just when it looked like he would crash into the old windmill tower, Edwin Boyd spun the dozer in its own length so that it was facing due north. The blade dropped into the prairie soil twenty yards from the windmill tower and the stack belched as he opened the throttle. From fifty yards away, I could smell the dirt as the bulldozer ripped open the earth.

He pushed dirt for fifty feet, then raised the blade, drove over the mound he'd made and pivoted for what looked like a return run. Just as suddenly, the heavy growling of the diesel died, ticking into silence. The two headlights continued to stare at the freshly scarred ground, their beams softened with power only from the battery.

"Now what the hell?" Johnny Boyd said, and he started toward the dozer. The rest of us followed.

We had fifty yards to cover, but Edwin Boyd took that long to dismount. He managed to step to earth at the same time we reached the dozer. He leaned heavily against the massive tread of the old machine and tried to light a cigarette. I could see his hands shaking, and he was gulping air.

"Just take it easy, Edwin," I said. "We're here now." His chest was heaving, and for a moment, I thought he would pitch forward on his face, taking all his answers with him.

He gave up finally, sitting on the cleats with lighter in one hand, cigarette in the other, staring at the ground. "Take your time," Neil Costace said. "Just breathe deep and take your time."

Johnny Boyd reached out and took Edwin by the left shoulder. "It's going to be all right, Ed. Talk to me now."

Edwin Boyd shrugged as if he had no idea of where to start, and it was Estelle Reyes-Guzman who helped him into gear. "Is this where it's buried, Edwin?" she asked, and his immediate nod was one of relief.

"You dig down three foot right here," he said, swinging a finger to trace the rip he'd made, "and you'll find one of them little foreign jobs. Roof's caved in, and she's kinda flat from having seven tons drove over her a few times, but it's there."

"Are you talking about a car?" Johnny Boyd asked incredulously.

Edwin nodded.

"Well, shit, whose car is it?" Costace asked.

"Belongs to a couple of hunters," Edwin muttered.

"And they're still in the car," Estelle added for him, and he nodded.

"Sure as hell are. You dig down right here and you'll find 'em."

"Finnegan buried them?" I asked.

"Sure enough did." He took a long, shuddering breath and held it for several seconds, finally letting it go with a little gasp. "I guess I had the bad luck to happen on him just as he was finishing up. About three weeks ago. I came over to fetch some tools from that toolbox up on the dozer. I didn't see much, but I saw enough. Saw part of the car roof, and through the back window, or where the back window used to be. Saw a hand."

"Did Finnegan see you?"

"He did. Don't think he knew that I saw the hand. Told me it was an old junker and that he was gettin' rid of it long as he had a hole. I made the mistake of sayin' something like 'Pretty fancy paint for an old junker,' and he told me to just forget it. Then I said something like, 'Looks like you're gettin' yourself quite a herd of antelope boxed in here,' and I guess that was the wrong thing to say, too. He got all huffy and told me to mind my own business." Edwin took another deep breath. "Pond, hell. That's what he was doing, is burying that car, and whoever was in it."

"The pond didn't make any sense from the very begin-

ning,'' Estelle said. "For one thing, he'd already scavenged
the windmill pump, and so digging a new pond without the
pump didn't make sense. And he'd started his project to run
pipe from the Forest Service spring on Cat Mesa to a stock
tank that's almost a mile east of here." She looked at me and
shook her head. "It didn't make any sense that he'd all of a
sudden spend his time digging a hole for a day or two, way
over here, and then just as quickly give up." She turned back
to Edwin. "Do you know who might have been in the car,
Edwin?"

He shook his head.

"When he saw you tonight in the Pierpoint...what was the
argument about?"

Edwin had enough control of his hands to finally light the
cigarette. "I figure it only one way. I was there first, just
minding my own business, trying to figure out what I should
do. 'Cause see, I knew damn well who fired that shot at the
airplane. If Dick thought someone was on to him about those
antelope, that's one thing. He could just shrug and say he was
plannin' to buy some summer lambs. If them antelope don't
like the fence, they can just jump out. But that car and whoever's inside it? That's something else. He gets real nervous,
thinkin' that somebody knows. Maybe he thought that I up
and told somebody. And so he figures, what the hell. Take a
shot. Who'd ever know?" He took a deep drag on the cigarette.

"Anyway, he come in to the Pierpoint, and I didn't want
to talk to him much, so I just left. Almost got to my truck
when he caught up with me. First thing he said was, 'You
remember what I told you.' He said he didn't like all those
federal agents pokin' around anymore than we did, but if I
made any kind of trouble, he'd fix it so that Johnny or the
boy, or maybe me, got blamed for it."

"The shell casings," I said.

"Don't know about that," Edwin said. "I kind of lost my
temper and said something like, 'You can just go to hell.' I'd
just about decided that I was doin' the wrong thing, not going
to the police. He kind of pushed me like, and then one thing

led to another. I banged my knee and damn near saw stars, and then he up and kicked me. I said something like, 'That's it. I can goddam crawl to the sheriff's office if I need to.' And then he jerked a jack handle out of the back of his truck and started to come down on me with that. I stuck him.''

"Your knife?"

Edwin Boyd nodded. "Sure as hell is. It's probably still in him, too."

"And then you drove back here?"

"Fast as I could. I figured the best thing to do was to tell you just exactly what I know, and mark the spot." He gestured with the cigarette. "And so there it is." He looked up at me. "I guess you got to arrest me, don't you?"

"Yes."

Johnny Boyd sat down on the dozer track beside his brother. "It's going to work out," he said. "You just tell that same story to Judge Hobart and you'll be home before first light."

I turned to Tom Pasquale. "Go ahead," I said. He started to reach for his cuffs. "Just be gentle." He nodded, and Edwin Boyd stood up and offered his wrists. As I walked back toward the car, I could hear the deputy intoning the Miranda rights.

I sat down on the front seat, my feet still on the ground. The sky overhead was as clear as I'd ever seen it, a vast wash of stars from one horizon to another. Estelle appeared by the door.

"Are you all right?" she asked.

"Sure," I said. "Ready for bed, I guess. I was just wondering who will end up with the Finnegans' ranch. Charlotte isn't going to be able to cope."

"The Boyds, I imagine," Estelle said. "Nothing worked out quite the way Dick Finnegan would have liked, if Edwin's story holds up."

"Oh, it'll hold up," I said. "But I don't much look forward to finding out who's in that car under there."

"Somebody who had an easy hunt out of season and then tried to pull a fast one by refusing to pay. Dick Finnegan was too strapped for cash to let that happen. That's what I'd be willing to bet,'' Estelle said.

"The one thing I've learned in all this time,'' I said, "is not to make bets with you.''

FORTY-THREE

EDWIN BOYD had been accurate as hell in what he'd remembered. Thirty-six inches down, the massive bucket of one of Posadas County's front loaders struck the roof of the car, and in another twenty minutes, the pathetic, crushed thing was hauled out and parked on the surface. Chris Lucero, the county employee who'd been shagged out of bed to dig up the prairie, shut down the machine and looked first at the car, then at me.

"Fun times,'' he said.

It wasn't, and the dozer had done a fair enough job of crushing the little tin can that it took Bob Torrez and Tom Pasquale nearly an hour using power jaws to pry part of it open. With a little imagination, the occupants appeared to be two men.

Richard Finnegan apparently had thought that the burial was adequate to cover his tracks without him having to attend to any other details. The Texas license plate was still intact, and came back as registered to a Vernon Dorrance of Houston. Mr. Dorrance had originally been seated behind the wheel—that much we could tell—before the weight of the dozer and the three weeks underground smeared him and his partner together.

The wallets were in place, in the hip pockets of Mr. Dorrance and his hunting buddy, Paul Friedel. A business card told us that Vernon Dorrance was actually Vernon D. Dorrance, Attorney at Law. There were credit cards and a blank check, but no cash.

Much of the rear of Mr. Dorrance's skull was missing, the sort of damage that would be done by a high-velocity rifle bullet. What had killed Mr. Friedel wasn't obvious, but I had no doubt that Dr. Francis Guzman would tell us within a few hours.

In the trunk of the car were two fancy, high-powered rifles and two boxes of ammunition, together with a few other odds and ends packed in two small suitcases, including a camera with ten photos taken in living color. If we were lucky, at least one of the exposures would show a proud great white hunter kneeling beside the antelope he'd stalked across the vast wastelands of Posadas County...a photo taken just before he stiffed his guide out of a day's pay.

I left the final inventory to Sergeant Torrez, but what the two men had been after seemed clear to me. How and why they'd tangled with Dick Finnegan was just a guess on our part, and only one person would know the answer for sure.

Charlotte Finnegan invited us in for coffee. That wasn't what I needed most at four o'clock in the morning, but playing hostess gave her something to do.

By then, she'd known for four hours that her husband was dead. Father Eugene Starkey had been with her most of that time after the deputies had left, but no one else had seen fit to pay her a visit—not that she had many neighbors who were on the night shift. One of the deputies told me that a sister who lived in Albuquerque was on her way down to stay with Charlotte until she decided which way to lean.

When Estelle and I arrived, we had known for two hours who was in the car.

I accepted the cup of coffee with a hand that wasn't all too steady.

"How about a sandwich?" Charlotte asked with that sort of eager brightness that takes so much effort when all you really want to do is puddle. "I've got some nice sliced ham and some of that wonderful dark rye bread."

"That would be nice," I said, and looked down at my

hands. Some of the prairie was still under my nails, and that brought back the image of the car and its ripe contents. "You mind if I wash up a little?"

The bathroom down the hall was neat as a pin, with the fake porcelain sink buffed spotless. I felt as if I were kicking Charlotte yet again as I watched the water and soap spot the finish. I used the dark towel with the roadrunner embossed on it and wiped out the sink when I was finished.

As I made my way back down the hall toward the living room of the mobile home, Charlotte stood with the sandwich on a paper plate in one hand and a mug of coffee in the other.

"Thank you," I said, and sat down with a sigh on the sofa beside Estelle. Charlotte wilted into a rocking chair next to the television.

"Charlotte, did you ever hear the names Vernon Dorrance and Paul Friedel?"

"Mercy, no. Are they coming by?"

"No." I took a sip of coffee. "Did you know anything about your husband's selling antelope hunts?"

"Oh, he did that all the time." She leaned forward and clasped her hands. "See, my sister's former husband is a travel agent, and he sometimes makes arrangements for guided hunts."

"Any time of year?"

"Oh, yes. That's the wonderful thing about it, my husband told me. If the game animals are on your own ranch, on your own land, you can hunt anytime of year without a license, just like the Indians do on the reservation. At first, I didn't believe that. I guess it sounded just too good to be true. So one day I called the sheriff's office—your office—and spoke to the sheriff himself. He told me that he didn't know, but that he'd find out for sure and call me back. He didn't, mind you. But I felt better just having checked."

"Is that right?" I said, and took a bite of the sandwich, reflecting that the Department of Game and Fish would be amused at the creative interpretation of their game laws. "Do you remember an incident about three weeks ago with any hunters?"

Charlotte looked puzzled. "Three weeks." She brightened, then almost immediately frowned. "Oh, my, he was so angry. If I'm remembering the same incident you are, that must be the one. My, he was angry. Two men had come to hunt, sure enough. On a Sunday. The first Sunday in April. I remember now. And then Richard said that after they took a really nice trophy antelope, they refused to pay. He showed them just where to hunt, and everything. And then they refused to pay. Honestly."

I leaned over and held out the two drivers' licenses to Charlotte. "Are these the men?"

"Oh, I never met them. He just told me that they'd argued, and that finally he'd been able to convince them that New Mexico laws were different than the laws in Texas. I remember that. So they were from Texas." She nodded and handed the licenses back to me.

"But you never saw them, or their vehicle?"

"I saw the car from a distance. A little blue thing. Really quite pretty."

Not anymore, I thought. Neither the coffee nor the sandwich sat any too well, and shortly after that, we left Charlotte to Father Starkey.

"With the jack handle that Torrez found beside Finnegan's truck in town, and with this, I can't imagine Judge Hobart wanting to bother with a Grand Jury," I said as we drove back down the hill toward Posadas. "Edwin Boyd just defended himself. It's as simple as that." I looked at the clock on the dashboard of the car and groaned.

"My God," I said, and Estelle glanced over at me.

"What?"

"The county commissioners' meeting is in about five hours."

"Are you going to it?"

"Oh," I sighed, "I don't know. What's the point? They'll do what they want to do whether or not I'm there. Besides, the service for Martin Holman is the day after tomorrow. I'm supposed to attend, and so are you. And Janice asked if I'd say a few words. I need sometime to think about that."

Estelle reached across and patted my arm affectionately. "You'll come up with something."

"If I'm awake."

"A Don Juan de Oñate breakfast burrito will see you through today and the commissioners' meeting," Estelle said. "And as far as tomorrow is concerned, I think Martin Holman would have been pleased to know that his photos provided the critical evidence to solve a quadruple homicide."

"Let me write that down," I said. "Maybe that will make Janice feel just a little better."

I showered, shaved, and managed a half-hour nap…enough to keep me awake long enough to meet Neil Costace and Estelle at the Don Juan for an early lunch. A blizzard of depositions and reports ruined the rest of the day, along with a twenty-minute meeting with the county commissioners. I was duly appointed sheriff of Posadas County, and Sam Carter looked satisfied. I didn't ruin his day by mentioning his tape-recorded hobby.

On Tuesday, despite Janice Holman's wishes, the memorial service for Martin Holman and Philip Camp filled the First Baptist Church on Bustos. At her request, the law-enforcement officers who attended were dressed in civilian clothes.

At the appropriate moment, Pastor Jeremy Hines motioned to me and I got up to face more than two hundred sober faces. Janice Holman, sitting in the front row, was looking down at her hands, and in a moment of cowardice, I found myself hoping that she would continue to do so. I knew that she had never thought much of her husband's midlife passion for law enforcement.

I looked down at the lectern where, if I'd had any sense, my notes would have been. I thrust my hands in my pockets. "You know," I said finally, "Martin Holman used to joke that he never seemed to be able to get anything done. Balky legislators, no money, not enough manpower, outdated equipment." I smiled. "All the rewards of winning a hard-fought political campaign." Five rows back, Sam Carter looked pained. "But I just want to say that Martin Holman accomplished far more than he would ever take credit for. He brought a small, rural law-enforcement department out of the Stone Age and into the modern world of computers and instant data checks. And he did that despite criticism from several dinosaurs, myself foremost.''

A light chuckle rippled through the audience, and I frowned. ''More important, he insisted on the up-to-date training that has created some of the finest law-enforcement officers in the country. The young men and women who work for Martin Holman's department receive job offers from some of the most prestigious law-enforcement organizations in the country.'' I hesitated, then added, ''He even made it possible for some of us to continue doing what we love best, long after some other administrator would have told us to go home and take up needlepoint.

''He would have been pleased to know that the evidence he gathered Friday afternoon also made it possible to resolve a most perplexing, tragic case.'' I saw Janice Holman shift uncomfortably. She looked up at me, and I nodded at her.

''But most important, Martin Holman was a good, honest human being who tried his best to make this world a better place for his family and his friends and his community. I don't think we can ask anymore of a man than that. I'm going to miss him.''

I nodded again and sat down. Estelle reached over and patted the back of my hand. Knowing the answer perfectly well, I leaned over and whispered, ''Have you talked with Sam Carter yet about the tape recording?''

Estelle Reyes-Guzman looked heavenward.

''I'll take care of it tomorrow,'' I whispered. ''It'll be a nice change of pace.''

After her husband is killed by a hit-and-run driver,
Minnesota police officer Claire Watkins takes her
ten-year-old daughter, Meg, and moves to a small
town in Wisconsin. Nine months later the crime is
still unsolved, but Claire, now working for the
local sheriff, is slowly building a new life.

Two things are about to shatter her fragile peace:
the murder of her neighbor, and the discovery
that Meg has a secret—she saw who killed her
father.

Available April 2001 at your favorite retail outlet.

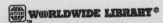

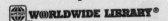

MICHAEL JAHN

A BILL DONOVAN MYSTERY

Murder in Central Park

When NYPD detective Bill Donovan spends a night in a crow observatory with an ornithologist friend—he wakes up to murder. It appears the victim, Harvey Cozzens, had been doing a little observing himself, namely the mating rituals of a couple of teenagers, both of whom are now prime suspects.

But the list of suspects grows as Donovan digs deep into the world he knows best: the underbelly of a city where rage, jealousy and secrets are the motivations for murder.

Available May 2001 at your favorite retail outlet.

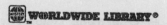

WMJ383

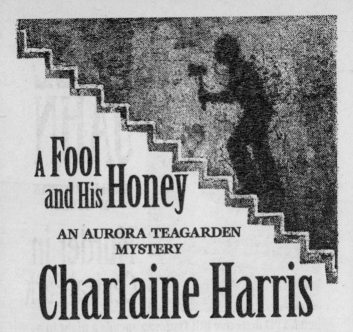

A Fool and His Honey

AN AURORA TEAGARDEN MYSTERY

Charlaine Harris

Sleepless nights, a cross-country chase and a temporary stint at motherhood turn Aurora Teagarden's life upside down. When her husband's niece Regina shows up unannounced on their doorstep with a baby and a secret, Aurora's perpetual curiosity leaps into overdrive—especially when the body of the girl's husband is found ax murdered in her own backyard.

Regina flees the scene, and Aurora is left holding the baby, struggling with the intricacies of bottles, diapers—and a mystery.

Available May 2001 at your favorite retail outlet.

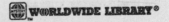

WCH384